Burnt Offerings

Books by Michael Lister

Burnt Offerings
Michael Lister

a novel

You buy a book. We plant a tree.

MYS

Copyright © 2012 by Michael Lister

This is a work of fiction. Any similarities to people or places, living or dead, is purely coincidental.

Inquiries should be addressed to:
Pulpwood Press
P.O. Box 35038
Panama City, FL 32412

Lister, Michael.
Burnt Offerings / Michael
Lister.
-----1st ed.
p. cm.

ISBN: 978-1-888146-89-9 Hardcover

ISBN: 978-1-888146-90-5 Paperback

ISBN: 978-1-888146-91-2 Ebook

Library of Congress Control Number:

Book Design by Adam Ake

Printed in the United States

1 3 5 7 9 10 8 6 4 2

First Edition

For Tommy
and Max who loves her

Thank You
Amy, Adam, Pam, and Jill

Chapter One

Scratch of a match.

Scrape of tip across striking strip.

He enjoys the sound, anticipates the light, the smell, the birth. The sand and powdered-glass surfaces create friction, cause spark, produce heat; the sulfur and oxidizing agent on the head mixing with the red phosphorus on the box.

A chemical reaction occurs.

Fire is born.

A tiny puff of smoke. A brilliant burst of flame.

The flame, blue at the base, orange at the tip, is small but filled with the potential of both creation and devastation. It waves in the wind of his movements, then rights itself when he becomes still again, hovering around the ember-red head beneath.

He can feel the tightness in his chest, the intoxicating effect of his arousal and adrenaline-spiked blood.

Building.

Expanding.

Consuming.

The light emanating from the single wooden match in the small, dark room is surprisingly bright, and the eyes of the woman kneeling before him widen in alarm. She raises her head slightly, her eyes pleading when not squinting against the liquid propellant trickling out of her hair, across her forehead, and down her face.

The smell of sulfur and smoke now join the fuel fumes filling the enclosure.

Outside, beyond the train tracks that now lead nowhere, the nocturnal noises of the deep woods are relentless in their repetition and volume. The dark sky is starless. There is no moon. The cool September air coils through the live oaks and slash pines, raining leaves and pine needles down onto the damp ground.

The flame of the match quickly reaches the tips of his fingers, and he lets it, feeling the burn on his flesh. He is a son of the Flame, begotten of Fire.

As the match burns out, he lights another, pausing for a moment to gaze into the small glow and breathe in the acrid odor of chemicals followed by the sweet scent of burning wood.

The whimper from the pathetic creature kneeling in front of him brings him out of his reverie, and he lifts the match upward, searching the darkness for the opening in the roof. Once he finds it, more by the flicker of the flame than sight of the opening, he moves the offering over, lining her up beneath it, steps back, and hesitates a moment, letting the tension, excitement, and expectation build inside him until it reaches its natural crescendo.

In the distance, he thinks he hears the lonely, haunting sound of a train whistle, as if an ancient echo of a lost locomotive. End of the line, he thinks. Last stop before hell.

Careful not to let the flame come in contact with the fuel, he lays his hands on the kneeling woman's head. The gesture is nearly tender, as if an ordination at a holy convocation, but it's something else entirely.

Ancient act.

Transference of transgression.

By laying hands on his sacrifice, he transfers the sin and guilt and shame of an entire people.

The second match burns out and he strikes a new one. He takes another step back and prepares to ignite his sacrifice, then remembers the final touch, the last act that adds meaning to his masterpiece.

He extinguishes the match between his forefinger and thumb, then steps toward the woman and begins to remove certain articles of clothing and accessories from her.

When he finishes, he steps back again, lights another match, says a prayer, and makes his presentation, tossing the lit match onto his offering.

As the spark hits its mark and flames run out in every direction, the kneeling woman is engulfed.

The small room fills with light and heat, and the son of the Flame is wracked with pleasure, flushed more from the blaze within than without.

It doesn't take long for the fuel to burn out and the fire to reach flesh, and he watches with great satisfaction as the smoke of his sacrifice rises to the rafters, through the rift in the rickety old roof, and to the heavens, a sweet fragrance in the nostrils of God who is the All-Consuming Fire.

He wants to stay, to be close to his gift, but he must go. The time of his ascension is near.

Chapter Two

On the morning Daniel Davis discovers what is left of the burned body, he and Ben Greene are running down the parallel railroad tracks in the heart of the North Florida Wildlife Preserve.

The tracks, once used by freight trains hauling pine chips to the paper mill at Pine Bay, run beneath a thick canopy of trees, providing a shaded path perfect for long-distance running. Unable to do much about the heat and humidity, the path provides protection from the sun's direct assault. No small favor.

It's late September, and lately the autumnal air has been perceptibly if only slightly cooler, carrying on its currents the first hints of change, but this morning is more a resolute step back toward summer than a stumble and fall toward winter.

—You don't miss it? Ben asks.

—What? Daniel says.

Daniel Davis still has his summer tan and sun-lightened brown hair. He's trim for forty-one and moves more like a natural athlete than a trained runner.

—Life, Ben says with a smile.

Smaller than Daniel's six feet by a few inches and lighter than his hundred and eighty pounds by about twenty, Ben has darker, thicker hair and pale skin that doesn't tan.

—I get a life, whatta you gonna do?

Moving at a perfectly synchronized pace, the running shoes of each man land in the gravel of the track bed between the crossties at the same time, roll forward, and push off again.

—I'd think of something, Ben says, his words, like Daniel's, coming out in bursts between breaths.

Weeds have popped up through the no longer maintained ballast, the creosoted crossties splintered, the railroad spikes loose and working their way up out of the rotting wood.

The two friends are fortunate to have found each other, and they know it. There aren't many men like them in and around Bayshore and Pine Key—small towns timidly transforming into resort communities, teetering between the rednecks and rebel flags of the Deep South Old Florida and the ticky-tacky little boxes and *Truman Show* perfection for hipsters with inheritances.

—You ever call that grad student staying at the Driftwood? Ben asks.

The Driftwood is a hotel on the beach in Bayshore, and while vacationing there, a former student of Daniel's had left a message saying how much she would like to get together with him.

Daniel shakes his head.

—That would qualify as a life.

— Exactly. Why not? She was so hot—and sweet and smart.

—And young, Daniel says.

—I *know.*

Married for many years, Ben is constantly attempting to help the single Daniel find true love again—or, in the absence of that, a night of debauchery he can hear the details of.

—*Too* young.

—If they can determine the outcome of elections and consume large amounts of alcohol, they're old enough.

—I'm not so sure, Daniel says. You see the clowns they're putting in office?

—They had some help.

—Probably from large amounts of alcohol. Besides, let's see if you still hold the same beliefs when you have a daughter that age.

—What about that lady cop? What was her . . . Had a dude's name.

Daniel's throat constricts as his stomach turns. Just thinking of Sam makes him nervous and excited and frustrated.

—She shut me down, he says, thinking that as true a statement as he's uttered in a very long time.

She had made him risk so much, dare to emerge from his self-imposed exile only to leave him, like Rick Blaine standing on a train platform, the rain rinsing a sick, gut-shot smile from his stunned face.

He sees Graham's lifeless face, Holly's pain-stricken one. For a moment, Sam had made them fade a bit, but then she withdrew so suddenly, so inexplicably, they began to haunt him even more.

—It's just running is such an obvious and inadequate substitute for sex, Ben says.

—And *you* do it because . . .

—I feel sorry for you.

Daniel smiles, but it fades the moment Ben looks away. He knows beneath the banter lies actual issues and genuine concern.

Thinking of Graham and Holly fills him with a despair that scratches at and worries with the dark edges of his soul. Remembering Sam fills him with the frustration of unfulfilled desire.

—How far we goin' today? Ben asks.

—Old depot.

The gravel crunches beneath their running shoes, the occasional rock shooting off the ballast to land in the dirt. The early morning is already hot, the humidity so high they look as if they've run through a light rain.

—How much farther is that?

—Few more miles.

—This shit kills us, sort of defeats the purpose.

—You're the one who keeps talking about the old depot.

—I *talk* about a lot of shit.

The two men stop conversing for a moment. The only sounds they add to the unseen creatures of the forest are their labored breaths and shoes striking the ballast.

After a while Ben stops, stepping off the track bed, hand to his side, leaning forward.

—You go ahead, he says. It can't be much farther. I'll be here when you get back. Sorry, but this is my limit.

Daniel stops, but continues running in place. So close. Almost there. Got to make it.

—This is good, he says. We can go back.

He wants to continue, but he hadn't realized until this moment just how much. And it has little to do with what reaching the old depot will require of him physically. It's what it means—actually what the desire to reach it means—about what's going on inside of him. He's waking up again, things dormant beginning to break through the fallow ground in little green shoots of hope and growth. Pushing himself, having a goal, caring at all is a sign of the very thing Ben was talking about moments before—life. He's sick of living in fear—sick of not living.

—Really, go, Ben says. I'm good. I'll be ready when you come back by.

—You sure?

—Positive. Couldn't run back now anyway.

Chapter Three

Every time her phone rings, Sam lurches for it, expecting it to be him. She can't help herself. It's instinctual, occurring instantly before her thoughts can catch up, which they quickly do—so that in the beat between the first ring and her hand actually making contact with the phone, she realizes it's not him and won't be.

He won't call with tearful apologies or admission of what a mistake it had been to leave her. Emotionally unavailable paramilitary law enforcement types, even older ones, turn off the spigot so that it doesn't drip (his actual expression about his last girlfriend), they move forward and don't look back. He wouldn't even call to see if she were okay, let alone in an attempt to work things out.

It's over.

In her more reasonable moments, she knows it and knows it's good that it is, that she's far better off alone by herself than alone with him, but the heart has reasons that reason cannot know and hers is wounded, and heavy, and, at the moment, unreasonable.

An agent with FDLE in the Miami Regional Operations Center, Samantha Michaels has returned home for a few days to her mother's house in the small North Florida town of Marianna to heal and to give him time to move his stuff out of her house—well, what she thinks of as her house. She actually house-sits for the owner of a mansion on Key Biscayne, an Internet billionaire who visits the place once a year and likes the idea of an agent with the Florida Department of Law Enforcement living in it the rest of the time.

She stands naked in her childhood room beneath a large Hunter ceiling fan, sweat trickling down the muscular curves of her taut, too pale body. She has just returned from an early morning run, and is, as the waiting room pamphlet put it, spending time getting to know her new body. She likes most of what she sees. Except for the scars, the paleness of her skin, and the sadness of her face, she has a better body than most women half her age. Knocking on the door of forty, she still has all her muscle tone and a tight little ass. And for all her strength and athleticism, there is nothing that's particularly masculine about her.

She finds her wounds disturbing, and wonders if she'll ever get feeling back, but tries to focus her attention on all that is good about what she sees.

Why doesn't Stan love me? Why can't he see how amazing I am? What did I do to drive him away? What can I do to get him back? Maybe if I hadn't been cut up, if I weren't maimed, if—

Stop it. It's not you. It's him.

She wants to believe that—it's what all her friends and his keep telling her—but she just can't.

When her phone rings, she steps over and grabs it off the bedside table, bumping the butt of her gun as she does, and looks at the digital readout. The call is from her office, and she actually considers throwing on her sweaty running clothes again before answering it. Shaking her head and laughing at herself, she takes the call, her fading smile causing her to sound deceptively upbeat.

—Sam?

Pale body flushing. Bruised heart beginning to bang breastplate.

—Yeah?

She wonders if Stan can hear the breathless vulnerability contained in that one small word. Maybe the four hundred miles and cell phone reception help mask it.

—Sorry to have to call, he says.

—It's okay.

She pictures him sitting at his large desk in his enormous office. Stan Winston in all his departmental glory. Head up. Shoulders back. Chest out. Deeply tanned skin peaking out of extravagantly expensive suit. Freshly cut, thick white-gray hair. Brilliant blue eyes.

At twenty years her senior and her boss, getting involved with him seems so self-destructive now, but at the time she really didn't think it was.

—I know you're, ah . . . he begins.

You don't know anything. Don't pretend you do.

— . . . spending time with your mother, he continues, but we've got a situation we need your help with.

He doesn't need me, *we* does.

—What's up? she asks, wondering if she sounds disinterested or defensive.

—Badly burned body. Over near Bayshore. In the wildlife preserve.

She can tell he's started smoking again. Probably never stopped.

—Small county, small department. Election year. Sheriff requested help.

With the exception of corruption within a department being suspected, FDLE normally doesn't get involved in cases belonging to a sheriff's office or police jurisdiction without an invitation.

—And?

She isn't going to make this easy for him.

—Would you go over and take a look?

He doesn't have to ask, and they both know it.

—Why not someone from the Tallahassee office?

It'd make more sense. Is he just trying to delay my return?

Mentioning Tallahassee makes her think of Daniel again. She plans to visit the campus of FSU, ostensibly to see former professors and friends, but actually in an attempt to bump into him.

Is that why I came home? Because it's so close to Tallahassee, to Daniel? It just might be. Maybe I'll get over Stan a lot sooner than I thought.

—You know how rare killing with fire is, he says. None of them have worked one. Sheriff called the department looking for an expert.

She doesn't qualify as that, but she's the closest thing FDLE has.

—Besides, you grew up there, he adds. Most of the agents in the Tallahassee office didn't.

She stalls, wondering how she can refuse without it becoming a big deal. She's just not up for it, but doesn't want him to know that.

—It sounds like a bad one, he says. They could really use you, but if you're not up for it—

—I'm up for it, she says, her voice defiant, defensive.

—Good, he says. If you hurry, you can help process the scene. Body was just found a few hours ago.

—I'm on my way.

—Thanks. I really appreciate it.

She can hear a change in his voice, a softening. He's about to ask how she is or say something personal, and she just can't take it.

—Thanks for thinking of me, boss, she says, amazed at the lightness and lilt she's able to pull off. I'll check in as soon as I know something.

Waiting in the woods alone, Daniel walks around, thinking, processing, careful to stay far enough away from the old depot to avoid the smell and to keep from contaminating the crime scene.

So much death, he thinks. So much suffering.

Life *is* suffering. These three words aren't just the place where Buddhism begins, but wisdom itself begins.

He can feel an attack coming on.

Heart pounding.

Head spinning.

Panic.

Pressure.

Fear.

Loss.

Seeing the horrific remains, smelling that unmistakable stench of charred body had forced the lid off a box in the basement of his subconscious. Images, smells, sounds of a child's ultimate waking nightmare fall like sparks and ash from a ravenous, rapidly spreading fire as it consumes everything in its path.

This's gotta stop.

He's lived in fear so long it feels far more than familiar—it's comfortable. Soon, if he doesn't get it under control, it'll be all he knows.

Taking a deep breath, he attempts to slow the progress of the panic attack he's teetering on the precipice of.

And then, just like when he was young, he's enveloped in something indescribably warm, loving, powerful, and he begins breathing normally again—almost immediately.

What just happened?

You know what. It's happened before.

It's been a while.

In his youth, following the most traumatic experience of his life, he'd felt something inexplicable, transcendent, ineffable—something that had put him on a path, a path that had ultimately led him away from the experience, obscured it to such an extent that he often doubted it had ever happened at all.

What he's feeling now merely hints at the long-ago episode, but it's enough of a taste, enough of a reminder, to renew his strength, restore his sense of—what? Possibility?

His thoughts return to the charred and ash mass no longer recognizably human inside the depot.

The patience required to so completely burn a human body, the investment, the experimentation that must have preceded it, the sheer force of will, is almost as disturbing as the act itself.

It's been a while since he's been involved in an investigation—yet another experience fear has robbed him of—and he realizes now just how much he's missed it.

Would he be asked to help with this one? Would he want to? Be able to? It does appear to be the type of case his particular expertise might be helpful in, and he'd enjoy the challenge, but doubts seriously he'd be asked, or, if asked, be equal to the task.

Chapter Four

A road-rail vehicle and a railroad maintenance supervisor borrowed from Bay County drives Sam and the Pine County sheriff toward the crime scene. The vehicle is a full-size standard pickup truck with steel rail wheels on a hydraulic system that lowers and raises as needed. Used for rail inspection and maintenance, the hi-rail can be driven on a road or rail tracks.

The tracks are uneven and the ride bumpy, and Sam, who as the smallest and the girl, sits in the middle, crushed from both sides by the two large men.

Not sure what the sheriff is willing to say in front of the driver, Sam considers the best way to proceed.

—What can you tell me?

—Not much left of the body, he says. I'm surprised the guy who found it knew what it was.

—Who made the discovery?

—Retired professor from FSU.

She wonders if she knows him, though it's unlikely if he isn't in the criminology department.

—What's his name?

—You went to FSU?

She nods.

—Daniel Davis.

Her eyebrows shoot up and a small smile forms on her face. She laughs at the irony. What're the odds?

Were my thoughts of him the universe's way of preparing me to see him again? Or just a way to fuck with me a little bit? Daniel would say the former, but in her experience, it's almost always the latter.

—You know him?

She nods.

—Not from school, but from a case.

—A *case?*

—He used to do some consulting for the department.

—A religion professor?

—If a crime appeared to be religiously motivated or cultic symbols were left at the scene.

—Oh.

—What was he doing out here?

—Running.

—From what?

He seems to consider this.

—Death, I think, the sheriff says. It's just something your generation does.

She smiles. That what I do when I run? In part, probably. Certainly seen death enough for the bastard to know my name.

A large older man with fine white hair and kind blue eyes, Sheriff Preacher Gibson reminds Sam of a kindly old grandfather who'd likely play Santa in the town Christmas parade each year. Like her own grandfather had, he smells of peppermint, Old Spice, and hair oil.

—Speaking of *my* generation, Daniel's too young to be retired.

The sheriff shrugs.

—I think maybe it was medical.

She makes a mental note of that. After a brief but intense connection and a flirtation that never went anywhere because of Stan, she had lost track of Daniel. She'd heard he had stopped consulting, but never knew why. She had always assumed it had just been too much for him—it was for most people—but if he'd taken medical retirement, maybe he'd gotten too close to one of the monsters he was helping catch.

—Sorry it's so bumpy, their driver says. Tracks ain't been maintained in several years.

The driver, a fifty-something white man in need of a shave, smells of sweat and motor oil and is wearing a soiled uniform of navy blue pants, a light blue shirt, and a white cap with Bay Line Railroad stitched in blue, beneath which too-long, oily hair pokes out in odd directions.

—No problem, Gibson says. We just appreciate you helpin' us out.

Everything he says is so polite, genial, and always with a smile on his face. No wonder he's been sheriff of Pine County so long.

Sam is excited. She's got that beginning-of-an-investigation buzz. Jangling nerves. Queasy stomach. Racing mind.

—What about the building they found the body in? Sam asks.

—Old train depot. Middle of nowhere now. Used to be a small community of turpentiners and loggers back in here at one time.

The old hi-rail's AC broken, the cab is stifling, even with the windows rolled down.

—And these tracks aren't used anymore?

—Not since the paper mill in Bayshore closed.

—Wonder how the killer got his victim back here? Sam says. And why he'd want to?

—That's why you're here. I'm good at a lot of things—keeping a clean, safe county, running a small sheriff's department, making a mean gumbo—but not something like this. I'm hoping you are.

—I'm not bad, Sam says.

Acts of arson to commit homicide and to cover up homicide had been on the rise for the past several years, and Sam had worked more than her share of them in and around Dade County. So much so that it had become a kind of specialty of hers, often advising her co-workers and being loaned out to other agencies.

Far from an expert, though.

—I'll assign an investigator to work with you and give you anything you need, he says, but you'll be in charge of this case.

Sam nods, wondering if she appears confident, wishing she were.

—I called the fire marshal's office, he says. Was told they really don't get involved in this kind of thing. They're more to do with arson—buildings, insurance, and the like. This is something way different. Said FDLE is much better equipped to deal with this kind of thing, and if it's beyond you guys, we've got to find a fed who specializes in it.

Sam nods again. She knows from her own research and training there're not many specialists in the field, even at the federal level. She also knows she's on her own, but perhaps her experiences as a female law enforcement officer and the girlfriend of the unavailable Stan Winston has prepared her that.

—We're almost there, he says. Any questions?

—Where'd you get the name 'Preacher'?

—I was quite a hell-raiser in my misspent youth.

—So it's ironic?

—Well, it was, but not anymore, he says. I guess I kinda grew into it. I pastor a small Methodist Church on the beach.

She suppresses a smirk. I don't even find that bizarre. Welcome home. Maybe Stan was right to send me after all.

She'd know soon enough.

As the lady agent talks with Daniel Davis, Preacher walks down the tracks several feet and pulls out his phone. From the instant he was notified a burned body had been discovered, he knew it was a call he'd have to make.

Reaching the moment when he can no longer in good conscience postpone the call, he thumbs in the familiar number of Frances Rainy, holding the damned thing at arm's length to make out the small numbers.

—Bayshore Counseling Center, Tiffany, the receptionist says, as if nothing makes her happier.

—Doc in? It's Preacher.

—Hey Sheriff, Tiffany says. Hold on a minute.

As Preacher holds, he thinks about what he's done, and wonders if it resulted in the mass of charred flesh and boiled blood on the floor of the small train depot.

Most people would understand that there are times when the chief law enforcement officer of a county might not adhere to the exact letter of the law. Most people realize that on certain occasions true justice can only be found outside the justice system. 'Course, if his asymmetrical application of the law had resulted in murder, they'd see him as an accessory, and rightly so.

—Sheriff? Frances Rainy says. Is everything okay?

An African-American woman in her early fifties, Dr. Frances Rainy is a skilled family counselor in private practice in Bayshore with a county contract to provide services for the school system.

—You tell me.

—What do you mean?

—How's our patient?

Though they've worked on many cases together over the years, he doesn't have to say more for her to know exactly who he's talking about. She's only treating one patient who could cause her to lose her license, him his job, and both of them to possibly face criminal charges.

—Making progress, I think, she says, doubt creeping into her voice. Has something happened?

—I've got a burned body out here in the preserve, he says.

She hesitates a moment, and the silence causes a shudder to run through him.

—You think he had something to do with it?

—I'm asking what *you* think, he says.

—I've got a session with him this afternoon, she says. Let me call you back afterward.

Chapter Five

Arson investigation, believed by some to be as much art as science, determines whether a fire was set deliberately, accidentally, or naturally. Of the several ways in which a fire can be proven to be arson, the use of accelerants, ignition devices, or there being more than one point of origin are the most common.

Accelerants can be solids, liquids, or gases.

Most arsonists use liquid accelerants.

A felony, arson occurs far more frequently in times of economic depression than during prosperity. It is estimated that arson accounts for as many as 267,000 fires each year, making it the leading cause of fire in the United States.

The clearance rate of arson cases is less than ten percent, the conviction rate far less.

Because of the nature of arson, its solitary, secretive, under-cover-of-night implementation, there are rarely any witnesses.

The various FDLE crime scene techs are processing the depot fire as if it is a standard arson investigation, collecting the three types of evidence—trace, possible accelerants, and documentation to help determine the cause and origin of the fire. Having already completed

a preliminary check of the premises, alert to signs and smells of accelerants, they are now carefully moving around the small room, pho-
tographing the scene from every possible angle, marking evidence,
taking measurements.

They are treating this like any other arson investigation, but it is
not. Sam knows before her part in the investigation has even begun,
she is dealing with a killer unlike any she has ever seen.

This isn't arson, it's murder—fire the weapon.

Though constructed of old and rotting wood, there is no fire
or smoke damage to the small train depot. Most burned bodies are
discovered in the blackened remains of torched buildings, attempts
at destroying evidence, but this act of fiery terrorism isn't meant to
cover a crime, it *is* the crime.

Far more frightening than the scene is the body at its center, and
the way the degree to which it has been consumed is juxtaposed with
the lack of damage to the structure. In all her years of looking at
burned bodies—both at crime scenes and in the explicit photographs
in textbooks and training manuals—she has never seen one as thoroughly devoured as this.

The formless mass on the floor is burned beyond recognition.
Beyond race. Beyond gender. Nearly beyond species. There is very
little left that is identifiably human, and it's hard to imagine another
human capable of such inconceivable inhumanity.

Daniel stands across the tracks from the old railroad depot, now
crime scene, beneath a tall pine tree. Behind him, the pine and hardwood forest extends for miles, thick with undergrowth, seemingly
impenetrable. He feels nearly naked in his running shorts and T-shirt,
vulnerable around the uniform-clad cops, emergency workers, crime
scene techs, and most of all, Sam.

The sweat in his clothes had dried as he returned back out here
on the hi-rail with the first deputy, but now nearing midday, he can
feel the trickle of moisture snaking down his back again.

He still can't believe this is happening. He smiles slightly as he recalls Ben's reaction. This is what I get for running on Rosh Hashanah, he had said, shaking his head.

After he and Ben had spoken with Preacher Gibson, Ben had been allowed to leave, while Daniel had been asked to accompany the sheriff and his men to the crime scene and hang around to talk to the FDLE agent who would be heading the investigation. It hadn't occurred to him it might be Sam. Seeing her so far from Miami and in the middle of the North Florida Wildlife Preserve had been as surprising as it was thrilling.

The small, dilapidated depot is a one-room wooden structure, missing its front door and windows, with a large hole in the rotting roof. Leaning, vine-covered, and overgrown with grass and weeds, the building looks moments from complete collapse.

Watching the crime scene being processed, he realizes how much he's missed being involved in investigations, and his mind begins to wonder about and worry with this one he just happened to stumble onto. Though only qualified to give input on crimes with cultic elements, and even then almost always as a consultant inside a safe office or conference room, he has always found all aspects of criminal investigation fascinating.

Why was the victim brought way out here? For privacy? To avoid interruption? Or were there other, more meaningful reasons? How long ago had it happened? From the fresh charred smell and the way the lump of ash and black liquid still smoldered, he couldn't imagine it had been very long.

He kicks at a rusted railroad spike and large splinter of wood on the ground in front of him, both of which have come loose from the rotting creosoted ties. Gravel scatters, pinging off the oxidized iron rail a few feet away.

When Sam had arrived, and he had recovered from his surprise, he was reminded again of just how attractive he found her, and how much he missed having someone in his life. When she asked if he minded waiting a few more moments while she took a quick look at the crime scene, he had told her he was happy to wait—and meant it.

As he waits for her now, he turns and takes a few steps into the woods, pacing around, too hot to stand still.

But it isn't just the heat that makes him fidget. It's the smell of the burned flesh, the sight of the charred body, and all the painful memories they resurrect. All this time, all the distance, and the odor that smells just the same takes him back again. All the repression and counseling and reprogramming, and in one moment, it all comes back—the horror, the loss, the fear that's never very far below the surface.

To his right, he sees a swath of tall grass and weeds bent and lying on its side. He imagines this being the way the killer came, dragging his victim, or the path by which he made his escape, and steps over to examine the area closer.

There's no question the depression of the grass has occurred recently, but it's obviously not the entry or exit used by the killer because it only goes a short distance into the forest and stops abruptly at the base of an oak tree.

Turning to walk back toward the tracks, he takes a few steps before he realizes how stupid it was not to examine the tree where the small trail ended so abruptly. He whips back around and reaches the tree in just a few short steps.

The base of the tree bears no obvious marks, and he feels foolish, guessing he's probably paying a lot of attention to the small path an animal made—if not one of the cops taking a nature call.

And then he glances a little higher.

About halfway up the tree one of the smaller branches is broken and there's a scrape in the bark. Moving to a spot directly beneath the tree and gazing straight up, he sees it. There, hidden among the leaves and Spanish moss covering the branches, is an old, green tree stand.

Had the killer hidden in it at some point? Could he be in it right now?

Chapter Six

—That look like a body to you? Sam asks.

She's inside the depot with the others, looking down at the blackened heap on the floor.

The small one-room structure is dusty and weed-filled, fallen
boards and bits of glass littering the floor.

The body lies beneath a hole in the roof. Extending out from it,
next to blood splatters, footprints, and fuel spills, are small yellow
evidence marker tents, each with a different number. In the corner
to the left of the open doorway, what appear to be a woman's belt,
shoes, watch, and ring are scattered about as if flung carelessly aside.

—Sure as hell don't to me, Gibson says.

A little surprised to hear Preacher sound more like a cop than a
clergyman, it makes her like him all the more.

The crime scene techs nod, but the deputies, firemen, and EMTs
shake their heads.

The sheriff's deputies, volunteer firemen, and local EMTs are
no longer needed, if they ever were, and in another moment she will
have to clear the crime scene, though it will be an unpopular thing to

do. They're so excited, most of them realizing that they're witnessing a once-in-a-career type case.

—So how'd Daniel know it was?

—Smell, one of the deputies offers.

—You suspect the professor? Gibson says.

—I'm just asking the obvious questions, but from what I know about guys who play with fire, they usually like to be around when their work is receiving the attention they think it deserves.

Nearly in unison, the small group of law enforcement personnel lean over and look through the opening where the missing door should be.

To their collective surprise, Daniel is standing there.

—If he offers to lend us a hand with the investigation, we'll know it's him, Sam whispers to Preacher.

—I think I might have found something, Daniel says.

Sam shoots Gibson a look.

—Oh yeah? Sam says. What's that?

He tells them.

—Just in case I'm not the killer, he adds, you might want to see if he's hiding up there.

With the various deputies fanned out around the tree, Gibson, using a bullhorn, addresses anyone who might be inside the stand.

Daniel stands on the opposite side of the tracks with Sam.

—Sorry about earlier, she says, speaking softly, looking straight ahead.

He shrugs it off.

—I was gonna say I've been called worse, but I don't think I have.

The fading camouflage tree stand is about fifteen feet in the air, mounted to an oak, a green aluminum ladder coming out of an opening in the bottom of it. Daniel didn't see the ladder at first because it is on the opposite side of the tree. Roughly three feet squared on a welded aluminum platform, the stand has painted plywood walls, a short, waterproof bench seat, and a shooting bar.

Inside the depot, the lab techs continue processing the scene.

—I was just referring to the percentages, she says. I don't think you're the killer.

A few moments and nothing. Gibson repeats his announcement.

—You haven't changed your mind that quickly, Daniel says. You're just hoping I'll let my guard down and won't lawyer up.

—Lawyer up?

He smiles.

—Cute.

—Just trying to speak your language. How'm I doin'? Besides helping you guys with a few cases and being pulled over for speeding, this is my only entanglement with five-O.

She smiles with what looks like genuine pleasure, the first time her face has looked anything but sad.

—Five-o? she asks, her smile turning wry.

—Fuzz, pig, cop, blue, piglet, bull, bear, bobby, heat, heavy, po-po, flatfoot, sweeney, smokey, Bayshore's finest.

She turns away from the tree stand to consider him.

He smiles and uses his best straight-up, nerdy white guy voice.

—I'm street like that, yo.

Her face lights up and she lets out a laugh.

—Oh, yeah. You're hardcore. 'Course, what professor isn't?

—Gots to be to get tenure.

Gibson warns anyone who might be in the stand that they're coming up, to sit still with his hands raised and he won't get hurt, then one of the deputies begins to climb the tree.

—So what happened in Miami? he asks.

—Whatta you mean?

—We had something. I wasn't imagining it. We were . . . whatever we were doing—feeling it out, testing the waters, and the next thing I know, you're pulling back, shutting down.

—That's how you remember it?

—That's how it was.

When the deputy reaches the stand, he gets his bearings, placing one boot on each of two large branches, draws his weapon, then quickly looks over the side of the stand, jerking his head back just as fast.

—Anything? Gibson yells up.

—Something, but no killer.

He holsters his firearm and looks in the stand again.

—He was up here. After he lit the body.

—How do you know?

—Footprints, he says. Traces of fuel and soot—and blood. Oh, fuck me.

—What is it?

—There's something up here, he says, grabbing a branch to steady himself.

Chapter Seven

The ancient Greeks believed fire to be one of the major natural elements of the world like water, earth, and air, which seems right, but it's not. Unlike earth, air, and water, which are forms of matter, fire is the result of matter changing forms. Not matter at all, but a devourer of it. Fire is the chemical reaction between oxygen and fuel when the fuel is heated to ignition temperature.

He is prostrate before the Flame, humbled and awestruck as he relives the pleasure and pain of his latest sacrifice, the small fire burning before him now merely a token, a symbol, for within its small blaze is all that is needed to consume the entire world.

Fire is self-perpetuating.

It will burn as long as it has fuel. The heat of the flame keeps the fuel at the ignition temperature, so all it needs is food. Fire spreads because its flame heats any fuel surrounding it, releasing gasses that aid in its mission to purify.

He has been fascinated by fire for as long as he can remember. As a child he lit up like the candles on his birthday cake in the glow of their flames. Since then, his interest in fire has consumed him. At first, and for a long part of his early journey, he wasn't sure of the purpose and calling of his gifts. He set fires, torched trash cans, burned buildings, offered sacrifices of a sort, but it was all so random, so meaningless. And yet he now realizes it was preparation for his true mission.

He loves fire, celebrates fire, *is* fire. He knows everything there is to know about fire.

He knows, for example, that gravity determines the shape of a flame. The hottest gasses of the flame have less density than the air surrounding it, so they move upward toward lower pressure. Thus, fire typically spreads upward, its flame pointed at the top. Fire without the effects of gravity forms a sphere. Different fuels ignite at different temperatures.

Every fire is unique because fire is alive.

As carbon atoms heat up, they rise and emit light.

The color of a flame varies according to its heat and intensity, the hottest part at the base glowing blue while the cooler tip flaring orange or yellow.

But more than any of this, he knows that fire is not merely chemical, not only physical, but spiritual.

Fire is a force.

Fire is life and light, creation and destruction.

Fire is God and God is fire.

Fire refines, purges, and purifies.

Fire consumes—wholly and without regard or respect.

Fire is relentless, imposing its will on the world.

Fire is an instrument, an implement, a weapon.

He is a weapon, forged in flame, born ablaze.

He is fire. His ash-charred heart burns in his chest to work its will. And it will. It will.

—Why would he take up there whatever it is he took? Gibson asks.

Lab techs are working the tree and stand. Gibson and Sam are standing nearby observing. Daniel Davis has been sent home and will be interviewed later.

Sam shakes her head.

—I have no idea. If the lab can tell us *what* it is, maybe we can figure out why, but probably not even then. Most ritual killers have an internal logic known only to them. We may never know—even if we catch him.

Sam stills herself, attempting to suppress the tremor deep inside her. She is gripped by an overwhelming fear when she considers the killer she is responsible for catching. She has no illusions. This will be dangerous and difficult, perhaps even deadly. She can tell from what she's seen so far that what she's dealing with is real evil. This guy has killed before, probably quite a few times. He's organized, methodical, and pitiless. She is no match for him. Maybe no one is.

—You really think it could be the professor?

—Davis? she says. I'm not sure. We'll have to watch him. It *is* interesting that he was so determined to make it to the depot today, even leaving his friend behind. And that he recognized that mass in there as a body.

The hi-rail truck approaches, returning from taking Daniel back to his car. Sam can see it has returned with a passenger—a plain-clothes cop from the look of him.

—Good, Gibson says, as he turns to see the truck. Steve's here.

Sam watches as the over-muscled young cop gets out of the truck and swaggers over toward them. Wearing expensive dress shoes, pleated and cuffed charcoal gray slacks, tight, tapered white dress shirt cut to display his efforts in the gym, and a gray-and-black silk tie, Steve doesn't look like a cop so much as someone who plays one on TV.

—Detective Steve Phillips, meet Agent Samantha Michaels, Gibson says.

—Well, hello, Samantha, Steve says, flirting though she has no doubt she's not his type. I look forward to working with you.

They shake hands. Though powerful, his hands are small, his fingers stubby. She smiles. He thinks it's at him, so he smiles back. His palm is sweaty, and when their shake is complete, she wonders how much testosterone and steroids are in the warm, wet residue in her hand.

—Steve'll be working the case with you, Gibson says. Anything you need, he's your man.

Sam nods, looking at Steve.

—I'd love a cup of coffee, she says.

There's an awkward silence for a moment, then both men begin to laugh.

—She's funny, Steve says. I like her. This is gonna be fun.

—There's a lot we won't know until we do an autopsy, Michelle Barnes says. There's a lot we won't know even then. Fire destroys evidence. And this guy used a lot of fire.

Michelle Barnes is the lead FDLE crime scene technician from the lab in Tallahassee. She is standing in the depot in her white bio protection suit. Sam, Steve, and Preacher Gibson listen attentively as she gives them her best and most educated guesses as to what happened here. She is pale with dark eyes and curly black hair that spills out from the hood around her face. Though not a thin woman, the suit makes her look bigger than she is.

—What do you mean a lot of fire? Gibson asks.

—It's not easy to burn a body, she says. A crematorium uses temperatures between fifteen- and eighteen-hundred degrees for a couple of hours, and still there's bits of bone and teeth left. Something like this took a lot of accelerant and a lot of patience. This guy loves fire and he takes his time with it. He would have to douse the body with the accelerant, light it, let it burn, and continue adding the accelerant to get as hot a fire as possible for as long as possible.

Sam thinks about it.

That's why you used this place, isn't it? So you'd have all the time you needed. But are there other reasons?

—Based on what I'm seeing here and in the tree stand, Barnes continues, I'd say the killer removes the victim's shoes, belt, and jewelry, douses him with the accelerant, sets him on fire, douses him with more accelerant, gets a good burn going, then goes outside, climbs the tree, and watches through the hole in the roof, going back and forth between the depot and the tree stand several times—he'd have to keep adding accelerant to get the kind of burn he did, and it'd take a while—and one of the times he removes part of the victim and takes it into the stand with him.

Steve shakes his head.

—Sick fuck.

—You just reaching that conclusion? Barnes asks.

—He just got here, Gibson says with a smile. And he's sort of slow.

—Why not take off all his clothes? Sam asks. Why just certain items?

Careful to avoid the yellow evidence markers, she steps over to examine the victim's watch, ring, belt, and shoes in the corner.

The others follow.

—It looks as if he just tossed them over here, Barnes says. It might be significant to him or it might have just been a habit or his way of preparing for the fire. I have no idea.

Sam considers this, hung up on the word *habit*.

—If the items were significant, like as sick souvenirs of his fuckin' fun, wouldn't he have taken 'em with him? Steve asks.

Michelle shrugs.

—I just process the scene, examine the forensics. You guys have to figure out what these twisted pricks are thinking—at least enough to catch 'em.

—I'm sure they have meaning of some kind—at least to him, Sam says. He wants us to see them. We just don't know what we're supposed to be seeing. And he could have left all this and still taken a souvenir to relive and fantasize about the kill.

—That's true, Gibson says.

—They appear to have just been tossed over here, Sam adds, but based on the patience it took to do what he did to the body, I think he's displayed them just how he wants them to be. Unless . . . I keep coming back to the word *habit*.

—I just meant— Michelle begins.

—What if the guy's a mortician or someone who works in a crematorium?

Gibson nods.

—That's good, he says. We need to check that out.

—Well, whatever he is, Michelle says, he's not new at this, so you might want to check other abandoned buildings and fire sites for more bodies.

Chapter Eight

As Gibson and his deputies investigate recent fires in the area, Sam and Steve interview Ben and Daniel. Convinced the men will be more relaxed in a familiar environment, they conduct the interviews at their respective homes.

Unlike Daniel, who lives outside of Bayshore, Ben lives on the barrier island of Pine Key. Referred to as the New Jerusalem by locals because of its large Jewish population, Pine Key is a seven-mile-long strip of land in the Gulf of Mexico, connected to the mainland town of Bayshore by a mile-long causeway. Less than a mile across at its widest point, Pine Key has beachfront mansions lining both the bay and Gulf sides, a resort on each end, and a small business district full of speciality shops and boutiques.

Though much smaller than the mansions all around it, Ben's beach house is far nicer than anything on the mainland. Built on stilts and overlooking the bay, the carport is on ground level, the living room, kitchen, study, and guest room on the second floor, and the master suite on the third.

Rachel, Ben's wife, answers the door and ushers the two cops into Ben's study. She is obviously younger than Ben, perhaps by nearly ten years, with black hair and eyes and olive skin.

—Would either of you like coffee or tea?

They both decline.

—Benjamin will be down in a moment. He's having a difficult time with all this.

When she leaves and closes the door, Steve shakes his head.

—Pretty tough on the guy that got roasted too.

One wall of the study has floor-to-ceiling built-in bookshelves, lined mostly with leather-bound editions. In front of it sits a large cherry desk that faces a plate glass window with a picturesque view of Pine Bay and, in the hazy distance, Bayshore.

—What's this guy do? Steve asks.

—Documentary filmmaker.

—For Stephen fuckin' *Spielberg*? He must have family money. Fuckin' Jews. They all got—

Stunned and incensed, Sam starts to say something, but stops when the study door opens.

—We all have what? Ben asks. Family money? Well, I didn't. I started with nothing. Less than nothing.

—Wait for me in the car, Detective, Sam says.

—What? Steve says. I just meant—

—Now, she says.

Flushed with what appears to be anger and embarrassment, he shakes his head and storms out of the room, slamming the door as he does.

—I'm very sorry about that. The sheriff just assigned him to help me. I had no idea he was anti-Semitic.

—Have a seat, he says. What can I do for you?

He sits behind his desk, motioning for her to take one of the chairs in front of it.

It bothers her that he doesn't seem more shocked or offended, as if it is merely what he expects from cops.

—What Detective Phillips said does not reflect my—

—Forget about that, he says. It's very common.

—Not in my world, she says. And I just—

—Where are you from?

—Well, here, but I live in Miami.

He nods.

—I love Miami, he says.

They talk about South Florida for a few moments, then transition into the real reason for her visit.

—How often do you and Daniel run along the tracks?

—Daniel pretty much does every day, he says. I join him a few times a week.

—Ever been as far as the depot before?

Ben shakes his head.

—Daniel say why he was so determined to do it today?

—No, he says, but he tries to go a little farther each time.

—But not you?

—We're different.

—Why did Daniel retire so early?

—Personal reasons. Doesn't really talk about it much.

—How was he able to?

—I'm not sure exactly, he says. He inherited the lodge where he lives. He writes books. I think he still teaches a few online courses.

—Did he mention how he knew it was a body?

He thinks about it, then shakes his head.

—He just told me there was someone inside the depot and we ran back and called the sheriff.

—What else can you tell me about him?

—He's not the killer. You don't really think he is, do you?

—I'm not thinking much of anything at the moment. Just gathering information.

—Daniel's a good man. I'd hate to see you waste a lot of time investigating him.

—Look at how they live out here, Steve says. I'm surprised he's even willing to jog on our ground.

—I've never been so embarrassed in my entire career, Sam says.

Entering the causeway, the car begins to make the rhythmic thu-dump sound as the tires pass over the seams of the cement structure. They are in an unmarked navy Caprice. Steve is driving.

—It's one thing to be a benighted bigot, but to express it on the job, Sam continues, *in* a witness's home . . .

—I'm not a bigot, he says. I just don't like rich people. And you know why? 'Cause they always think they're above the law—that the rules don't apply to them.

—You didn't say 'fuckin' rich people,' you said, 'fuckin' Jews.'

—Well, I meant fuckin' rich people, he says. Just around here, all the fuckin' rich people are fuckin' Jews.

—Take me to the station.

—One little comment and you're not gonna work with me any-more?

—I didn't say that, but I'm surprised you want to work with me, she says. Me bein' a fuckin' Jew and all.

—No way, he says. Oh, shit, I'm sorry. No offense. I didn't mean to—I just meant—

Before she can say anything else, her phone rings.

—We've had a lot more fires in the last year than I realized, Gib-son says.

—We need to talk to anyone arrested for or suspected of arson.

—I'm working on a list now, and I've got men checking all the sites.

—Just men?

—Huh?

Even good and kindly old cops are sexist. No wonder a young redneck like Phillips is racist.

—Steve's about to check out the morgues and crematoriums in the area, she says, and I'm gonna go interview the professor. Be okay if we all meet back at the station tonight to discuss everything?

—Whatever you want. It's your investigation and I already have overtime approved.

—Thanks.

—Are you sure you should interview Davis alone?

—Yeah, she says. I can't take the chance that Steve'll call him a mick or a spick or a shanty Irish bastard.

Chapter Nine

Driving along the small dirt road toward Daniel's lodge, Sam calls a friend of hers at FSU to find out why he retired so early. To get to the dirt road she is now easing her way down, she had to travel five miles outside of Bayshore on an empty rural highway. She has been on the dirt road for nearly two miles and has yet to find the entrance to Louisiana Landing.

When she finally does and turns onto what is more path than driveway, it's nearly another mile before she reaches the rustic old house, all of which gives her plenty of time to explain to Tweeta, her friend and the secretary to the Dean of the Criminology Department who became like a mother to her when she was there, what she needs to know and why.

The ancient two-story French Colonial house in need of painting is white clapboard with a steeply-pitched black shingle roof and tall, narrow windows and doors. As she approaches it, Davis steps out onto the large screened-in porch.

Who are you hiding from back here? she wonders.

—Is this place as old as it looks?

—My great granddad built it. It's based on a house he had in St. Martinsville, Louisiana. He lived there before he moved his family here.

Out of his running clothes, wearing blue jeans and an untucked white button-down shirt with the sleeves rolled up, he's even more handsome than he was this morning. He might be a compulsive killer, but he's the first man she's found attractive since she and Stan broke up.

Ted Bundy was handsome and appealing.

He holds the screen door open for her, and she steps up onto the porch.

—It's been empty a long time, he says. Needs some work. Unfortunately, I'm not much of a handyman.

He gestures her into the house and follows her inside.

—What brings you back here? she asks.

—That's a long story.

—What's the short version?

—Needed a change.

—That's pretty short.

The house's exterior has not prepared her for its interior. She's stepped into a beautiful great room with polished hardwood floors, high ceilings, bookshelves on every wall, and large plate glass windows along the back that overlook a backyard that slopes down to the Dead River. Unlike Ben's books, Daniel's are not leather and have obviously been thoroughly used.

—It looks like a different house on the inside.

Very faintly, barely perceptible, she hears the soothing sound of music playing. It sounds like the score to an emotionally intense film, but she can't place it.

—I had it remodeled, then ran out of money, he says. Would you like something to drink?

As he fixes each of them a glass of a sweet tea, she walks along Oriental rugs to the camel-colored leather sofa and love seat in the center of the room and sits down.

The cool, quiet house is peaceful, and sinking into the sofa, she finds herself relaxing, a response that surprises her.

—This is quite an environment you have here.

He hands her a large glass of sweetened ice tea with a napkin wrapped around the base and sits across from her.

—It's conducive to writing, which is what I mostly do these days.

—What're you writing?

—Couple of things. Another book on investigating religious crimes.

—I read your first one. It was very interesting.

—Thanks. The other thing I'm working on right now is more of a general religion title called 'Disorganized Religion: Meandering Paths for Marginal Souls.'

She nods.

—I like that. How're they coming?

—Very slowly.

—That because it's *too* good an environment? Or because you run so much?

He smiles.

—Nice transition, he says.

—But not perfect, or you wouldn't have known that's what it was.

—My friends laughed their asses off when I told them you thought I was the killer.

—I don't think—

—*Could* be the killer, he says, and after what we had in Miami. We gonna talk about that?

—What's there to talk about?

—What happened.

—Whatta you mean?

—Why you pulled back when we were just getting started good.

—I was involved with someone, she says. I thought it was over. Turned out it wasn't.

—Would've been nice to know.

—Sorry. I wasn't in a very good place.

—And now?

—I'm much better.

—I'm sure you are, but I meant are you still involved with someone?

She shakes her head.

—It's over.

—Really over? he asks. Or Miami over?

—It's over over.

—Good.

—Actually, irrelevant. Well, you managed to fuck up my smooth transition—

He smiles.

—Sorry.

—So I'll just ask. What made you run so far today?

He shrugs.

—Nothing in particular. I just try to go a little farther every day.

—What made you go over and look in the depot?

—I probably would have anyway, but the smell was what caught my attention.

—You always investigate strange smells?

He nods, suppressing a smile.

—It's a hobby of mine.

She is unable to keep from laughing.

—This thing seem ritualistic to you?

He nods.

—Any thoughts?

—A few. It's definitely ritualistic—the act itself, using fire, removing the articles of clothing he did, whatever he did in the tree stand.

—Why would he remove part of the body and take it up there?

—I'm not sure, but there's a reason. If it were just a souvenir, he'd've taken it with him. Let me think on it. It's important. We find out why he's doing what he is, we'll find him.

—We?

—Then there's the body.

—Yeah?

—He's not just robbing them of their lives, but of their identities—completely obliterating them, wiping them out, making it as if they were never born.

She starts to say something, but her phone rings.

—I'm sorry, she says, but I need to take this.

—No problem.

—Opening the phone, she stands and walks to the window.

—Agent Michaels.

—Samantha, it's Tweeta. I've got the goods for you.

Through the window, she sees that the river is low, its receded waters exposing far more of the thick bases of the cypress trees at its edges.

The Dead River, named for its many deadhead cypress trees, curls around Pine County before dumping its fresh water into the bay.

—How involved is it? Sam asks. I might need to call you back.

As Tweeta answers, Sam's phone beeps, alerting her to another call and blocking out Tweeta's response.

—Hey, she says. Let me call you right back. I've got another call.

—Sure, sweetie.

She clicks over to hear the labored breathing of Preacher Gibson.

—We've got another one, he says. It's in a field not far from Louisiana Landing. Right around the corner from where you are.

Chapter Ten

Rimmed with several rows of pines on all sides, the blackened field is only visible once past the trees. If it weren't so large, the area would be considered a clearing rather than a field. Having parked behind the sheriff's car just off the dirt road and walked a hundred yards or so in, Sam enters the charred area as the sun descends beneath the tips of the tall pine trees along the horizon.

As she hurries across the field, tiny plumes of ash and smoke rising off the ground with every step, she realizes they will be out of daylight soon. Nearing the center of the large pasture, she can see that Gibson and one of his deputies are standing by the remains of an abandoned old barn that the earth has long since pulled down to herself.

Though the field is almost entirely burned, the pile of unvarnished wood and corrugated tin appear not to have so much as a scorch mark.

—Whatta we got? she asks.

—Another one, Preacher says.

He steps around the largest part of the fallen roof and she follows. On the other side, beneath rusted sheets of tin and rotting boards, an old white porcelain bathtub with brass claw feet peeks out, and in it, partially burned, badly decomposed remains of an adult male.

—How'd you find it? she asks.

—Got close and smelled it. Just pulled a couple of boards out to take a look underneath, and there it was.

—This is Greg Carr, Gibson says.

—But what made you walk all the way out here?

—Sheriff told me to.

—I was told this field had burned recently—from lightning I think, 'cause the rain put it out pretty quick. But just in case I was wrong, I told Greg to check it out.

Sam nods, thinking.

—Crime scene unit's on the way, Gibson adds.

—This was a barn, right? Greg says. Not a house. So what's a bathtub doing out here?

—Feed trough, Sam says.

Gibson smiles.

—You *are* from around here, aren't you?

—A lot of farmers use old bathtubs for feed troughs, she tells Greg. They're sturdy and don't rust.

Not as thoroughly burned as the train depot victim, the man in the bathtub is only partially consumed by fire, his body assuming the classic pugilistic position as a result of the coagulation of his muscles, though decomposition is well underway.

—It'll be dark soon, Gibson says. We better get a generator and some lights set up.

—And some coffee, Sam says. Gonna be a long night.

Gibson shakes his head.

—Wonder how many times we're gonna say that?

It is not without a little embarrassment that he watches as the sheriff and the lady agent poke around one of his first feeble attempts. As much experiment as message, the mess they're examining is like the discarded sketches of a young artist, not meant to be found.

He had burned things for years, beginning with objects and small animals when he was young, buildings and human beings when he was older, but this—this was something new. What they're seeing are his first steps toward becoming. What he's been testing, trying, figuring out, is not burning, but consuming.

It's as if they've invaded his private studio, stumbled upon early drafts of his work—a work in progress, an early version, necessary, but never meant to be seen.

How many more such scribblings will they happen upon?

Not that it really matters. The only thing that concerns him is that they don't get distracted, that they don't lose sight of the masterwork right in front of them. The best by far is yet to come—it's in front of them. Not behind. Quit wasting time on the past, on the drafts. Look in front of you. See what wondrous works I will do.

He's disappointed that they haven't involved Daniel yet. He thought for sure they would have at least glimpsed the significance of what he's doing. He thought he had been so obvious, but maybe he's giving them too much credit.

He thought Daniel a worthy interpreter of his work, a seer of his dreams, a witness to his visions. Was he wrong? No. He knows he wasn't. But how can Daniel explain and interpret if he's not involved?

He's got to make Daniel part of the investigation, keep him close, and he knows just how to do it. He'll get Daniel's attention—and won't let it go.

As the FDLE crime scene unit processes the scene in the dim light of the portable halogen lamps, Preacher walks out of the circle of illumination and into the darkness, the charred grass crunching beneath his boots.

Trying to avoid appearing suspicious, he nonetheless turns his head, looking over his shoulder, then side to side. Satisfied no one is around, he withdraws his cell phone, scrolls down to the recently called number, and presses the button.

This time Dr. Rainy answers the phone herself.

—You're working late, he says.

—Makes two of us.

—I hope we're not working on the same thing.

—I really do too.

—I thought you were going to call me right after the session.

—He never showed.

—He ever done that before?

—Not without calling, she says. I'm trying to reach him now. If I can't find him, I may have to ask for your help tracking him down.

—If you can't find him, you won't have to ask, he says. Call me as soon as you know something.

—There's a guy over at the corner of the field, Greg says.

Sam turns from watching the techs work to look in the direction he's indicating.

—Says he owns the place and that he knows you.

—Thanks, she says, and walks over to where Daniel Davis is standing.

—You own this land?

He nods.

—Is it like this morning?

—How long has it been since you were back here? she asks.

He shrugs.

—Haven't been since I moved back. You think I did this?

—What're you doin' out here?

—Just checking on things, he says. Need anything? Sandwiches, drinks?

—We're good, she says. You go on back home and we'll finish our interview as soon as I can.

—Didn't expect to see you again *quite* so soon, Michelle Barnes says.

—But you knew you'd see us again, Sam says.

She nods.

—The one we worked this morning wasn't a one-off. We all knew that.

The boards and tin of the fallen roof laid to one side, the body and the bathtub examined, photographs taken, measurements made, evidence gathered.

—I won't be able to tell you much until we do an autopsy, Michelle says, but if it's the same guy—

—It is, Sam says.

—Then this was him learning. I'd say this was done a few weeks ago at least.

—Why'd he burn the field? Steve asks.

—He didn't, Sam says.

Michelle nods.

—I agree. I think the field was burned far more recently—a matter of days, not weeks—and could very well have been natural or unintentional. Lightning strike or someone tossing a cigarette.

—Division of Forestry told me it was caused by lightning, Gibson says. That's what brought us out here.

—The body isn't nearly as badly burned as the previous one we found because the fire didn't burn as long or as hot, Michelle says. The killer has probably been experimenting with different accelerants. He either used a different one on this body or just didn't use as much. He was smart to do it in the bathtub—contain the fire, prevent it from igniting anything else, and keep it concentrated on the body. My guess is there're more bodies scattered around the area, and the more we find, the more we'll know. This one would have told us more than the other one since it's not nearly as burned, if it weren't for the decomposition. I wish we'd've found it sooner.

—You workin' a lot of missing persons? Sam asks Gibson.

—Not a single one.

—If these woods are filled with bodies, she says, we'll need to call FBI in. Probably go ahead and give them a heads-up anyway, but we've got to begin a search.

Preacher nods.

—Will do.

—I'm hoping the fallen roof covering the body's gonna help us out, Michelle continues. I'll rush the autopsies and lab work and let you know something just as soon as I can.

—Can you believe she thinks I'm the killer? Daniel says.

—Probably didn't help that you were lurking around the crime scene tonight, Ben says.

—I wasn't lurking.

It's not late, but it's been a very long day. The two men, talking on the telephone, sound tired, their voices soft, flat, quiet.

—Why *were* you there?

—It's my property. I have a vested interest. And I was curious.

—And that's it?

—What else could it be?

—How about an attractive girl with a gun? Ben says. She's very tough so it might mean you're gay, but I think you like her.

You don't know how right you are.

—It's her, he says. The one from Miami.

—Really? Wow. I can see why you'd be interested in her.

—She was interested in me too—for a while. Told me today she was seeing someone back then. Thought it was over, but it wasn't.

—Let me guess. Now it is.

—Uh huh.

—I understand you wanting to see her again and all, but don't you think burning people is a little extreme?

—Not for true love.

Ben laughs.

They are quiet a moment, then Ben clears his throat.

—You been drinking?

—No. You?

—A little.

—How are you? Ben asks. It was one hell of a stressful day.

Daniel takes a long time to respond, and when he does, his voice is different—distant, small.

—I did have some strange thoughts today. Actually, they seemed like memories. They're really freaking me out.

—Your parents?

—Yeah.

When he was only seven, Daniel's parents both died when their house burned down. Just a few days before, a friend of Daniel's father had fixed a short in the wiring of their old wooden home, and everyone assumed the cause of the fire was electrical.

—It's not surprising, Ben says, his voice understanding, kind.

—Smell took me right back to it.

—Makes sense.

—No, it doesn't, he says. According to what my uncle has always told me, I wasn't there.

Chapter Eleven

—Where were we? Sam asks.

—You were trying to trick me into confessing, Daniel says.

It's late.

Sam has returned to Daniel's after processing the crime scene. A nocturnal creature like herself, she finds him on the computer, chatting with one of his students about an assignment.

—How was I doing?

He is seated at the small wooden table that holds the monitor, mouse, and keyboard, she hovering behind him.

—You almost had me, he says. Of course, now you're gonna have to start all over. Give me just a minute to finish this up and we can get back to it.

He types a couple of lines, then clicks a couple of times and turns back toward her, his foot bumping the CPU beneath the table as he does.

—How many students do you have?

—Two classes with about twenty in each.

—All online?

He nods.

—You've never seen them?

He shakes his head.

—You miss the classroom?

—Sometimes.

—Why did you quit teaching at such an early age and move out here in the middle of nowhere?

Tweeta had given her a lot of information about him. If he lies, she'll know it.

—I enjoyed teaching, but the call of pyromania was just too strong.

She laughs.

—Seriously, she says.

—I've come to the woods because I want to live deliberately, to front only the essential facts of life, and see if I can learn what it has to teach—and not, when I come to die, discover that I have not lived. I don't want to be one of those men who lead lives of quiet desperation and go to the grave with the song still in them.

She can tell he's quoting something, and it's vaguely familiar, but she can't quite place it.

—What's that from?

—Walden. They're Thoreau's words, but I mean them.

She nods.

—So that's why you're here? Climbing off the treadmill.

He nods.

—And it doesn't have anything to do with Graham Russell and Holly Bailey?

The change in him is obvious, though not overt. She had found her mark, pierced through the armor of his denial and defense.

It takes him a moment to gather himself, but once he does, he nods.

—I'm sure it does. Anything else you need to know?

She decides to leave that alone for now. He's too hurt, too closed for further questions on the subject to do any good. To continue pressing him about his best friend and girlfriend would only be cruel.

—So far you're the only person with any link to the murders. Any idea why?

He shakes his head.

—None. You wanna sit down?

—I've got to go. Any enemies?

He shakes his head again.

—A student unhappy with a grade maybe.

—Anybody fixated or obsessed with you?

—With *me*? he asks with a laugh. Haven't had any more problems with that since we shut down the fan club.

She laughs.

—What about someone from a case you consulted on?

—It was just a few, and as far as I know they're either dead or in prison.

—So you think it's a coincidence?

—That I happen to stumble onto one of the bodies and another one was hidden in a secluded field on a thousand-acre parcel my family happens to own? Yeah, I think it's a coincidence. If it happens again, I might be open to amending my position, but . . .

—It's not really your family's land, is it? she asks.

—What?

—It's just you now, right?

He nods.

—One person really isn't a family, is it?

She feels especially cruel, knowing she's hurting him, knowing part of it is personal curiosity, wondering how he'll respond.

—I just meant it's been in my family for a while now.

—You don't have any siblings?

He shakes his head.

—Parents?

—Dead.

—How?

His face lights up.

—Now I see where you're going, he says. You really are a—

—How'd you inherit this place and the money to live on? she asks. How'd your parents die, Daniel?

—You obviously know, he says. It was in a fire. They burned to death in a fire.

Sam gone.

Daniel alone.

Filled with equal parts anger and attraction, he's surprised at the response she evokes in him.

Though aware he's focusing his thoughts on Sam to keep memories of his parents at bay, it's nonetheless effective.

Since shortly after the accident that killed them, he's experienced images, flashes, fragments of memories, which according to his uncle are merely the product of his intense imagination.

As a child he had trusted his uncle more than his memory.

As an adult he has repressed what he convinced himself was just a form of childhood trauma.

Now because of the jolt delivered by his more recent experiences, he can no longer so easily dismiss his reawakened memories, but he can, for the moment, occupy himself with his conflicting responses to Sam.

He had been honest with her. He has come to the woods in an attempt to see what life can teach him, to discover what he should do with the remainder of his days. When Graham died he decided to do it for himself rather than let it be done for him.

At forty-four, just three years older than Daniel, Graham had suffered a massive heart attack, leaving his best friend behind, shocked at the shortness and random nature of life, determined to determine his own destiny. And it wasn't just Graham's death, but Holly's revelations and the disillusionment they brought.

The tiny paperback edition of Viktor Frankl's *Man's Search for Meaning* on the coffee table catches his eye, and he lifts it, easing it open, removing the small scrap of paper used as a bookmark, and begins to read. If Frankl and others could find meaning in a Nazi concentration camp, surely he could find it in the comfortable life he's carving out of the North Florida slash pines.

He's only read a few paragraphs when his computer alerts him to an incoming message. Dropping the book back on the table, he crosses the room to the computer and opens the message.

Immediately, a video pops up and fills the screen. Though the quality of the image is poor, what he's seeing is unmistakable.

Ben.

Bound and gagged, his hair and clothes wet, Ben is strapped to a chair in a dim room. Overturned gas cans litter the bare concrete around him, their contents pooling at his feet, shimmering with the glow of short and shrinking candles, their flames flickering near the flammable substance as they burn toward the floor.

Chapter Twelve

—Rachel? Hey. It's Daniel. I'm sorry to call so late, but I really need to speak with Ben.

Sam speeds through the empty streets of Bayshore, the unmarked's lights flashing, the siren silent, Daniel in the passenger seat on his cell, computer printouts in his lap.

Sam hadn't even made it to the highway when he called with news of the video, and she was back at his house in less than three minutes.

Now they're racing toward Pine Key, as an FDLE tech pulled from the crime scene is back at Louisiana Lodge examining Daniel's computer.

—You sure? Daniel says into the phone.

Sam frowns and shakes her head.

—You have any idea where he could be?

As he talks, Sam lifts one of the printouts of the video from his lap and examines it again.

—Okay. I'll call over there. Thanks . . . I will. You too . . . Okay. Good night.

When Daniel clicks off the call, Sam looks over at him, eyebrows raised.

—She went to bed before him. She thought he just hadn't come up yet, but now she can't find him. Said he might be at the office. He goes over sometimes late at night to edit. I'm calling over there now.

The dark night is damp, condensation clinging to the car as it cuts through the low-lying fog. All the traffic signals have been turned to caution lights, their warnings blinking to no one. Beneath streetlamps, the dew on the empty sidewalks shimmers, and Bayshore appears deserted.

Sam holds the picture and the steering wheel with both hands, glancing back and forth between the printout and the road.

—What kind of room you think that is? she asks.

—It's just too dark to—

—Could it be a garage?

He nods.

—Joel? It's Daniel. Is Ben there?

—What else has a bare concrete floor? Sam asks.

—Have you seen him at all tonight? . . . Really? What is it? . . . Okay. I'll be there in a few minutes.

—What? she asks as he ends the call.

—Haven't seen him but he did leave something for me marked 'urgent.'

He could die any minute, could be burned alive, engulfed in excruciating pain, and all he can think about is what he's left undone.

He'll never get to finish the Passover Project. Will it continue? Will Brian, Joel, and Esther get it completed? Or will all his work be for nothing?

Will Rachel remarry? Who'll replace him? Don't let it be David. Anybody but David. Is there enough life insurance? Savings?

His head throbs. The blow that had rendered him unconscious was bad enough, but now with the fumes it's unbearable.

Eyes stinging.

Nose and throat burning.

Brain feels swollen to several sizes too big for his skull.

It's like he's on a bad drug trip, and he continually swallows in an attempt to suppress the vomit pushing its way up his esophagus.

Who will find his porn? If it's Rachel, it'll be bad enough, but if anyone else—he can't even think about it. Daniel. He'll go and find it and get rid of it before anyone else sees it. He'll take care of Esther too. Probably even make sure my project gets finished.

Poor Esther. She's so fragile, so dependent on him.

He glances down at the candles. They're nearly burned down, their flames dangerously close to the floor and his fate.

Why is this happening? Who would do this?

A few more minutes and he'd never find out.

—What's going on? Brian Katz asks when Daniel and Sam rush into Pine Key Productions.

—Did something happen to Ben? Joel Reeves asks.

The two young men look like artists—Brian with long, wavy black hair, Joel with narrow black-frame glasses and a soul patch. They are dressed casually and act cool, but the tension in their voices contradicts their personas.

Joel is holding a manila envelope.

—Is that what he left for me?

—Yeah, Joel says, and hands it to him.

Daniel quickly glances at the front of the envelope before flipping it over and tearing into it. It reads: To Daniel From Ben URGENT!

—Who left it and when? Sam asks.

—I guess Ben did, Brian says. It had been slid under the door when I got back from grabbing some food.

—What time was that?

He shrugs.

—Hour ago, maybe.

Inside the envelope, Daniel finds a single sheet of printer paper with a typed letter on it.

Dearest Daniel,

I have even heard of thee, that the spirit of the gods is in thee, and that light and understanding and excellent wisdom is found in thee.

I know thou canst make interpretations and dissolve doubts. Read the writing on the wall. Interpret my dreams. Bear witness to my visions.

Don't fail me again, my friend.

To find Benjamin, read what the fingers of the man's hand wrote over the candlestick upon the wall upon the plaster of the wall of the king's palace.

—Come on, Daniel says to Sam.

Without waiting, he turns and leaves, Sam following after him.

—What's going on? Brian asks.

—If you hear anything from Ben, call me, she says, slinging a business card at them.

She quickly backs the car out of the oyster shell parking lot, the tires crunching, popping, shooting out shells.

—Where're we going? she asks.

—Ben's. Hurry.

She guns the car and it lurches onto the empty main road of the island.

—What is it? she asks.

—He's giving me a chance to find Ben before the candles burn down.

—You understood that shit in the letter?

He nods.

The island of Pine Key appears as empty as Bayshore, its fog-covered streets and the sand dunes surrounding them bathed in pale moonlight. Sea oats wave in the wind.

—Well?

—Take a left here, he says. It's quicker.

She does.

—It's from the biblical book of Daniel, he says.

—Cute.

—King Belshazzar made a great feast and during it a man's hand appeared and wrote a message for him on the wall. Daniel had to interpret what it said.

—Why're we going to Ben's?

—My guess is the message is written on his living room wall behind the menorah.

—The what?

—Seven branched candelabrum of Judaism.

—Oh.

—Hurry. He doesn't have long.

Chapter Thirteen

As Daniel tries to get Rachel to the door, Sam is on her phone lining up backup and forensics support.

The island is breezy, the air around them thick with the briney smell of the bay and the monotonous sound of the surf as the Gulf's tide rolls rhythmically in and out. In and out. In and out.

—What is it? Rachel asks as she opens the door. What's wrong?

—It's gonna be okay, he says, putting his arm around her. I promise. But we think someone has Ben and we're trying to find him.

—*Has* him? she asks, panic in her voice. Whatta you mean?

As she continues to press Daniel for information, he gently leads her into the dark living room. She is wearing a sheer white nightgown and negligee that shows off the curves of her lovely body, the light color complimenting her olive complexion. Sam watches how he is with her, the way he gives comfort and keeps her from falling apart. She appreciates what he's doing, admires his skill, but experiences an irrational jealousy at his arm being around her, his hand on the dark skin of her arm.

Don't be silly. You have no right. Get a grip.

When Daniel flips on the lights of the living room, Rachel passes out.

Catching her, he eases her down to the floor and rushes over to read the message.

Above the mantle, on the wall behind the large menorah, written in what looks to be blood are these words: Then the king went to his palace, and passed the night fasting: neither were instruments of music brought before him: and his sleep went from him.

—What's it mean? Sam asks.

Daniel reads it again, then closes his eyes.

As he does, Sam says a little prayer.

—Grab me a Bible, he says.

They begin looking around the room.

—I don't see one, she says.

On a built-in mahogany bookshelf in the corner, he finds a Hebrew Bible and begins to flip through it.

—That's a Bible? she asks.

—Hebrew.

—You read Hebrew?

—Yeah, but it's in English. I meant it's a Hebrew Bible.

—What is—

—As in Judaism.

—Huh?

—Old testament.

—Oh. What is it?

—I'm pretty sure it's when King Darius had Daniel put in the lions' den and couldn't sleep. Here it is, he says. Daniel six-eighteen.

—How are *you* in a lions' den? I don't get it.

—I don't think he's being that literal. It's a clue to where Ben is.

—Which is?

—A lions' den.

—Where would that be? A zoo?

—Maybe.

—Are there any around here?

He shrugs.

She punches in Preacher's number.

—Are there any zoos around here?

As she talks to the sheriff, Daniel looks around the house, stepping over and peering into the garage. Both Ben's and Rachel's cars are inside, leaving little room for anything else.

—Zoo World on Panama City Beach, she says.

—Anything closer?

She repeats the question into the phone, then waits.

—Would they have lions? she asks, then to Daniel, There's a family outside of Bayshore who have an animal farm and petting zoo. He thinks they have some lions.

—We need to get someone over there.

—He's on the causeway headed over here, she says. He'll get a deputy dispatched.

—Better get Bay County Sheriff's Department to check Zoo World just to be safe.

They both jump as someone bangs on the front door. Turning, they see Rachel is coming around.

—I'll see to her, Sam says. You get the door.

He does. It's Brian and Joel, both men looking awkward and anxious.

—What's going on? Brian asks.

They follow him into the living room, stopping as they see the writing on the wall.

—What the fuck? Joel says.

—Stay with Rachel, Daniel says. We don't have time to explain right now.

—Pine County sheriff's on the way, Sam adds. Wait for him.

—Where're we goin'? Sam asks when they're back in the car.

—I'm not sure, but I had to get out of there.

—Why?

—I need to think.

—You don't think it's the farm?

—In case it's not, he says. Let's drive back into Bayshore. I don't think there's anything on the island that would be it.

Lights flashing, siren on this time, she speeds through Pine Key and onto the causeway.

A few minutes later, her phone rings. She answers and listens.

—They have lions, she says, but no den, no Ben.

—Fuck.

—It's okay, we'll find him.

He closes his eyes. Think. Come on.

As he tries to figure out what it might be, Sam explains to Preacher more about what they're looking for.

—Have them search Ben's house and office, Daniel says.

—I've already told them.

—And get everyone to look at the video—or at least a picture of it, he says. See what we're missing.

—It's taken care of, she says. I've got this. You just concentrate on the meaning of the message.

Think. Where. Where. Where. The more he tries, the more blank his mind becomes. Fear seizes him and he can feel the panic begin.

—We're out of time, he says when she hangs up. I let him die.

—No you didn't. Now, don't think about anything but figuring out the goddam clue. Okay?

—Lions' den.

Her phone rings again.

—Agent Michaels, she says, then is silent for a few moments before saying, That all we're gonna get? . . . Okay. Thanks.

She looks over at Daniel.

—What is it? he asks.

—The video came from Ben's email account, she says. It was forwarded through several free Yahoo accounts. No way to trace it.

Daniel nods.

—That's no surprise. We knew he was smart.

—He'll fuck up, she says.

—I wouldn't count on it.

—Just hoping.

—If it's not an actual lions' den, what else could it be? As soon as he says it, he has a thought. What about a school mascot?

—That's good, she says, but Bayshore's the Sharks. What about Franklin County schools? Or Gulf? Or Bay?

—Gators, rams, bulldogs, tornadoes, sea hawks. No lions. That's it, he says.

—What?

—Bayshore Christian Academy, he says. They're the lions.

—The Christians are the *lions?*

—And they're not even being ironic, he says, shaking his head.

—But they don't have a football team.

—They've got other sports, he says, and I bet you somewhere on that campus they've got a lions' den.

Chapter Fourteen

They reach the small school just behind Preacher, a Pine County deputy, and a Bayshore patrol car. Preacher's trunk pops open, and when he gets out of his car he goes directly to it. He reaches into it and comes out with a sledgehammer.

—You better be right, he says to Daniel. Fundamentalists feel persecuted enough as it is. I break down their doors for nothing, I'll lose votes.

—This is it, Daniel says. It's got to be.

—Well, just keep thinking, in case it's not, Sam says.

—Where do we start? Preacher asks.

—The gym.

The glass doors of the gym are chained. Preacher tries to bust open the padlock, but after three attempts decides to break the glass.

When the door shatters, he clears away the jagged shards with the wooden handle of the hammer and they step through.

They find the gym dark and empty, their footfalls echoing on the hardwood court.

The patrolman flips on the lights, but the gym remains dim for a long time as the florescent lamps warm up.

—Check the home locker room, Preacher says.

—It'd make more sense if it's the visitors, Sam says. Entering the lions' den.

—Right, he says. You're right.

And so she is.

From beneath the locked door, they can smell the fumes of gasoline and see what looks like the flicker of candlelight.

—What if it's booby-trapped? the deputy asks.

—It won't be, Daniel says.

—How the hell do you know that? he asks.

—This isn't one of his murders, he says. He's doing this for a different, very specific reason.

—Oh, yeah? What's that?

—To get Daniel involved in the case, Sam says.

Preacher swings the sledgehammer at the lock and the door swings open and bangs against the wall behind it.

Ben is there, moments away from being burned to death.

As they rush in, the deputy kicks one of the candles, and an airy whoosh is followed by flames spreading in every direction.

—Get out. Get out, Preacher yells.

The two cops turn and rush out. Daniel and Sam continue toward Ben, but stop as they see Preacher grab his chair and begin to pull him out. Each taking a side, they help pull, all four of them falling into the gym, the wooden chair breaking as they crash to the floor and the locker room behind them is engulfed in flames.

—So I guess you're on the case, Sam says.

Daniel smiles.

They're leaning against her car in the school parking lot as firefighters put out the last of the flames in the locker room and EMTs make sure Ben is okay.

—Will you work with me on this? she asks. I know you're retired or whatever.

He nods.

—I don't how much help I can be. And there's something you should know.

He doesn't want to tell her, hates for her to hear how weak he is, but knows he must.

The parking lot is full of emergency vehicles. The school buildings and the church beside them are bathed in bright white light, accented by rapid flashes of red and blue, the elongated shadows of first responders dancing through them like figures formed from a child's hand and a flashlight inside a sheet tent.

She turns from watching all the activity in front of them. She looks so tired, so small and vulnerable, yet so beautiful.

He wants to kiss her.

—Yeah? she says.

He decides not to tell her and tries to think of something witty to say, but is too tired to come up with anything.

—Nothing.

—I'm too tired for this shit, she says. Just tell me now and get it over with.

—Sometimes . . . I, ah, get . . . I have little episodes.

—*Episodes?* she says, her voice so loud a couple of emergency workers turn toward them. Sorry, she adds, lowering her voice. Whatta you mean by *episode?*

He hesitates another moment, then just blurts it out.

—Panic attacks.

—How often?

He shrugs, attempting nonchalance.

—Couple times a week.

—What causes them?

—They come out of nowhere and at odd times.

—How long they last?

—Not long, he says. Ten minutes, maybe.

She nods.

—Thanks for telling me.

—They're not as bad as they sound.

—We all have shit to deal with.

They are quiet a moment, watching as Preacher works the crowd that has gathered, looking into eyes, pressing flesh, listening to concerns, and answering questions.

—So why you think this guy wants you involved in the investigation so badly?

He shrugs.

—According to his message tonight, to interpret what he does.

—Wonder how he got fixated on you in the first place? she says. You work any high-profile cases, do any media back when you were consulting?

He shakes his head.

—I was always way, *way* behind the scenes.

—It could be a former student of yours, or someone whose case you worked. More likely someone who read your book.

—I did a little media for the release.

—We'll have to search for a connection.

Daniel's phone rings. He withdraws it from his pocket and answers it.

—Do I have your attention now?

Eyes wide, Daniel motions to Sam.

—It's him, he mouths.

The voice on the phone is digitally altered and sounds distorted and demonic.

—You certainly do.

—Good. We have important work to do. Tonight was nothing. Just a little fun. The silly little cops can investigate, but they won't find anything. Ben was unconscious the whole time, it's not real blood on the wall, I used candles and gas from Ben's house and the school, and I didn't leave any prints or trace evidence behind.

—What—

—Oh yeah, and I'm calling from a stolen cell phone. I'm on the move and when we finish our little conversation I'll toss it in the bay, but they can waste their time trying to trace it if they want to.

—I'll pass that along. What exactly do you want me to do?

—Read the writing on the wall. Be worthy of your name and bear witness to the mighty work I will wrought. I have a vision. Oh, you should see what I see—and you will. Be faithful, Daniel, and I will show you great and wondrous works you knowest not of.

Before Daniel can say anything else, the connection is severed, the caller gone.

—Wasn't long enough for a trace, Sam says.

—It was a stolen cell phone. From what he said, he's aware of investigative techniques.

She nods.

—Who isn't, these days? He's not going to leave us anything to work with, is he?

—Nothing physical, he agrees, but plenty psychological and religious—he'll leave us clues without meaning to.

—You want the fuckin' feds taking over your case? Stan Winston is saying, voice thick with sleep, tone sharp with irritation.

She woke him up, but is that all? Was someone sleeping beside him? Does he feel guilty? Doubtful. He might feel caught, though, his privacy invaded.

—Of course not, but—

Exhausted, she's driving back to her sad, lonely little room at the Driftwood after having dropped Daniel off at Louisiana Lodge. They'd had a good talk on the drive back from the crime scene, and she had enjoyed watching him work earlier, liked the way she could see his mind teasing at the strands of the puzzle—and now he's all she can think about.

She'd called to give Stan a quick update and to suggest they go ahead and call in the FBI for help with what looked to be a methodical, compulsive, ritualistic killer, but she should've known better.

—That's what'll happen, he says. You call them in and we're out.

That's not true, but she can't say it. Any problems Stan's had with federal agencies has more to do with his ego than how they operate.

The night seems even darker now, and she fights to keep her eyelids open as her high beams pierce the remaining wisps of fog scattered along the rural highway like small gatherings of ghosts.

—I just want their help, she says.

She knows enough to know when to ask for help—when to call in reinforcements. It's early, true, but she can already tell that this will require far more than just her, and as much as she's longed to have a case like this, she'd rather lose the case than lives because she tried to lone wolf it.

—They don't help, they take over. And how many times you think that's gotta happen before someone says we're not needed? You don't even know what you've got yet.

—Yes I do. I do.

—You don't even know if the two victims are part of the same case. They're pretty damn different. They may have nothing to do with each other.

—They do. I know it. This one's big and bad and it's gonna get a lot worse.

—If you can't handle it, I'll send someone else, but no feds. I wanna keep this in-house.

How could she have let this prick prevent her from having something with Daniel? How could she have ever been with him at all?

—I can handle it, she says. But I'm gonna need help.

Why do I always go for the egotistical, narcissistic assholes? Not always. What about Daniel? What *is* that about? Maybe I've finally learned a few things.

—Fine, Stan says. Use our people. Hell, you're supposed to be the expert in cases like this one. Feds should be calling us. Anyway, call in favors from individual feds if you have to, but nothing else. See what you've got before you start giving cases away.

Chapter Fifteen

—I'm not sure how much of this will apply, Sam says. I think we're dealing with the rare exception that makes what I'm about to share with you the general rule, but it'll help if we all have a basic understanding.

It's the following morning, and they are gathered in the conference room of the sheriff's department—Preacher Gibson, Steve Phillips, a couple of deputies, a couple of Bayshore and Pine Key police officers, and a volunteer fireman who's studying to be an arson investigator.

—I've contacted state and federal agencies. For now, they will assist us, but if this turns out to be what we think it could be, the FBI will come in and take the lead. For now, I'll be working with criminal profilers, forensic psychologists, and other consultants and experts. We'll study every behavioral and forensic detail of this case and develop a personality snapshot of our unknown subject, or UNSUB. What I'm sharing with you is just general background info on serial arsonists. It's very important that you remember that.

She has had only a few hours' sleep, her eyes sting and her head throbs, but she's excited, adrenaline pumping through her. She can't believe this is only the beginning of the second day of the investigation. So much has happened. It's all moving so fast. Too fast.

A speakerphone sits in the center of the long conference table. In approximately half an hour, it will ring and Michelle Barnes will share with the assembled task force the lab findings so far.

Sam passes out a report she's prepared on serial arsonists, and everyone begins to read through it. As in most of these situations, she's the only woman in the room.

When she had first walked in, she had undergone the usual inspection, the eyes of the cops lingering on every inch of her body, checking her out, sizing her up, making faces and whispering to each other followed by little bursts of laughter.

If they only knew what's hidden beneath these clothes, they'd find it difficult to keep their eggs and bacon down, and I wouldn't have to put up with this shit.

—As you can see, arson is the fastest-growing crime in America. Over fifty percent of all fires are incendiary or at least suspicious.

The conference room is long and narrow, the side walls marred by the conference chairs scuffing them when people push back from the table. On one end an enlarged framed version of the Pine County Sheriff's logo hangs between the American and Florida's flags. The opposite wall holds a projection screen and a large map of Pine County.

Steve raises his hand, and she begrudgingly acknowledges him.

—Aren't most fires started by firemen? he asks, his face full of mock sincerity.

A couple of the cops snicker.

—Bite my big long hose, Jerry Douglas, the volunteer fireman says, giving Phillips the finger.

Even in his seated position, it is obvious Jerry Douglas is a very tall man, which along with his curly hair and bushy mustache makes him look like a fireman. All he needs is suspenders and he could be a poster boy, or, if suspenders and no shirt, a calendar boy—Mr. September. Though not particularly attractive, from the size of him, especially his hands, she guesses his comment about the length of his hose is no exaggeration.

—I'm serious, Steve says.

—Oh, fuck you, Phillips, Douglas says.

Gibson doesn't say anything, and Sam is grateful. To truly have the authority and respect to lead the task force, she's got to demand it for herself.

—There's a monster out there killing people in the most painful manner imaginable, she says. I'm here to stop him. You're here to help me. If you can't do that like professionals, then leave now. We don't have time for anything else.

—But Jerry here's not a professional, Steve says.

—You're gone, Steve, Sam says. Go work your other cases.

Shock fills his face as the room grows quiet, and he whips around toward Gibson.

Back my play, old man. If he doesn't, she might as well resign now. Why did it always have to be this way? She hated having to prove herself every single day, hated the way assholes like Phillips felt the need to test her.

Gibson nods and she exhales, relief emanating from deep within her.

—But Sheriff— Steve begins.

—I don't have time for this right now, Detective, Gibson says. We'll talk about it later.

Steve stands, seething, and slowly walks toward the door.

Without waiting until he's gone, Sam continues.

—Notice the age of most arsonists, she says. Half are under eighteen and half of those are between ten and fourteen. If adults, they're usually in their twenties and rarely over thirty-five.

Having to pass Sam to leave the room, Phillips walks even more slowly, his shoulder brushing against her.

—Ninety percent of arsonists are male, she continues, ignoring him, and seventy-five to eighty percent are white. Most arsonists are from lower-income or working-class families where the father is absent or abusive and the mother has a history of emotional problems.

She pauses, but no one says anything. There's palpable tension in the room, and she's not sure how to relieve the pressure. Did what just happened earn her respect or make her enemies?

—Serial arsonists are typically social misfits and have interpersonal relationship issues—especially with the opposite sex. They are usually physically and emotionally weaker than their peers, choose work that is subservient, but resent it and feel oppressed by bosses or authority figures. They often have learning problems and a vast majority of them have a subnormal IQ in the seventy to ninety range, with about twenty percent mentally handicapped. A few—and this is important to remember, especially in this case—are geniuses, which negates nearly everything else I've just said.

At first, Steve sits at his desk, fidgeting, the angry energy coming out as constant movement.

Fuckin' uptight cunt. Who the fuck's she think she is?

He's waiting for an apology. Surely Gibson'll send her out here to make things right or come himself.

Stick up her ass. Can't take a joke. Bitch's got no business being a cop. And why the fuck would she take up for Douglas anyway? Fuckin' loser.

After a while, he realizes no one's coming out to ask his forgiveness, and he's too pissed to sit still any longer.

She's gonna regret this. They all will. He's got a pretty good idea who the killer is, but they kicked him out before he could tell them. He was waiting for the best moment to play his hand. He just wanted to see what the dealer had first.

Standing and snatching up the file folder from his desktop, he thinks, I'll just catch the bastard myself. Wrap him up in a bow and bring him back here. Then they can all kiss my ass.

—When you hear why most arsonists set fires, you'll see why what we're dealing with is so different, Sam says. Look on page three. Forty-one percent of arson is committed as an act of revenge, thirty percent just for excitement, seven percent is vandalism, five percent is for profit, and seventeen percent is to conceal another crime. Of course, it's early and we don't know a lot yet, but even if one or two of these apply to what our perp is doing, they're secondary. He may be seeking revenge, but fire isn't a way to conceal his crime. It *is* his crime. The act itself is the thing. It's significant and meaningful to him.

—There really doesn't seem to be a category for what this guy's doing, Douglas says.

—Exactly, Sam says. I'm not so sure we're dealing with an arsonist as much as a compulsive, ritualistic killer whose weapon is fire.

—You saying these are motiveless murders? one of the Bayshore police asks.

Sam shakes her head.

—There's no such thing. Just because none of the usual motives apply doesn't mean there isn't one. Compulsive ritual killers have motives every bit as strong as any other criminal, maybe more, but they are only known to the perp. They're internal. They have a reason for everything they do.

—How the hell do we catch a killer like that?

—It'd help to figure out what's driving him, she says. His compulsion. His pre-crime stresser. His trigger. What sets him off.

—How?

—Through the clues he's intentionally and unintentionally leaving. The crime scene tells us everything we need to know. We've just got to read it right.

—You said 'crime scene,' singular, Gibson says. I take it you think the depot is the one we need to be trying to read.

She nods.

—The Louisiana Landing one was him getting ready, practicing, experimenting, preparing.

—If it was even him.

—It was, but the depot is his beginning. I'm not saying the other can't tell us anything, just not nearly as much.

—Thank God you're here, Gibson says.

She laughs, pauses a moment, then continues.

—We've got to ask questions of our crime scene. Why were things arranged the way they were? We've got to develop a victimology. Who are his victims? Why does he choose them? We need to reconstruct as best we can the behavior of our UNSUB at the scene. Was the body left where it was killed, or dumped in another location? Michelle will have to tell us for sure, but I'm betting our victim was killed at the depot. Why did he choose the depot? What's its significance?

She pauses another moment, but the only sound in the room is the scratch of pen on paper.

—We generally ask what damage was done to the victim. In this case, he almost completely destroyed the body. Why? Why is he wiping out their identity? If the Louisiana Landing victim is connected, and I believe he is, it's obvious he was attempting to get the accelerant and timing just right, practicing—for this. This is what he's been working toward. Why? What does it mean? How does he choose his victims? We don't even know who the victims are yet, but once we do, we'll be able to tell a lot more.

—Remember, everything he's doing is meeting a need. What is it? And then there's the physical evidence at the scene. Why leave what he did? How much was intentional, how much was accidental? Why did he remove only the victim's belt, watch, ring, and shoes? He's got a very specific reason. This is particularly important. What did he do at the scene he didn't have to? What did he go out of his way to accomplish that was not necessary to the murder? This is his signature, and we've got to interpret it to catch him.

Chapter Sixteen

After a quick break, everyone gathers back in the conference room, joined by Michelle Barnes via speakerphone.

—I wish I had more for you, Michelle is saying.

—We'll take anything you got, Sam says. And we're grateful to get it.

—The problem is the body from the train depot is too badly burned, Michelle continues, and the other body, which is less burned, is far more decayed.

—Fuckin' Florida, one of the deputies says. So hot and humid it melts the flesh off corpses.

—I'm surprised the dang mosquitoes didn't carry the body off, another one says.

—Well, like I said, our external findings were nearly nil—of course, that's not that uncommon in cases of fire. We've got no way to identify the victims except through dental records, and we've got to have some idea whose to look at.

—What about gender?

—One woman, one man, she says.

—The body in the depot?

—Female, she says.

Michelle pauses a moment, and the sound of turning pages comes through the phone.

—I do have a couple of goodies for you, though.

Sam thinks *goodies* is an odd choice of words for autopsy and lab results on burned and rotted bodies, but tries not to show it.

—We found soot deposits in the respiratory tract, esophagus, and stomach, Michelle says, and elevated CO-Hb values in the blood.

—Which means? Gibson asks.

Sam knows, but she lets Michelle say it.

—The victims were alive at the time they were burned. They breathed in the smoke and heat.

—God have mercy, he says.

—He's burning them alive, Michelle says. He's watching them in unimaginable agony and enjoying himself. There's no sign of ligatures or cuffs and shackles on either of the bodies.

He's drugging them. Incapacitating them so he can concentrate on what he's doing.

—I think he's giving them something, Michelle says. And I hope to know what it is within another day or two.

—Good. That's good.

—And we might just have something we can get an ID from.

—Oh yeah? Sam says, her quickening pulse and breath showing in her excited voice. What's that?

—The Louisiana Landing victim. Since he wasn't burned as badly. Gives us more to work with. He was wearing a necklace under his shirt. I think there's enough left. We're working on it. Will let you know as soon as we have something.

—Thanks, Michelle, Sam says. I really—

—There's one more thing, and I think you'll find it very interesting. The killer used accelerants in both instances, but different ones—the first was an easy to find fuel like you'd expect, common gasoline—but on the body in the train depot, he switched to diesel consistent with the kind used in locomotives.

—What the hell're you doin'? Ben asks.

—Research, Daniel says.

They are in the editing suite of Ben's Pine Key Productions studio with Esther Behr, the producer, Brian Katz, the camera man, and Joel Reeves, the editor. The room is dark and cool, track lighting mounted on the ceiling illuminating only three spots—the editing desk the three employees are huddled around, a bookshelf holding mostly owner's manuals for the editing hardware and software, and the computer table in the corner where Daniel is scrolling through pages and pages of information about pyromania and ritual killers.

—For the Passover Project?

He can see that it's not. He's making a point. Ben has hired Daniel to write the introductions and endings for the Passover Project, a documentary on the miraculous survival of the Jewish people throughout history.

—I really didn't think you'd come in to work today, Daniel says. You feeling okay?

—I thought you came by to check on me, Ben says. Your internet out again?

—I still can't believe you guys didn't call me, Esther says.

—Things were happening pretty fast, Brian says.

Joel turns and looks at Daniel's screen.

—He's obviously doing research so he'll have something to talk to Agent Michaels about.

—Discovering bodies, Ben says, showing up at crime scenes, researching the murders, playing cat and mouse with the killer, she'll be happy to talk to him—in an interview room.

The others laugh.

—Still don't remember anything? Daniel asks.

—I was unconscious. I'm not going to.

Esther rolls her chair over next to Daniel and begins to read.

—Approximately eighty-five percent of compulsive killers are white males.

The men look at each other.

—If you go to death row, she says to Daniel, I'll stand by you. Even marry you.

Her flirting with Daniel is as continuous as it is harmless, and at ten years his junior, married, and devoutly religious, he wonders how she would act if he ever responded to her overtures.

—You'll have to get in line, Brian says. He'll have all kinds of groupies wanting to get all conjugal and shit.

The others have turned from what they were editing and are listening intently.

—Sixty-two percent kill strangers, she continues, and seventy-one percent operate in a specific location and don't travel around. To fit the FBI profile, you have to complete three separate murders with a cooling off period between them and have a particular method.

—Doesn't it bother you that someone like that is right here with us? Joel says.

Esther and Brian laugh.

—I didn't mean Daniel. Here in our community.

—Well, actually, he appears to be working over around Bayshore, Daniel says. I think you Pine Key cats are safe for now. I'm thinking I should move out here.

—No goys allowed, Joel says.

—Even the one who saved Ben's life? Daniel asks.

—Depends if you're the killer, Brian says. What else does it say?

—They typically have over-productive imaginations that started in their dysfunctional childhoods when they began to fantasize because of feelings of isolation and inadequacy. Usually don't bond with anyone because of some sort of abuse by their families. The three most common behaviors in the childhood of a budding serial killer are daydreaming, compulsive masturbation, and isolation.

—Uh oh, Joel says.

—Yeah, Brian agrees. That's all of us.

—They're virtually impossible to detect, appearing quite normal in their day-to-day lives. That rules you guys out. Not a normal one in the lot of you.

Daniel nods.

—It's a misconception that they're psychotics hearing voices and hallucinating, he says. They're people without consciences who have a need to control and dominate. They have violent and abnormal behaviors, but wear masks of sanity in their everyday lives.

Chapter Seventeen

—I looked into getting a crematory a few years back, Joe Kent is
saying, but the consultants I spoke with said I'd have to do a hundred
and twenty-five cremations each year just to break even. Hell, I don't
do that many more total funerals.

Joe Kent, a fourth generation funeral director at Kent's Funeral
Home in Bayshore, is an enormous man, too large for Steve to say
with any accuracy, but well over four-hundred pounds. He's crammed
into a large La-Z-Boy recliner, his bulk billowing his blouse around
him, in the parlor of his three-story Victorian house that serves as
both his business and living quarters. A box fan on high is directly in
front of him, but in spite of it and the arctic air whistling out of the
loud, monotonous window unit nearby, he is sweating profusely.

—No, I take all my cremations over to Panama City, he adds.

Thick glasses help further obscure hooded eyes beneath long
hairs swooped over a mostly bald head. The oversized mitts of his
hands hold a cane, which he taps on the floor often, and a sweat-
soiled handkerchief, which is constantly used to dab his forehead,
temples, and upper lip.

—Only one place over there'll do it for me. Most of them'll only
do their own. They say it's liability, but I think they think they're too
good for us small-town boys. Same's true of Tallahassee, except no
one over there'll do it for me. Crazy as it sounds, I got a body in Tallahassee needs cremating, I gotta drive it all the way back to Panama
City, have it done, then transport it back to Tallahassee.

Like many truly elephantine people Steve has been around, Joe
Kent smells of BO and shit, and he wonders if they're just too big to
be able to clean themselves very well.

—They got special technicians or whatever to do the, ah, proce-
dure? he asks.

—Oh, yes sir, indeed, Joe Kent says, his words coming out in the
labored breaths of the obese. Damn EPA and the state are so far up
a man's ass these days. The operators of the units have to be certi-
fied. They get special training and then go for continuing education.
Crematory itself is subject to a goddam mountain of codes and regu-
lations. A goddam mountain. They have to be inspected and maintained ever so often. Upgraded constantly. You know how crazy the
damn state and federal governments are these days. Not too long ago
they came around worried about mercury poisoning from cremated
decedents' teeth fillings. It's always something.

Though originally designed by his great-grandfather as a funeral
home downstairs with family living quarters upstairs, Joe Kent, too
large to climb the stairs, lives in the parlor on the first floor. Hidden by sliding panel doors, the dim room is filled with dust-covered,
outdated furniture and the clutter of clothes scattered about, piles of
newspapers, and carry-out cartons from local eating establishments.

—Any of those technicians live over here?

—None I know of. But there was a retired fellow over to the
home at Sue Ann's.

Sue Ann Grambling converted her house into a retirement home
and had six or ten old people living with her.

—Asked me for a job while back. Said he could do cremations,
but he was an odd bird. Had an accent. Stared a lot. Held his mouth

open slightly when he wasn't talking. Would make my customers uncomfortable, and like I said, I didn't need no cremator 'cause, well, I got no crematory.

—You remember his name?

He looks up at the high ceiling, squints for a minute, then back down and shakes his head.

—You tell me who's staying over there and I'll tell you which one he is.

—Will do, Steve says. And as far as you know there's never been a crematorium in Bayshore or hereabouts?

Joe Kent shakes his enormous head, his jowls jiggling from side to side.

—I didn't say that, he says. I said *I* never had one. My competition did before he shut down. Come to think of it, that may be why he went out of business—losing so much damn money on his crematory. He had no head for business whatsoever. Dumb bastard. His crematory was a piece of shit too. Tried to sell it when he closed up, but no one would have it.

—Who was it? Steve asks, excitement in his voice. He still live here?

—Believe he moved up to Alabama. Didn't last here too long at all. No, sir, this business is a lot harder than it looks. Let me tell you.

—What was his name? Any kin still livin' here?

—Wendell Marshall. Had no relations I'm aware of.

The synapses in Steve's brain arc as he thinks about the old Marshall building out on County Road 232.

—Where was his place?

—That's the other thing. He was too far out of town. No one wants to drive all the way out past the city limits when they're bereaved. They just don't.

—Thanks, Mr. Kent, he says, rising up from his chair, trying to keep from running.

—No problem, young man. This about those burned bodies y'all found?

—Did we make a mistake with this one? Gibson asks. Maybe they all can't be saved.

—They can all be saved, Hugh Wilson says. Just takes longer for some than others.

Preacher's experience as a sheriff, even of a small county, has taught him differently, but he doesn't argue with the older man.

The two aging men, one in the fall of his life, the other in winter, sit beside each other on a front porch swing in early evening, the heat of the day giving way to a fallish breeze winding its way through the cypress trees down near the river.

—You have any idea where he is?

Wilson shakes his bald, wrinkled head.

When River Scott had been caught setting fires, Hugh Wilson had pleaded with the sheriff not to arrest him, to instead let him come be a resident of the Wilson Family Boys Home. On the condition that he undergo regular counseling with Dr. Rainy, Gibson had agreed. Had he known then the extent to which the troubled teen had torched his world, including large buildings and small animals, he probably wouldn't have agreed, but couldn't say for sure.

Having been instrumental in helping Preacher remove the irony from his name, Wilson has no small influence on the man that the boy he helped so long ago became.

Perhaps too much. I trusted him over my own judgment.

He had allowed himself to be manipulated because of admiration and appreciation of this man, hoping he could have the same effect on River Scott as he had on him and so many other boys over the years.

A retired superintendent of schools, Wilson's dream of operating a home for troubled boys became a reality nearly twenty years ago when he left the school system. Since then, a few hundred boys had passed through—most of them on their way to better lives.

As Hugh Wilson slowly raises his arthritic, misshapen hand to rub the top of his head, Preacher is startled to realize just how old he is.

Hell, *I'm* old. He's ancient.

—He have any family in the area? Preacher asks.

—Mother's in prison. He never knew his father.

The creaking swing holding the two men hangs on the front porch of the boys home, a huge, three-story dorm-style house with a gymnasium built onto the back of it. The wooden house, built of boards made from cypress trees growing on the property, is flawed, filled with faulty wiring and plumbing, and has very few straight lines. It was raised in a few consecutive weekends by several people in the community, some of whom had worked for Hugh, all of whom loved and respected the man.

—Any thoughts on where he might go?

Hugh shakes his head.

—I was sad to see him leave. Wish he'd've at least said goodbye, but he turned eighteen recently, so like I told Dr. Rainy, he's not a runaway.

—You hear from him, you let me know.

Usually asking and entreating, it's the most direct he's ever been with his mentor, and it feels odd, like disrespecting a parent for the first time.

—And find out which of the boys he connected with here. I wanna talk to 'em. It's in all our best interests that we find him first—especially his.

Chapter Eighteen

The old Marshall building on County Road 232 sits back off the road, a weed-infested circular drive in front of it. A large For Sale sign near the road hangs at an angle, the scattered pockmarks of buckshot splintering the wood beneath the paint.

In need of a good cleaning, a few coats of paint, and some yard work, the place is not in bad shape for as long as it's been empty.

It's late evening, the sun quickly descending, when Steve pulls around back, parks, and gets out.

Walking toward the back door, he unsnaps the thumb break on his holster, letting his hand linger next to the butt of the comforting .45 semiautomatic.

Even if the perp is using this place to burn the bodies, he's probably not here. Still, you can never be too careful.

His heart is racing nearly as fast as his mind. If he's right and this is the place, everyone'll see what a cunt the state cop is. Vindication.

When he reaches for the knob of the back door and finds it unlocked, he almost calls for backup, but fuck 'em. He can handle whatever's on the other side of the door.

The dusty room he steps into smells of mildew and is shadowy in the little sunlight able to penetrate the sliver of smeary window showing through the faded curtains.

—Pine County Sheriff's Department, he yells. Is anyone here?

There's no response.

—If you're staying here illegally, I'm not here for you. You can come out and be on your way. I won't jam you up. I'm here on another matter.

There's still no response, and though everything is perfectly quiet and still, he believes he senses someone in the darkness, a presence that makes the hair on his arms stand up.

Stepping back outside and to his car, he returns to the room with a large flashlight, his gun drawn this time.

The room has a tile floor with a drain in the center and large stainless steel counters and sinks along one wall. Obviously used for embalming, the room is now empty except for a single gurney in one corner.

With his back to the side wall, Steve lets the beam of his flashlight play across the room, over the counters and sinks, and along the other walls. The front wall has two doors in it, one on each side, both open into dark, empty carpeted hallways. To his left, through an archway in the back corner, he sees another room with a large steel object his beam reflects off of.

Figuring it's the crematory, he moves toward it, edging along the wall, surprised at how frightened he is. The place is eerie, but it's not that. It's the fact that he knows he's not alone. Well, doesn't know it, but believes it.

Stepping into the room, he sees that the door of the crematory is open. In his excitement, he rushes over to it and looks in.

And this one impetuous act costs him his life.

Movement.

Spinning.

Turning.

Flashlight beam. Illumination. Overexposure.

Frightening.

Ghostly face.

Rushing toward him.

Striking. Stabbing. Piercing.

Final image—light-flash and heat seared on his retinas.

Bizarre. Haunting. Horrific.

He fires a shot but it ricochets off the block wall behind his attacker. Then he feels the scorching rip, split, and tear of his flesh as the long metal object is thrust in repeatedly, then shock, then he's falling backward onto the tray, being shoved into the crematory, then nothing.

—Why use train fuel as part of the accelerant? Sam asks. It's highly significant, right?

—Highly, Lars Darcy, the FDLE criminal profiler says. He brought it with him, right? There was none at the scene.

—Right.

Sam is on her cell phone as she walks into Jordan's, the small café in downtown Bayshore. Though the sign says that the hostess will seat her, she seats herself at a table in the front next to the plate glass window with an expansive view of Main Street. She needs privacy and no one is seated in the vicinity. She's come to grab a very quick bite to eat before returning to the office—a desk in the records room Gibson had given her the use of.

—It helps make the location even more significant, Lars says. Ties the tracks and the depot together with the act. It has something to do with a train. It could be as simple as his victim's last journey—he's sending them on a train ride to hell—or something so elaborate we can't even begin to imagine.

—What about the things he removed before he burned the guy, and the way he left them?

—Again, I'd say highly significant. I'm sure in his mind it connects to what he's doing, relates in some way—i.e. these things aren't allowed where you're going. Something like that. Of course, it could be anything. I'm just saying it's meaningful for him and a message for us.

—What should I do?

—Let Daniel help you. I've worked with him before. He's good—and not just on the religious stuff. The last time I talked to him he was working on a degree in forensic psychology. I'd do some research on trains and depots and tracks. What about the crime scene? Have you been back?

—Not yet.

—You need to go during the estimated time of death, he says. Was it at night?

—Yeah.

—Take someone with you.

Suddenly, she wishes she'd handled things differently with steroid-enhanced Steve.

—See what it looked like to him. Take it all in. What stands out? He chose the place for a reason—probably several. See if you can discern what they are. See if he's been back for a visit. Has he left anything, taken anything?

—I hope you don't mind, but I mentioned what you told me to Brian, Ben says.

He and Daniel are sitting at a table near the back of Jordan's. Unlike Daniel's health-conscious choices, Ben's plate is piled high with fried seafood and french fries. The two men often meet here for secretive meals at odd times. Rachel can't cook for shit and Ben doesn't have the heart to tell her.

—What I told you?

—About your memories. Whether you were in your house when it burned down or you've just been imagining you were. About your panic attacks.

—They're not related.

—Brian's got a degree in psychology.

—I do too. It hasn't helped.

Ben smiles.

—He was in private practice for a while. He's very good, very understanding.

Daniel lets out a long sigh.

—You mad?

—No.

—Didn't think you'd mind. I wouldn't have told him if I did.

—I don't mind.

—You wanna talk to him?

—Don't have a good reason not to.

Spotting Sam across the restaurant, Daniel smiles.

—Still, he adds, you should've asked me first.

—I know, Ben says, I just thought—

—Wanna make it up to me?

—Yeah, I guess. If there's anything to make up.

—Get a to-go box for your food and sneak out the back door.

—It's not good to eat alone, Daniel says.

Sam looks up from her plate to see Daniel standing there with his plate and glass in hand. She has been so distracted, she hadn't noticed he was in the restaurant.

—Mind if I join you?

She's genuinely happy to see him.

She shakes her head.

—Probably won't be good company.

He places his half-eaten plate of boiled shrimp and steamed vegetables on the table and takes a seat in the chair across from her.

—Sure you don't mind? he asks.

—Yeah, she says. Sorry. I'm just sleep deprived and preoccupied.

She takes another bite of her cheeseburger.

—Best seafood in the world and you're eating a hamburger?

She smiles.

—Not really hungry. Just knew I needed something.

They are quiet a moment, as outside streetlights flicker on and traffic thins out. All around them regulars, friendly, small-town folk, are enjoying their supper, comfortable with one another, safe in their little corner of the world.

She had forgotten the simple pleasures of small-town life, the relaxed pace, the friendly environment created by neighborly people connected by common interests and relatedness.

—This is nice, she says.

He smiles.

—I can see why you moved back here.

He nods slowly, as if not so certain.

—It working for you? she asks.

—What?

—Living deliberately, fronting the essential facts of life, all that bullshit you were slinging yesterday.

He smiles.

—It has its moments, he says, hesitating before going on. You were right. I'm here because of Graham and Holly. Mostly Graham. I meant what I said about the other. I think Thoreau was onto something and it has improved my life, but . . .

She listens intently, genuinely interested, forgetting momentarily the case and the killings and the feelings of fear and inadequacy.

—Have you had less panic attacks since you moved back?

He shakes his head and frowns.

—Just the opposite. They started when Graham died but have gotten worse since I moved out here.

—Any idea what causes them?

He looks at her more directly, his eyes unflinchingly locking onto hers.

—I'm afraid, he says. That's the truth. I'm so afraid. Not ready to die.

Preacher was right. He is running from death. Then again, aren't we all?

—I'm eating boiled this and baked that, I'm taking vitamins, running my ass off, searching my books and the fuckin' pine trees for the meaning of life. In the process living a sort of half life.

She doesn't think a man has ever been as honest with her, perhaps not a woman either.

—Seeing Graham die so young really freaked me out. I just . . . I'm not ready. I haven't done enough with my life yet.

So you moved out here to do nothing.

—Sorry, he says. Don't know why I feel compelled to tell you all my secrets.

—Don't apologize. Your honesty's refreshing.

She thinks of how closed, repressed, and emotionless Stan is.

They are quiet for a moment.

—Techs confirmed everything the killer told you. Fake blood, stolen candles and gas, and the phone was stolen from a woman who works at the gift shop in the Bay County airport.

He nods.

—You think he took Ben because he's your best friend? No other reason?

—Such as?

—If I knew I wouldn't be asking.

—I'll have to think about it. I had assumed it was just because of our connection.

—I just thought since we don't know who any of the other victims are, he might help us establish a victimology.

—It's possible. Maybe.

—It might be nothing, she says. Either way, it's scary he knows so much about you.

He nods.

—I'm trying not to think of that.

—He seems to have a purpose for you, she says, so I think you're safe enough for now, but you need to be careful. And if we don't catch him soon, we should probably assign you some protection.

—That your way of telling me you want to sleep over?

She smiles.

—Nice try, slim, but no cigar.

—Sometimes a cigar is just a cigar, he says.

—Huh?

—And sometimes it's not.

—Is that like a Lewinsky thing?

—More a Sigmund thing.

She smiles.

—I remember that from being around you.

—What's that?

—Having to look shit up.

—Sorry, he says. I'm not trying to—

—No, I like it. Well, I better get back.

As they stand, his phone rings.

She tries to pay, but he shakes his head, drops money on the table, answering his phone as they walk out the front door.

—I'm not interrupting anything, am I?

Different number, but same digitally deranged voice. He motions to Sam.

—Not at all, he says. I was hoping you'd call.

—Just wanted you to know that after tonight there'll be more writing on the wall for you to read.

—What wall?

—You'll have to find it, now won't you?

—That's all I get?

—For now, he says, and ends the call.

—You're handling him so well, Sam says. Very natural—and you're stroking his ego without sounding patronizing.

—I want to do more. Let me help. What can I do?

She thinks about it, twisting her lips as she does.

—Run with me tonight.

Chapter Nineteen

Only negligibly cooler than the day, the night is less humid, and a gentle breeze rustles through the trees and whistles down the long, narrow natural tunnel surrounding the tracks. Low on the horizon directly ahead, a full, caramel-tinged moon casts shadows and dapples the damp ground with complex patterns caused by tree branches. So low is the inconstant orb, it appears the tracks end into it, as if the two runners will eventually reach it if only they run far enough before morning.

After a mile or so, Sam and Daniel, loose and comfortable, find a rhythm that matches one another, their strides in sync, and glide together down the tracks.

As she runs, Sam can feel the tension of the day, the stress of the investigation inside her breaking apart and drifting away, as if she is actually sweating it out of her body.

Even with the illumination of the full moon, the tracks and the woods surrounding them on both sides have an eerie quality, and she wonders if it's because she knows the horror that has happened here.

—I've never run out here at night, Daniel says. Now I know why.

—It bothers you?

—Little bit, yeah.

She laughs. His honesty and lack of false bravado is a pleasant change from most of the men she knows. Neither effeminate nor macho, she's yet to see him act as if he has something to prove.

—It's more disturbing than I thought it'd be, he says. I'm sure it's my imagination, but it feels like there's a presence here. Almost like the violence of the act is lingering.

She nods, finding the weight of her snub-nosed .38 inside her neoprene runners pouch comforting.

He's right. The darkness of the environment around them isn't merely the absence of light, but the presence of something—something that feels like fear and pain and loss.

—I need to see how it looks out here as close to the estimated time of death as possible, she says, but I can come back with a deputy tomorrow night.

He laughs.

—None of those fat deputies could run this distance.

—They could walk it.

Their words are choppy, the phrases they form coming out in staccato bursts between breaths.

—I'm not sure they could even do that. We better keep going.

As they run, she tries to concentrate on the crime scene.

Why'd you bring her out here? What is it about this place? How'd you find the old depot? How'd you get her out here? Why set her on fire then climb up into the tree stand to watch? Why take part of her up there with you?

—How far would you say we are from the depot? she asks.

—A mile, maybe. Not positive. Wonder how he got the victim out here? Why did he even want to? Had to be for far more than just privacy.

—It's significant to him. I just don't know why.

The chirping of crickets and other nocturnal noises sound like the back and forth of a handsaw attempting to cut through metal, and is so loud they have to nearly yell to hear one another.

—Was there a full moon the night of the murder? he asks.

—Pretty full, yeah, she says. Probably about as bright as this.

—Still pretty dark.

They run in silence for a few moments.

—Is this our first or second date?

—Huh?

—We were together a lot last night, he says, but it didn't feel like a date.

—And *this* does? I can't believe all that was last night. It seems like a week ago. That had to be about the longest day of my life.

She's been in law enforcement long enough, been involved in enough cases, studied enough other ones to know that what they're dealing with is rare, unique, maybe even in some ways unprecedented. As tired as she is, as long as yesterday was, she's glad things are happening so fast. Maybe, just maybe, she can catch him before he sets fire to someone else's life.

—And this *isn't* a date.

He turns to look at her, his eyebrows raised, though he doubts she can see his expression.

—That came out kinda harsh, she says.

He laughs.

—I didn't mean—

She stops abruptly as she sees the crime scene tape stretched across the track, the small depot beyond, the tree stand in the trees above.

He hears them before he sees them, labored breaths, snatches of conversation, running shoes striking railroad ties, crunching gravel.

Should I run or be perfectly still and hope they don't climb up here?

If they're close enough for him to hear them, then they could hear him. Best to stay. Hope they pass on by. If they don't, if they stop and discover him, he'll have to burn them. He doesn't want to.

Whoever it is, they're not a part of his plan, but he can't let them get in the way of it. Can't let anyone.

As the voices draw closer, he rises up and looks over the edge of the tree stand, but the joggers—who would jog out here at night?—are blocked by the branches of a small oak.

He waits. Another few steps and they'll be visible.

When they do emerge into clear view, he sees it is Daniel and the female agent. Not them. I need them—at least him. It's too early for him to be offered. Not yet. Daniel is his best chance for understanding, for uncovering his message and deciphering it for all the other imbeciles. But he can't let anything stop him from his mission—not even them. Far better to complete his masterwork and have no one interpret it than not finish it at all.

He can tell from their body language that they're nervous, can actually smell the fear on them—and something else. What is it? Attraction? Might be able to use that.

They stop and begin to look around the train station. She withdraws a small flashlight from the pouch she is wearing. What else is in there? A gun? He can't take the chance.

A few minutes before, he had put his knife away in preparation for running. Now he withdraws it again, snapping it open, the moonlight glinting off the blade.

As they look around, Sam becomes aware of the physiological signs of her fear. Body tense. Heart pounding. Breath labored. She steps onto the wooden porch of the old depot and shines the small beam of her flashlight around, Daniel beside her.

Was the killer scared when he was out here? Does anything scare him?

Careful to avoid the evidence markings still on the floor, she moves around the small room, her light illuminating one tiny spot at a time.

Did he fear interruption? Someone seeing his smoke or flame?

Why wait so late to light the fire? Was it simply a matter of logistics, or is it meaningful?

She appreciates how Daniel can sense her need for silence, for uninterrupted thought.

As far as she can tell, nothing in the small room has been disturbed. It looks as if they are the only ones to return to the scene since it was taped off.

—Okay, she says finally, let's take a quick look at the tree stand, then we can go. I want to see what it looked like to him.

Chapter Twenty

He shakes his head in disbelief. They're actually coming up here.

He'd like to avoid being shot and keep from having to carve them up, but doesn't see how he can. He looks down at the ground, wondering if he can jump to it without breaking a leg. It's about fifteen feet. He thinks he can do it, but knows if he does, they'll see him.

Relax. Take your time. You can figure this out. Just don't rush, don't do something stupid.

Looking around, he gets an idea. He'll crawl out on one of the branches and hide there until they're gone.

Easing out of the stand, he shimmies out onto the branch, trying to make as little noise as possible. If they hear him, he'll have to kill them, and it's too early for that. It'd be all wrong. Still, the mission is what matters. It comes first. Ahead of everything. Including him.

Climbing up the ladder of the tree stand, Daniel behind her, fatigue sets in and Sam is again weary and spent. Now emptied of adrenaline and endorphins, she is exhausted and ready to leave, to get back to the comfortable bed at the Driftwood and collapse into it.

I'm here. Might as well take a quick peek. Besides, it'll postpone the run back—something she's now dreading.

Reaching the small, square opening in the floor of the stand, she braces herself, planting her feet firmly on one rung, locking her elbow around another, and shining the light in and looking about.

—Anything? Daniel asks.

She gasps.

—What is it?

—He's been back.

—You sure?

—He's carved something into one of the boards.

—The writing on the wall, Daniel says.

—Looks like—

—Let me see your light, he says.

—What? Why?

—I heard something.

—You're just spooked, she says. There's nothing—

Just then, a figure jumps off one of the limbs to the ground and begins to run down the tracks.

At first, Daniel freezes, watching the man run away.

—Move, Sam yells. Get down.

Daniel takes a few steps back down the ladder before jumping off to the side, landing out of the way.

On the ground nearly the moment he is, Sam pulls her gun and cell phone out of her pouch. Tossing the phone to Daniel, she heads down the tracks behind the man in the distance, yelling over her shoulder.

—Call nine-one-one. Tell them where we are and what's happening.

When Daniel opens the cell phone and sees there is no signal, something he would've remembered if not for being dazed, he begins to run after her.

The man she's chasing is way out in front of her and getting farther with every stride. Daniel can catch Sam, but neither of them will
be able to catch the other man.

—What're you doin'? Sam asks when Daniel catches up to her.

—There's no signal out here.

—Fuck. Run back to your car and go get help.

—It'd take too long. I'm not leaving you alone out here.

She returns her attention to the figure quickly vanishing in the
distance.

—Why doesn't he go into the woods? Daniel asks.

—Probably going somewhere in particular. Or knows how hard
it'd be to get through the woods and how easily he can outrun us.
Where do the tracks lead?

—Nowhere, now that the mill's closed, he says. I guess they eventually end at the bay where the mill used to be. Way before that they
cross over the Dead.

—Maybe he's just trying to make it to the river, she says. He may
have a boat. How far is that?

—Several miles.

—Oh.

They run for a while longer, the distance between them and the
man they're chasing growing.

—You're not gonna shoot him? he asks.

—He's way too far away for my little .38.

—I was kidding. We don't even know who it is.

She runs a few more feet, then stops abruptly.

—I can't go any farther, she says.

—We couldn't catch him if you could, he says, stopping beside
her.

Sam holds the small pistol up, pointing it toward the sky, and fires
off a round.

—Stop, she yells. FDLE.

In the moment following the loud pop of the gunshot, the crickets and other nocturnal noisemakers are silent, leaving only the haunting whine of the wind.

The man doesn't stop, doesn't even slow down or look back.

She fires again and repeats her warning, but in another few moments the man is no longer visible.

—Think he was here to relive the murder? Daniel says.

They are walking back down the tracks in the direction of the depot, Daniel looking over his shoulder often.

Sam nods.

—It's all about fantasy. They take something from the victim, a souvenir, or they revisit the scene. Contact with the object or return to the scene fuels the fantasy.

He nods.

—What can you tell me about fire and religion?

—Nearly every mythology includes an account of how humanity discovered fire—usually by stealing it from the gods. In Greek legend, Prometheus stole it from Mount Olympus.

When he looks over his shoulder again, she shakes her head.

—He's not coming back for us. He could've killed us back at the stand. We didn't even know he was there. We're not part of his victim profile or plan.

As with her comments about killers returning to crime scenes or taking souvenirs, what she's saying now is something Daniel knows well, but he doesn't remind her.

—Fire has been used in the rites and rituals of virtually every religion in human history, he continues, from large bonfires to candles. It has to do with its power and mystery, the way it consumes, creates, and destroys, and the way the smoke rises up toward the heavens.

—Is that why he went up into the tree stand the night of the murder? she asks. Watch the smoke rise.

—Probably. Could've been to get a god's-eye-view.

—So, if they all use it, knowing his use of fire is religious doesn't give us any clue as to what religion he is?

—Not in itself, but what he does with it, what clues he leaves, should help us narrow it down. I keep coming back to identity. He's not just using fire ritualistically, but also to annihilate them.

—Is he just hiding their identities from us?

—I don't think so, but let's think about that for a minute. Why would he need to?

—To keep us from identifying them.

—No, to keep us from identifying *him*. Could be there's something about them that'd reveal too much about him.

—Makes sense, but what?

—Let me think on it. What'd he carve in the tree stand?

—I'll show you a photo after I get someone out here to process it, she says, but it looked like a body on a fire near train tracks, a priest in a robe and tall hat with a torch and a book, and a symbol like a cross with an extra prong or two.

—Some Eastern Orthodox Christian crosses have extra bars.

—That's good, she says.

—But so do papal, patriarchal, Lorraine, Crusader, Jerusalem, Coptic, Dobbs, and a lot of others.

Chapter Twenty-one

In a roadside motel in the small town of Pottersville, a cell phone rings, breaking the silence, waking the two lovers in the cold, dark room.

Naked beneath the wrinkled, bleach-scented sheets, her dark skin pressed to his pale flesh, they are sound asleep.

He wakes first, disoriented, not sure where he is. It dawns on him quickly and he reaches for the bedside lamp. She stirs, her enormous black breasts trailing across his back.

Sheriff Preacher Gibson and Dr. Frances Rainy, he white and in his sixties, she black and in her fifties, love each other with a passion and intensity they've not experienced with any of their previous lovers—something nothing in their lives until now had prepared them for.

Her mother used to be his mother's maid and cook. They are about as far apart on the political spectrum as two people can be, and they live in the deep, still mostly segregated South. As a politician and part-time preacher, it would be social suicide for him to reveal his love for this woman. As a public person with county contracts, the effects would be nearly as unfavorable for her. So they meet in out-of-the-way motels, hidden from the world the way their love is, biding their time until, no longer able to contain the euphoria, one of them breaks and makes a public profession, something they both have a nearly adolescent urge to do.

—Is it mine or yours? he asks. I can't tell the damn things apart.

—Yours, I think, she says, but let me check. Neither one of us can afford to answer the wrong one.

She climbs out of bed and he turns to watch her walk toward the dresser, enjoying, as he always does, the way her large hips sway and her thick bottom bounces.

—It's yours, baby.

—You sure?

—Positive.

—It won't be good news, he says, shaking his head, rubbing his right eye. I can guarantee that. Just hope it's not another body.

She's standing in front of him now, attempting to hand him the phone. He gets distracted by her breasts and doesn't take it.

She smiles.

—Nigger lover, she says.

He laughs.

—Nubian queen lover, he corrects.

—I like that, she says. You catch on pretty quick for a redneck cracker-ass motherfucker. You sweet-talkin' me so you can hit this again?

He smiles his answer and takes the phone.

—Sorry to bother you so late, Sheriff, Sam says.

—Just don't tell me we've got another body, and it'll be okay.

—We don't have another body, she says, then tells him what they do have.

—You think it was our perp?

—Don't know who else it could be.

—Get a look at him?

—The backside of him from a distance as he sped away. He's like Olympic-medal fast.

River Scott had been a Bayshore High track star, setting school records in several events.

—Any sense of his age?

—Can't be too old, she says. Run like that.

—I'll be out there as soon as I can.

—Crime scene tech from Tallahassee is on her way. Roadblocks are in place, got a couple of deputies in a boat patrolling the river, and a K-9 unit from the prison over in Pottersville's gonna run the dogs through here and see if they pick up his trail, but as fast as he runs, he could be halfway to Ebro by now.

When he closes his phone, Frances raises her eyebrows over her worried face.

—Is it him?

—Runs like him, he says.

She sits down on the bed beside him.

—We made the best decision we could at the time, she says. We took a chance trying to save a kid.

—Well, it didn't work.

—Even if that's true, she says, I hope we'd do it again.

Since before recorded history, many humans have believed fire to be an earthly manifestation of the divine. In Hinduism, fire is seen as one of five sacred elements all living creatures share and an essential element to all sacred ceremonies. In Zoroastrianism, fire is the symbol of the god Ahura Mazda, and their places of worship are known as fire temples. In the ancient Roman religion, Vulcan, the son of Jupiter and Juno and husband of Venus, is the god of fire. At his forge, he uses fire to create art, armor, and weapons for other gods and heroes. His counterpart in ancient Greek mythology is Hephaestus.

In ancient Judaism, Yahweh is depicted as a pillar of fire, a burning bush, the eternal flame. In Christianity, fire is the symbol of the Holy Ghost. When the Spirit first fell at Pentecost, those present were said to speak with tongues of fire.

Fire is also a vital part of alchemy, witchcraft, Halloween, and, of course, hell.

It's very late.

Daniel is exhausted.

His room dark, his bed uncomfortable.

Sleep is just moments away, but until it comes, he wants to recall as much as he can about how fire relates to religion. He wants to help catch the killer, to stop him before he lights another human being on fire for the pleasure of watching him burn.

Fire, as a religious symbol, is as common as water or wind, and until Daniel has more specific details and sees a picture of the carving in the tree stand, it's impossible to narrow down the significance. For now, he decides to focus on the priest from Sam's description.

Is the killer a priest? Is that how he sees himself?

A priest is a representative, a conduit connecting humanity and divinity. He—they're almost always men—intercedes on behalf of humanity to God and pleads on behalf of God to humanity. In most religions it's the priest who keeps the fire in the temples burning, ensuring it never goes out.

And then it hits him. Priests are also the ones who offer sacrifices. A priest makes a sacrifice, igniting it, letting the flames consume it, as an offering to God or the gods, its smoke rising up from the earth as a sweet fragrance in the nostrils of the deity.

This thought leads to another.

The fullest expression of fire worship, of devotion to the divine flame, was in ancient Persia where the primary responsibility of the religion was to care for and keep the eternal flame. In fact, the term *priest* in Zoroastrian scriptures is *athravan*, which means belonging to the fire.

He wants to call Sam, to tell her what he's remembered, but he's just too tired, he just can't make himself get up. Then he's asleep.

Chapter Twenty-two

With only a weekly paper and a community cable show on local access, the Bayshore media had not posed a problem yet, but Sam knows every day that passes brings the likelihood that reporters and broadcasters from larger media outlets will discover the story and descend on the town and her investigation, which will in turn increase the likelihood that the case will be taken from her.

She can't let that happen. So with just a few hours' sleep, exhausted, edgy, yet euphoric, she's back in her basement office working the case.

Wonder how media attention will change our guy.

—Agent Michaels?

She turns to see Travis Brogdon, a young, shy deputy with a buzz cut, bad skin, and bifocals, standing in the doorway. Sweet, but slow, his continuous attempts to serve have been more hindrance than help.

—Morning, Travis.

Her basement office is humid and smells of mildew. More storage closet than records room—Christmas decorations, traffic cones, old computers, and an assortment of plaques and framed photographs litter the space not taken by the large filing cabinets.

For a moment, Travis just stands there, staring at her.

—You need something?

—I found out who the tree stand belongs to.

She recalls asking Steve to look into that before he went AWOL.

—Steve ask you to do that?

—No, ma'am. But since Steve quit and I know most of the hunters 'round here, I just thought . . .

—No, you did good.

He smiles, his face reddening.

—Did Steve quit?

—I just figured.

—What'd you find out?

—There's an engineering firm here that has a big hunting lease out near the wildlife preserve. Stand belongs to them. Was stolen 'bout a month ago. They filed a report and everything.

So he was planning this for over a month. He's even more patient than I realized.

Her phone rings.

—Good work, Travis, she says as she answers it. I really appreciate it.

Blushing again, he turns to leave.

—See if you can find out about Steve, she says, where he is, what he's doing, if he really quit.

—Yes, ma'am. Be happy to.

—Sam? the voice on the phone says.

—Yes.

—It's Lars Darcy.

—Hey.

—I got your message. Sorry I couldn't get back to you sooner. They're sending me to Gainesville. Got a guy cuttin' up coeds with a big hunting knife.

—We found a carving of religious symbols he made at the scene.

—That's helpful. Go ahead and e-mail 'em to me, but Daniel's who you need. Did you talk to him?

Every chance I get.

The mention of his name suffuses her skin with a warmth that seems to emanate from her soul, but it's soon followed by a sinking sensation. Am I up for this again? And so soon? Do I really have it in me to give it a real chance?

—Yeah, she says, trying to sound nonchalant. So is the reason he burns them so utterly and completely a religious thing?

—Could be. Could be rage or just a matter of prolonging the fantasy.

—Any suggestions? I'm wide open. Will try anything.

—The Phoenix is housed right down the road at PCI.

Potter Correctional Institution, the state's largest prison, holds the Phoenix, the state's most prolific serial arsonist. She had no idea, but she should have.

—You could do worse than driving over and talking to him.

Preacher is known for his patience, especially with the group of men known as his boys, the Pine County deputies, who feel like his own children and who treat him like a father. He understands that cops have a certain kind of temperament and ego, and that giving them room is the best way to handle them. Let a man cool off a while and he's more likely to listen to you, to really hear what you have to say.

He'd like to be able to give Steve more time, but he just can't, which is why he's banging on the front door of the little lakeside cabin he lives in. Steve's old pick-up truck's in back, but his unmarked is missing, which is mostly what he drives on duty or off.

More like Steve when he was younger than he cares to admit, Preacher can't help but think that if Hugh Wilson had reached out to him earlier, he might have come around a lot sooner and dealt a lot less misery to those in his path.

He's only given Steve a little over a day, but a lot is happening and he needs him, needs every available man and then some.

After banging for several minutes, he steps off the porch and walks around toward the back.

—Hey, Preacher, Minnie Clay says. You lookin' for Steve?

Steve's neighbor, a retired teacher, is walking up from behind her cabin with a black plastic trash bag slung over her shoulder.

—Yes, ma'am, I am. You seen him?

She shakes her head.

—He didn't come home last night, and he ain't been home all day today.

—You sure he didn't slip in and out real fast? he asks. Maybe for a quick shower and change of clothes?

—I ain't sayin' it's an impossibility, Sheriff, but I don't sleep much and when I do it's light and I wake easily. I sleep in this front corner right here and always hear Steve when he comes home—no matter the time.

—Any ideas where he might be?

She shakes her head again.

—Steve's a homebody. Likes to sleep in his own bed. Even when he's out with one of his lady friends he always comes back home and gets in his own rack—as he calls it—no matter how late it is, and I always hear him. This is the first night since I've lived here that he hasn't come home.

—May I talk with you a minute, ma'am?

Sam turns from the squad room coffee pot to see a middle-aged black deputy approaching her tentatively. He's tallish and thick, with close-cropped, uneven hair that has receded to nearly the halfway point of his head.

—Sure, she says, glancing up at her watch.

—Won't take but a minute, he adds, blinking his heavily lidded eyes behind his big blue-framed glasses.

—No. Sorry. It's fine. I've just got to head to PCI in a few. What's up?

He looks around.

—Can we step down here?

He nods toward a quiet hallway, and they step down away from everyone to stand in front of a bulletin board filled with state-generated notifications, flyers, index cards listing items for sale, and cop cartoons cut out of newspapers and magazines.

—I . . . ah, well, I'd like to be assigned to your task force, he says.

—I appreciate that, and we'll probably use everyone in one way or another before we're through, but the sheriff's the one allocating manpower for our team and his department.

—The sheriff's a good man, he says. Gave me a job a long time ago. Some say it was just political . . . Maybe so, I don't know, but I should be an investigator. Should've been one way before Steve. Preacher gave me a job, sure, but even that only go so far. Can't advance, can't really live up to my potential.

—I'm sorry, but—

—You have any idea how racist this area is?

—Actually, I have. And I know firsthand how sexist it is.

—It permeates the culture like the stink from the damn paper mill. It's in the air we all breathe and the water we drink. Do you know where I live?

—No.

—The quarters. What everybody calls the part of town I live in—like we're still fuckin' slaves, and I ain't so sure they ain't right. He scrunches his nose like he's trying not to sneeze and pushes his glasses up.

—I know what you're saying is true, she says, and I'm very sorry, *and* I'm trying to do my part to change things, but—

—One thing you can do is put me on the task force. Give me a chance to help, to show what I can do. Somebody gave you a chance. How 'bout givin' me one?

—I'll talk to Preacher. See what I can do.

—All I'm asking.

Back in his car, Preacher radios his dispatcher.

—Sally, see if anyone knows where Steve Phillips is.

—Sure, Sheriff. He missin'?

—Maybe, but don't say that. Just have everyone looking for him. Tell them I need to talk to him. Make it sound important, but not like an emergency.

—Ten-four. I'll do it right now. I hope he's okay.

—I'm sure he is. Just need a word with him.

Chapter Twenty-three

When Daniel walks into the editing suite, Ben, Brian, Joel, and Esther seem genuinely happy to see him.

—Told you he'd come through, Brian says. Pay up.

—Gladly, Ben says. Money well spent.

—What'd I miss? Daniel asks.

—Ben bet Brian you'd forget about the intro for Rabbi Gold, she says.

Daniel was supposed to have written an intro about Rabbi Irwin Gold, the son of German Jews who survived a Nazi concentration camp. The rabbi will be arriving tomorrow from Miami to shoot the story of his parents' survival and to be interviewed, and Ben wants to record the voice-over intro today.

Brian is examining the crisp, new fifty-dollar bill Ben has just given him.

—Anybody got a marker? he asks.

—Doesn't matter, Daniel says. You've gotta give it back.

—What?

The others laugh.

—I'm here to borrow a computer. My Internet's out again.

—You lived anywhere near civilization, you wouldn't have that problem so often, Esther says.

—But wouldn't get to see you as much.

She blushes.

Brian hands Ben the bill back, then pulls another one out of his pocket and, turning to glare at Daniel, holds it out to Ben also.

—Do I know human nature or what? Ben asks. Bet your use of the computer has something to do with the investigation and nothing to do with my project.

—Sorry, man, Daniel says to Brian.

—How long will it take you to write the intro? Ben asks.

—Not too long, he says, but I'm not sure when I can get to it.

—How about right now? Ben says. Rabbi Gold is gracious enough to fly up here during the Days of Awe, and you can't be bothered to write a short intro for him?

—I'll do it in a minute, he says. I will. I just need to check some pictures Sam sent me first.

—Nudes? Esther asks.

—No, you're the only one who sends those to him, Joel says.

—Crime scene. There might be a religious component to the killings.

Driving down the long, empty rural highway that connects Pine and Potter Counties, Sam has a file folder propped open on the steering wheel. In preparation for her interview of the Phoenix, she is reviewing pyromania, arson, and antisocial personality disorders.

According to the literature, pyromania is an impulse control disorder that brings about a release of tension when the person sets a fire. Someone suffering from this disorder is unable to resist setting fires, gains great gratification from watching them, and feels no remorse, regardless of the destruction and death they cause. Pyromania, one of the most misunderstood and undertreated disorders, differs from other impulse control disorders in that it is often planned in advance—something that brings the fire-setter enormous pleasure.

Pyromania comes from two Greek words meaning fire and loss of reason or madness. She lingers on the language for a moment. Fire madness. She's pursuing a person infected with fire madness.

Predominantly a male disorder, pyromania often begins in childhood or adolescence. Freud noted that fire has a special symbolic relationship to the male sexual urge, and at least one of the studies attributed fire-setting to a reaction to the fear of castration in young males and as a way to gain power over adults. Pyromania, along with cruelty to animals in childhood, is an early predictor of violent behavior in adulthood. A number of serial killers, including David Berkowitz and David Carpenter, were fire-setters in their teenage years, Berkowitz admitting to starting over two thousand fires in the Brooklyn-Queens area in the early 1970s.

The complex, often misunderstood causes of pyromania can be categorized as individual and environmental. They include antisocial behavior, sensation seeking, attention seeking, poor supervision, parental neglect, poor early learning experiences of watching adults misuse fire, and peer pressure.

When her phone rings, it startles her, but she smiles when she sees it's Daniel.

—I've been thinking, he says.

—I love it when you do that. It's so sexy.

How'd that slip out?

—Especially when it's about you. If you only knew the things I do to you in my mind.

—Like I said, Professor, I really, *really* love the way you think.

—I should share some of my thoughts with you sometime.

—Yes, you should.

—Sometime soon before you disappear again.

That one stings a bit, but she's earned it. And she's not so sure she won't do it again.

—I explained that.

They are quiet a moment.

Nervousness needles into neuroses and she begins to panic. It's too soon. She's not ready. Especially for something so real, so intense. And just the thought of him seeing her naked makes her nauseous.

—So, she says, what have you been thinking about that you called to tell me?

—Huh? Oh. Identity.

—Yeah?

—You know how identity is whatever makes an entity definable and recognizable, distinguishes it from other entities?

—Okay.

—In the philosophy of identity, it's all about the things that make something the same or different. I think this plays into why he's destroying their identities.

—How? Help me. I'm lost. Hope the same doesn't happen when you tell me your sexy thoughts—not that these aren't sexy.

—I'm not doing a very good job of explaining. I should've organized my thoughts before I called. I was just too excited.

—No. I'm glad you didn't wait. Just break it down for us short-bus kids.

—By burning them so thoroughly, he's obliterating their sameness and differences—at least in one sense. In another, he's making them all the same. Either way, he's robbing them of that which distinguishes them from us, from others, and I think that might help reveal his motive too.

—How? I'm lost again.

—Who is most identifiably different among us?

—Those most not like us?

—Yeah, but there're visible and invisible differences—a homosexual person is different from a heterosexual person, but it's not necessarily identifiable by appearances.

—Huh?

—What are visible differences?

—Well . . . the most obvious would be race.

—Exactly.

—You think these are racially motivated killings?

—I don't think anything. I'm *thinking*. It's a process. Of course, he's robbing them of everything else too, but I think there's something central to his theft of their identity.

—I thought you guys had to get ready for Rabbi Gold's arrival? Daniel asks.

All four of them, Ben, Brian, Joel, and Esther, are gathered around him, hovering over his shoulders, peering at the pictures of the carvings.

They had been working on the Passover Project when he came back in from calling Sam, but quickly abandoned it in favor of watching him.

—Gold-schmold, Joel says.

—We do need to get back to work, Ben says. Just a few more minutes.

The elaborate carvings depict a robed figure wearing a hat and holding a torch and book next to a large fire, the tips of its flames embracing a splayed body atop it. Not far from the fire is a cross with two extra bars and a set of train tracks.

—I'm probably not even supposed to let you guys see this stuff, Daniel says. This is police evidence.

—If it's a problem we could start sleeping with one of the investigators too, Esther says.

—Hey, I'm like an expert in my field, serving as a consultant to the task force, Daniel says. I haven't so much as held the lady's hand.

—Okay, Mr. Expert, Joel says. Enlighten us.

Daniel smiles.

—In my expert opinion, those are train tracks, that's a fire, that's a body on it, and that's a priestly figure.

—Wow, Joel says. You're good. It's downright humbling to see a master at work.

—Seriously, Esther says. What kind of priest is that and what does that symbol mean?

—The figure could be from any number of religions.

—He looks Catholic to me, Brian says.

—Like a pope or cardinal or something, Ben says.

—Could be, but a lot of clergy wear robes and hats.

—And the symbol? Esther says.

Drawn at a slight angle, the symbol looks like a seven with a crossbeam.

—I think it's a cross of some sort, Daniel says.

—Now that's just spooky, Joel says. How did you do that?

—I'm just not sure what kind, Daniel continues, ignoring Joel. There're several it could be—and see those little marks there?

He clicks the point of the picture he's indicating with the small magnifying glass icon and it enlarges on the screen.

—It looks like he didn't get to finish it, Daniel says. It could just be the pixelization, but I think we interrupted him.

Chapter Twenty-four

Parking in front of the admin building of Potter Correctional Institution, Sam removes her cell phone and handgun, leaving them in the car, locking the latter with its holster in the glove compartment. There are no weapons allowed inside the institution, and the only reason she can get away with having one on the property is that she's a state law enforcement officer here on official business.

As she walks toward the control room, she has two thoughts, one warm and nurturing, the other cold and frightening.

Her first thought is of Daniel. She finds herself thinking of him a lot lately, remembering their times together, both in Miami and now here, anticipating being with him again.

As she nears the main gate, thoughts of Daniel and all the complications he brings to her life are replaced by the more troubling and chilling thoughts of the Phoenix. Excited to talk to him, she is also nervous and scared. She has no idea what she's going to say or what she even needs from him. She just doesn't know what else to do at this point.

After signing in, showing her badge and ID, and clipping the body alarm to her belt, she is escorted through the pedestrian sally port and into the security building, the loud buzz-pop of the electronic locks preceding her, the deafening bang of the heavy metal doors slamming shut following her.

Taking a couple of quick breaths, she tries to shake off the trapped, helpless, claustrophobic feeling she always gets when she comes weaponless to a place like this.

At the beginning of each shift, the captain assigns an A team and a B team to respond to body alarm alerts. These six- and five-person teams, respectively, consist of correctional officers throughout the institution who respond to the zone the alarm signal indicates on the display in the control room. The second team is in case the alarm is a diversion in one zone for an escape in another or is actually an ambush on the first response team.

—Right this way, ma'am, the lieutenant, a dumpy white female with masculine mannerisms says.

She is led down a long, narrow hallway lined by offices, a storage room, and a holding cell, and into a small visiting room with a folding table and four plastic chairs around it.

—You can have a seat in here, the lieutenant says. Miss Lopez will be here in a moment, and they're working on gettin' the inmate up now.

—Thanks.

When asked who to talk to about the Phoenix, she was told by the warden that DeLisa Lopez, a psyche specialist, and John Jordan, the senior chaplain, were her best bets. Out of town this week, the chaplain is unavailable, but the psyche specialist had agreed to meet with her.

When she arrives, DeLisa Lopez is a surprise. Colorful, Cuban, and sexy, Sam knows there's a story behind her working as a psyche specialist in a North Florida state prison and wonders what it might be. Like Sam, something has drawn her to this unusual and dangerous job.

The two women, who have more than a little in common, spend a few moments getting to know each other.

—Why'd the warden say I should talk to the chaplain about Chabon? Sam asks. He get religion?

Lisa laughs.

—No, she says. We have a very unique chaplain. Used to be a cop. When Chabon escaped, he's the one who got him back.

Sam nods, thinking John Jordan sounds like someone she'd like to meet.

—You investigating a serial arsonist? Lisa asks.

—It's serial and it involves fire, she says, but it's no ordinary arson.

Sam tells her about the case.

—There's so much we don't know about these crimes, Lisa says. I'm not sure if there is an *ordinary* arson. The DSM, *Diagnostic and Statistical Manual of Mental Disorders*, classifies pyromania as a disorder of impulse control, but I'm not sure that's right. I'd much rather it were a subset of the obsessive-compulsive disorders.

Sam nods, though she's not sure she understands.

—Most experts say that fire-setting is far more common among adolescents than adults, but I think there are far more cases of adult pyromania or arson or fire-setting than we know. Some research suggests that repeated fire-setting may be less a disturbance of impulse control than a manifestation of psycho-infantilism, which when supported by drug and alcohol abuse extends into adulthood. That's the thing about pyromania in adults, it has a high rate of comorbidity.

—Of what?

—The presence of other disorders—OCD, anxiety, mood disorders, and, of course, substance abuse. Freud said that it—fire-setting—represented a regression to a primitive desire to demonstrate power over nature.

—How do you diagnose someone with the disease?

—The DSM specifies six criteria that must be met. The subject must set fires deliberately and purposefully and on more than one occasion; he must experience feelings of tension and emotional arousal before setting the fire; he must be fascinated by and attracted to fire; he must experience relief, pleasure, and satisfaction as a result of setting the fire; he can't have other motivations—financial, political, revenge; and his condition cannot be accounted for by antisocial personality or other disorders.

—I don't think my UNSUB is a pyromaniac.

Lisa smiles and nods.

—I don't think the Phoenix is either.

Over a two-year period, Ian Chabon, the compulsive killer known as the Phoenix, reigned over the Tampa area with fiery terror, was convicted of killing more than twenty young women—how many more no one knows.

Trapping his victims in a variety of places, Chabon would set fire to that which was imprisoning them. Locking coeds in their dorm rooms, single women in their apartments and houses, teenagers in their cars, delivery workers in their vans, teachers in their classrooms, he would light the fire and watch them squirm as the world around them was consumed in flames that inched ever closer to where they were tied, cuffed, or taped into place.

—It's why I'm working with him, studying him, Lisa says. He's a hybrid—a cross between a pyromaniac and a compulsive killer. He loves fire, is aroused by it, but only burns something when a person is inside it.

—Mine does one better, Sam says. He *only* burns his victim. Doesn't bother with the surroundings at all.

—My uncle always told me I had been at his house the night our house burned down and my parents died, Daniel says. And it makes sense—I mean, if I was in the house, how'd I get out?

With Ben, Joel, and Esther busy with various parts of pre-production on the next segment of the Passover Project, Brian and

Daniel have stepped out of the editing suite and are now sitting on chairs in the small soundstage.

—Have you tried talking to him? Brian asks.

—He died several years back, and my aunt has Alzheimer's.

Brian nods.

With the large production lights off, the soundstage is dim, its backdrops soaking up the little light in the room the way the acoustic treatment absorbs every sound. Since much of the work for the Passover Project is done in post-production, the simple set is comprised of two chairs in front of a large green screen.

—Why'd you get out of private practice?

—Too structured, Brian says. I think every artist has a bit of the anarchist in him. I want to explore humanity—our minds and our motives—but in the archetypal sense, through film, not listening to clients all day.

—Like you're doing for me now.

—Not at all. I'm happy to talk to you. I like you. I know you. I find you interesting. It's a lot different than with strangers, and I didn't say I didn't enjoy it, just not enough to do it all day every day.

Daniel nods.

—How can I figure out whether I'm just imagining or if I was really there?

—Why do you want to?

The question surprises him and he's not sure he's got an answer.

—I've wanted to know since I started having them—the memories or whatever they are—and with what's happening now . . . They're more frequent and more vivid.

—Are they having an adverse effect on your life?

—Not really. That mean I shouldn't try to figure out if they're real?

—I don't think you're going to be able to—unless you find someone who was there, he says. From a therapeutic perspective, it's irrelevant because the result is the same. Go to any counselor and he or she will work with you as if the memories are real, because whether they are or not, they're having the same effect on you.

The two men are surrounded by silence, their soft words falling inaudibly once they travel a short distance past them.

—What if I just want to know?

—Sounds to me like they're so much a part of your psyche and have been for so long that you'd never really be able to—not for sure anyway. Memory is a mysterious thing. Even when we have no doubt about whether or not something really happened, it's not as if we remember exactly every detail or that we don't add layers as time goes by. It's the Rashomon effect. You seen it?

Daniel nods.

—Kurosawa is a genius, Brian says. Anyway, four different people recalling the exact same event will have four different memories of it—sometimes radically different.

—What about hypnosis?

—Whether what you're experiencing is actual memory, complete fantasy, or some combination of the two, it's so deep in your psyche it'd come out during hypnotherapy. Besides, a person under hypnosis is in such a vulnerable and highly suggestive state that I just don't trust it.

Daniel nods and thinks about that.

—If what you're remembering isn't having a negative effect on your life, why is it so important that you know?

Daniel takes a deep breath and lets it out very slowly.

Say it. Just get it out. What's the worst that could happen?

—For a while now, I've let fear control my life.

—Ben told me about the panic attacks.

—A very good friend of mine died and it really messed me up, he says. I just can't stop thinking about dying—or couldn't. Seeing the burned body—or smelling it—has brought up even more fear. I've always been afraid my house would burn down or I'd burn to death in a fire, and now it's intensified.

Brian nods.

—I think your time would be far better spent dealing with your fears than trying to figure out whether or not you were in the house when your parents died.

—What I've been wondering is if maybe all my fear—and there's a lot of it—goes back to that event or my memories of it. If maybe it's the root of this thing that has me in its grip.

Brian nods.

—But something you said sounded like you're not thinking about dying all the time now.

—I haven't had a panic attack in a while.

—How long?

—Since I found the body.

—And you're not thinking about dying all the time?

—Actually, not at all, he says. All I think about is Sam and the killer.

Ian Chabon, the Phoenix, in full restraints, including handcuffs and shackles connected by chains wrapped around his waist, is escorted into the small visiting room and placed in a chair across the table from Sam.

Escorting officers exit.

Door closed.

Alone with a monster.

Sam tries to steady her breathing, controlling her fear before she speaks.

Burns.

The only parts of Chabon's skin not covered by his blue inmate uniform, his head and hands, are parchment thin, as if his flesh has been melted over the frame beneath it. The scars are the result of the extremely rare act of self-immolation.

As FDLE and Tampa PD closed in on him, Chabon became his last victim, dousing himself with what was left of the gasoline he had just used on Claire Hoffman and lighting himself on fire, convinced, like a phoenix, he would rise anew out of the flames.

—Hello, Mr. Chabon. I'm Agent Michaels with the Florida Department of Law Enforcement. Would you mind if I asked you a few questions?

—Call me Phoenix.

His voice is hoarse and gravelly, fire-damaged, sounding of char and ash, as if smoke should issue forth as he speaks.

—If I do, will you let me ask you a few questions?

—Try it and see.

—How'd you pick your victims, Mr. Phoenix?

—Just Phoenix.

His scars make his age indeterminate, he has no hair whatsoever, not even eyebrows, and the skin grafts over his left eye droop down to partially cover the ocular orb.

—Okay, she says, not repeating the question this time.

—Why do you want to know?

One ear is completely missing, the other a shriveled mass, like part of a dried apricot. His nose is virtually nonexistent, just a small piece of tautly stretched skin, like a tiny tarp spread over an opening. His entire head is so small, so inhuman, it is bat-like in its resemblance to a partially melted wax figure.

If only they could all look like what they really are, it'd make my job a hell of a lot easier.

—I'm fascinated by you, she says.

If what they say about most men like him is true, he will have no problem believing it.

—Well, I wouldn't choose you, he says.

—Why not?

—Wouldn't be worth the effort. You're a scrapper, I can tell. Besides, you got too much muscle and not enough fat. I like the burn I get from the fat. Plus it smells better. Why I always picked the cows.

Through the window a group of inmates, mostly young black men in wrinkled, ill-fitting light blue uniforms, are lined up in front of the mail room. They look like kids. How much of her career has been spent chasing young men just like them? In this environment, they seem so tame, so small compared to the massive machinery of the department of corrections, but they are dangerous, and she knows it all too well.

—Did you have a plan? she asks.

—What do you mean?

—Were you trying to accomplish something? Did the cops interrupt your work?

He doesn't understand what she means, but she can see him thinking, trying to come up with something.

—I was becoming what I am. I am the Phoenix.

Unless she is really mistaken about the guy she's after, there's not going to be much that Chabon can help her with. They're too different, their motivations and methods too dissimilar for Chabon to do her any good.

As scary as Ian Chabon is, the guy she's after is far more frightening. He's more patient, more exacting, and he's on a mission. He has a vision.

—Look at me, bitch, he says.

He seems aware that her interest is waning, and his ego just can't take it.

—Behold the Phoenix. Don't be distracted by lesser men.

—Thanks for your time, Mr. Chabon, she says. I really appreciate—

Before she is finished, he is diving over the table, on top of her, chairs and table crashing down around them.

Her legs are beneath the table, his full weight on it bearing down on her. She cannot move.

—I'll burn you, bitch.

He moves something around in his mouth, a small plastic object. Biting down on it, he spits on her hair, the acrid smell of gas mixed with his foul breath. Scratching a match off the chain at his waist, he flicks it toward her head. It lands on the floor next to her hair, flame finding fuel, beginning to run.

She can feel the heat next to her neck, smell her hair as it burns.

—Burn, bitch, burn.

There's a small poof and her hair ignites.

Chabon lets out a wicked, gleeful cackle.

She's fighting, but can't move. He's too heavy, the table too wide.

Twisting her head, rolling it from side to side on the floor, she attempts to put out her hair, but the carpet next to her is burning too, and it only makes her hair burn all the more.

Remembering the small body alarm she had been given when she entered the control room, she stops fighting him and reaches for it. Finds it, still there, clipped to her belt, and presses the small single white button that sends a distress signal to the control room.

Help will come now, but how soon, and how much of her head will be left by the time it does?

Chapter Twenty-five

His next sacrifice chosen and all preparations completed, he has now but to anticipate, which he does with the expectation of a lover's first touch.

This is the best part—the waiting, the savoring, the building.

He has everyone right where he wants them, several steps behind but beginning to put a few clues together. They have no idea who he is. His identity is as much a mystery to them as his mission, his masterpiece. They're nowhere near him, and won't be—ever.

The other night was close, but even that proved his superiority, his invincibility. He would've liked to have finished his carving, but otherwise the little interruption was exciting, their impotent chase amusing.

Enough of that for now. He can't let the daydreaming drain all his time again. He's got to focus, to prepare. He has been chosen. He can't take that for granted. He's got to live a life worthy of his calling.

Honor the flame. Serve the fire. Offer the sacrifices. Become one with the one who turns mountaintops to molten ash and billowing pillars of smoke.

—Still no word from Steve? Preacher asks.

Stacy, the admin lieutenant, shakes her head.

Preacher is leaving for the day. It's a little early, but he's exhausted and in need of sleep. Between Frances and the case, he hasn't gotten much lately.

—Does everyone realize he's not in trouble, that I just need him? She nods.

—I really think they do. I'd've heard if someone was just trying to cover for him. No one knows where he is.

—Anybody talked to his folks?

—His folks, his sister, his ex-girlfriend. No one knows.

—Who should I talk to? he asks.

—He's not really close to anyone here. Wouldn't know where to begin.

—Okay, he says, sighing in frustration.

—Sorry.

—Not your fault. Let me know if you hear anything.

He walks out the front door of his department and through the corridor of the courthouse, speaking to everyone he passes along the way—and not just because he'll be up for reelection again in two years, but because he genuinely likes people, likes being their sheriff.

He's almost to his truck when his phone rings.

—Sheriff, it's Stacy, she says. Phone started ringing almost the moment the door closed behind you.

—Steve?

—Sort of, she says. They found his car.

The unexpected knock on Daniel's door fills his heart with hope. He has no reason to believe it's Sam, but why not her?

It's dusk, the September sun low on the horizon, its softening or-ange light filtering through the tops of trees lining the Dead, lengthening the shadows in Louisiana Lodge to oblong shapes bearing little resemblance to the objects that cast them.

When he opens the door, he doesn't recognize the face at first, then realizes it's who he was hoping it would be, only she's different. Her beautiful blonde hair has been chopped off and her face is red and puffy, a darkening disc developing around her right eye.

Without realizing what he's doing, he steps onto the porch and wraps her up in a gentle embrace.

She breaks down and begins to cry, her body heaving as she sobs.

They remain like this for a long time, then, putting his arm around her, he leads her into the house, sits her down on the couch, and fixes her a strong drink.

Eventually, when she's able, she tells him what happened, how the fire had singed much of her hair but had not burned her scalp. Physically, all she needed was ointment, a bandage on the back of her neck, and a haircut. Emotionally, she needs much more.

—I like you with short hair, he says. You're just as beautiful and perhaps even more sexy.

She smiles, rubbing her hair down with her hands.

—You're sweet.

—I'm honest. It's the truth.

—I'm sorry to come here like this, she says.

—I'm *so* glad you came.

—I need to go, she says. I have so much to do, but I just—

—Not yet. Please. Just stay a little longer.

She takes another sip of her drink.

—How'd he get the gas and the match? he asks.

—The best they can tell, he bought them from an inmate who works in the mechanic shop. He's a maximum-custody inmate in lockdown, which means he's locked in a cell, so a food service or library orderly had to sneak it to him. He had saved the capsules from his meds, emptied them out, sold the medicine, and filled them with gasoline. No tellin' how long he's had them, waiting for an opportunity like today.

—I'm so sorry, he says. I wish I could do something.

—You are. She starts to say something else, then stops.

—What?

—I'm sorry for the way I treated you in Miami.

He shakes his head.

—It's okay.

—I was trying to get out of a bad relationship—bad for me, anyway—and I got sucked back into it. I wish I'd at least given us a chance.

—That's just the liquor talking, he says with a smile.

She smiles and her face returns to normal for the first time to-night, her eyes twinkling. She punches him in the arm.

—I haven't even had a whole drink.

He wonders if he should kiss her, but decides she's been through too much today for anything but comfort.

—I've really got to go, she says.

—Only if you'll go back to the hotel and take a long, hot bath and get in bed.

—I can't, she says. Too much to do.

—It can wait. All of it.

—Someone else could die.

—Not because you get a good night's sleep.

—I don't think I'll be able to sleep. Too wound up. Too scared. Afraid of what I'll dream. Afraid he's coming after me.

—Stay here, he says.

—I can't.

—Just to sleep. Hide away for a while.

—I wish I could. It sounds so nice, but I can't.

—Then I'll come back to the Driftwood with you.

—You can't—

—I'll sit in the hallway next to your room. Read. Keep watch. Let you sleep.

—That's so . . . Thank you, but I can't let you do that.

—Actually, he says, you can't stop me.

Chapter Twenty-six

—Any sign of a struggle? Preacher asks.

—No, sir, Travis Brogdon says. It's just empty.

Margaret Glass, a thick, white thirty-something deputy with frizzy hair clears her throat.

—The keys're still in it, she says.

They are gathered around Steve's unmarked near a clearing along the river where local teenagers gather on the weekends. The area around the car is filled with litter. Charred logs, soot, and ash where bonfires have been; beer bottles, soda cans, potato chip bags, condom wrappers, and carry-out food containers are scattered about.

—You don't think any of these fires were set by the—

—No, Preacher says. I don't.

The sun is setting. There's very little light in the clearing—even less in the woods surrounding it. With no direct sunlight to illuminate them, the waters of the Dead look black and menacing.

—What was Steve doing out here? Margaret asks. Who would he leave with?

—Maybe he didn't leave willingly, Travis says.

—Maybe he didn't leave at all, Preacher says. We need to search the woods around here. Call the K-9 unit at the prison in Pottersville and line up some deputies. We'll start first thing in the morning. If we don't find anything, then we'll have to drag the river.

Sitting alone in the dim, empty corridor of the Driftwood in the middle of the night, Daniel wishes he'd have thought more carefully about the reading material he chose to bring.

Before leaving the lodge, he grabbed several of his old textbooks to review information about psychopaths and sociopaths, but reading them is beginning to spook him. Convinced they're not pursuing a pyromaniac or arsonist so much as a psychopathic killer who uses fire as his weapon, he wants to immerse himself, once again, into the dark matter of the little we know and understand about them.

Mixed in with the other texts is a relatively recent book by Matt Grann titled *The Sociopath's Mask*, which posits that one in twenty-five Americans is a sociopath or someone without a conscience. The claim is staggering, but Grann isn't the only one making it. He's not arguing, however, that four percent of the population are monsters like the one they're after, but people unable to feel shame, guilt, or remorse.

Sam and Daniel are in pursuit of a psychopath, and though one psychologist says both *sociopath* and *psychopath* describe someone with an antisocial personality disorder and are often used interchangeably, it's important to note that the psychopath's disorder makes him act aggressively or violently, whereas the sociopath's doesn't necessarily.

His assertion, which makes sense to Daniel, is not supported by the DSM. According to it, both terms refer to an antisocial personality disorder, a pervasive pattern of disregard for and violation of the rights of others that begins in early childhood or adolescence and continues to adulthood.

The key symptoms of this disorder are often divided into two categories—interpersonal and social. In his interpersonal relationships, the psychopath is glib and superficial, egocentric and grandiose, deceitful and manipulative, shallow, lacking guilt, remorse, and empathy. In the social sense, the psychopath is impulsive, antisocial, has poor behavioral controls, refuses to take responsibility, and has a need for excitement.

As he reads, movement seen in his peripheral vision causes him to whip his head around, peering down the long hallway for what caught his attention. Nothing's there. No psychopath running toward him with accelerant and flame.

Sam's room is at the far end of the hall, next to the stairwell. Without climate control or ventilation, the muggy corridor stinks of cigarette smoke-tinged body odor, its carpet worn and filled with sand, its baseboards scarred, many of its light bulbs missing—a distressful setting for such disturbing late-night reading.

Often deceiving even the experts, psychopaths can be attractive and charming, popular and admired. But beneath their mask of sanity, they are not human—at least not in any kind of fundamental way. They are people without restraint, who have uninhibited internal liberty, and no pesky pangs of guilt or conscience.

Psychopaths view the rules and conventions of society as not applicable to them. Inconvenient and unreasonable, the rules and laws of a society only impede their lifestyles. They are self-serving, impulsive, and deceitful, making their own rules up as they go along.

Though many criminals have some of the same traits as psychopaths, they are different in that they can experience remorse, feel guilt over what they've done, empathize with their victims.

Psychopaths have a condition that causes them no such discomfort. Often satisfied with their lives, they see no need to change—even if they could.

Continuing to see phantom figures out of the corner of his eye and growing too jumpy to continue comprehending what he's reading, Daniel closes the book, stands, stretches, and stifles a yawn.

Picturing the traumatized, shorthaired Sam, bruised and vulnerable, he's overcome with the desire to hold her, to reassure her, and simultaneously so enraged he wants to choke the life out of Ian Chabon's scar-ravaged body with his own hands.

When the rage subsides, the fear returns, and he realizes he is no match for the Chabons of the world. What would he do if one did show up, throw one of his books at him? He is weak, impotent, powerless. Who's he kidding? Sam can defend herself better than he can. Words on the page of a book and figments in an empty hallway have him frightened. Real monsters with or without masks of sanity would swallow him whole.

And then it begins.

It pounces on him, an overpowering predator, he, its defenseless prey. All at once, he has palpitations, severe chest pains, and he can't catch his breath.

Awash with adrenaline, he is trembling and shaky, sweating profusely as his body temperature spikes.

He's gonna die. Right now. Death is here, has come for him, and there's nothing he can do. Sam's gonna die, her skin split open by the intense heat of a hellish fire, and he's powerless to prevent it.

Jumping up, trying to run, he experiences extreme vertigo. He reaches for the wall to steady himself, but loses control of his legs and falls to the floor. Suddenly, he's being crushed by an unbearable weight as the whole world collapses down onto him.

Paralysis sets in and he can't move so much as his mouth. Can't scream. Can't yell for help. Can't do anything but stare up into the demon-like face of the killer.

He's come for me. I'm dead. Then he'll break down the door and burn Sam in her bed.

You're out of your mind. No one's here. Look. Do you see anyone? No one's here.

Eventually, the attack ends, his mind and body righting themselves, returning to their previous settings, but he remains on the floor for a long time, disheartened, disgusted, depressed.

After a night of virtually no sleep, Preacher sips on coffee he can't taste, as deputies and dogs spread out in the woods around him search for a man he knows is dead.

Though the sun has yet to make an appearance, the morning is bright and hot. The river is calm, seemingly still, the surface of its green-tinged waters smooth and glass-like. The air is thick with humidity, the hushed forest and sandy landing damp with dew.

He can't explain it, but he had a revelation last night, at which point he lost his ability to smell or taste, and he knows with certainty that Steve is dead.

In all his time as sheriff, he had only lost two men—one to cancer, the other to a car accident. Never like this. Nothing so strange or as yet unexplained.

The only thing he can hope for now is that when they find Steve's body, it won't be black and charred, that he wasn't burned alive in unimaginable agony.

—You stayed, Sam says.

The morning sun is streaming into the already hot hallway. She is standing in the narrow strip of her partially opened door, a thick robe wrapped around her. Her short blonde hair is mashed flat against her head on one side and standing out on the other. Her face has lost its redness and puffiness, but her right eye is still slightly blue and swollen.

He stands.

—How'd you sleep?

At some point during the long night, he had managed to make it back to the chair.

—Very well, considering, she says. It helped knowing you were watching over me.

He laughs, feeling embarrassed and foolish.

Is she making fun of me? Mocking my ridiculous gesture?

—Seriously, she says. Thank you. That was so sweet.

He nods and gives her a small, it-was-nothing shrug. Feeling ridiculous and self-conscious, he's anxious to leave, to get away, flee the scene of his humiliation.

What would he have done if someone intending to harm Sam had shown up? It's laughable. A friend's heart attack sent him into hiding, gave him debilitating attacks that make him even more weak and impotent than he already is.

—Let me get changed and I'll take you to breakfast, she says.

—Thanks, but I've got to go.

Though her robe is tied tightly around her, she holds it in place with her left hand. With her right, she rubs at her short hair self-consciously.

—Come on, she says, her voice airy, flirtatious. It's the least I can do.

—I really can't, but thanks, he says, and begins to gather his books.

—What is it, Daniel? she asks. Did I do something wrong?

Chapter Twenty-seven

An early model conversion van pulls into the landing and parks.

Preacher turns to look. He recognizes the van. It belongs to Joe Kent, the local funeral director the sheriff doesn't care for. It's not just that the grotesque creature campaigned heavily against him and for a truly crooked man in the last election. The Kents and Gibsons have a small-town family feud going back more than three generations, and though no one presently living remembers any of the particulars, their dislike and distrust of one another is no less vitriolic.

After a few moments, the side door of the van opens and a hydraulic lift lowers into place. In another moment, Joe Kent rides out onto the lift ramp on a uScoot powered chair, his enormous girth draped around the seat like the ballooning of a loose blouse, nearly eclipsing it.

Preacher could cross the landing over to the man, but feels no compunction to make things any easier on him. So he stands, watching as Kent is slowly lowered to the ground and then drives his motorized vehicle across the sand and debris of the clearing.

—You got a license for that? Preacher says when the man who reminds him of a large bear on a tiny tricycle finally arrives.

—Witty, Joe Kent says. It's good to know you don't let the indignity of others get in the way of your own amusement.

—Gotta find fun where you can in a small town.

—Indeed.

Joe Kent looks out across the river and Preacher follows his gaze.

—Lovely morning. Wish we could enjoy it under better circumstances.

Preacher nods.

Starting at the clearing and moving outward, the deputies and K-9 unit have progressed so far into the woods they are no longer visible, their presence evidenced only by the occasional bark, laugh, or yell.

—I hesitated coming to you, Joe Kent says, our history being what it is.

—What is it exactly? Preacher asks.

—But I understand Steve Phillips is missing.

Preacher nods again.

—He is.

Beneath his green sheriff's cap, Preacher's head is sweating, the moisture not absorbed by the band, trickling down his temples, onto his cheeks. He wipes it with his fingertips, which he then rubs onto his jeans.

—Well, if you're willing to accept it from me, I may be able to offer some assistance.

No matter how much she tries, Sam just can't concentrate on her work.

It's not Chabon or what he did to her. It's not even the enormous pressure to clear this case and the fear that if she doesn't come up with something soon, she'll be replaced. It's Daniel. Why had he acted the way he did this morning? Why the change? He hadn't been mean or hateful. It wasn't as if she had closed the door to Dr. Jekyll last night and opened it to Mr. Hyde this morning. He was polite and courteous, but distant, distracted.

She could understand if he had second thoughts or lost interest, but why after such a loving act? Why after being so kind and attentive would he be so aloof and disinterested?

Concentrate. You can't afford to—

She realizes it's futile, so since she's no use here at her desk going over evidence and conducting research, she decides to join those walking through the woods looking for Steve.

Not sure if Joe Kent's information is to be trusted, and not wanting to waste a single moment of manpower in the search for his fallen deputy, Preacher comes alone to the old Marshall building out on County Road 232.

It's a longshot. Steve's car is clear across town, but it's got to be followed up like every other lead, and it should take no more time than a chicken jumping on a June bug.

Nothing seems amiss with the place. This is a waste of time.

But since I'm here, might as well look inside.

He thinks it's a little odd that the front door is not locked, but not enough to be alarmed.

Stepping through the doorway, he enters a large, empty room with thick, dust-covered drapes and carpet that smells of mildew. There are rooms off each side, once used for viewings, now empty like the bodies they once held. Three doorways line the center wall in front of him—the two at each end open into hallways that lead to the back, the center to a small chapel.

—Anybody here? he yells, then listens very carefully.

He gets no response, but continues standing very still for a few moments to see if he can hear anything.

—River? You here? Steve?

As silly as it is, he's actually a little hesitant to walk down one of the hallways to the back. He tells himself it has more to do with what the room was used for and how close he is to being in one than the possibility someone is actually here now, but he's not sure if he believes it.

Looking at the two end doors, he thinks of a story he read in high school titled 'The Lady or the Tiger'—at least, that's what he thinks it was called. He can't remember much about it, just that it involved a choice and the man making it—choosing between the lady who would marry him or the tiger who would eat him. The man stood before two doors, having to decide if the woman he loved would rather him be happy with another woman or dead if she couldn't have him.

Just pick a damn door and come on. You've got too much to do to be wasting time like this.

Opening the right-side door, he withdraws his gun and his flashlight, shining the latter down the dark corridor. Near the end there are two doors, one on each side. Both they and the one on the end are open—at least that's what it looks like from here.

—Pine County Sheriff. Anybody in here?

No answer.

—River? Are you here?

He begins to walk down the hallway, the barrel of his gun following the beam of his light. He turns occasionally to look over his shoulder, wishing he had closed the door behind him.

The hall is dank. The building obviously has a leak somewhere.

When he is a little over halfway down the hallway, he smells it— the smell unlike any other.

Death.

Nearly the moment the stench wafts into his nostrils, he hears the flies.

Deciding to go back outside and wait for backup, he yanks the radio from his belt, spinning around to leave.

As he turns, he sees a figure just a few steps away, running toward him with a long, narrow stainless steel embalming tool, its tip black with blood.

Dropping his radio and flashlight, he brings his left hand up to join his right for support on the butt of his gun and begins to fire.

Pop.

Pop.

Pop.

He can still hear the steps rushing toward him.

Pop.

Pop.

The beam of the flashlight on the floor illuminates the bare, blood-covered feet as they close in on him.

Last shot.

Last chance.

Pop.

Daniel wakes depressed.

Late afternoon. On the sofa. Fully dressed. In the same position he collapsed into after returning from the Driftwood.

He hasn't had enough sleep, but can tell he's not going to get any more at the moment. He knows his body well enough to know that.

Groggy. Eyes swollen and stinging. Head throbbing. Irritable. Out of sorts. Beneath it all the dull, empty ache of depression.

What had he been thinking? Why had he acted like such a jerk? Why was he so goddam afraid of everything?

He wants to do nothing with the rest of his day, just take a shower, eat something, and get back in bed, but there's something bothering him, something scratching at the edge of his subconscious.

He had it—then lost it again. What was it?

In his morose, sleep-deprived condition, his ability to think seems thick and slow, the thoughts themselves labored, lumbering.

His phone rings.

At first he's not going to answer it, but when he doesn't recognize the number being displayed, knows he must.

—You didn't let me finish my message, the digitally demented voice says.

He remembers that Sam has set up a trace on his phone and realizes their conversation has an audience.

—Sorry about that. Didn't mean to interrupt.

—You think you can figure it out with what you have?

—I'm working on it.

—Well, hurry. You don't have much time.

Daniel doesn't say anything, and they fall silent. After a while, Daniel thinks the man is gone, but waits to be sure. As disturbing as the altered voice he's using is, there's something about the silence that bothers him even more.

—Were you scared?

—Yes, Daniel says. When?

—When you beheld me.

—Very.

—Why'd you say yes before you knew what I was talking about? Are you patronizing me?

Daniel hesitates a moment.

—Not at all. I . . . I just meant . . . I'm afraid most all the time these days.

—My, how honest of you, but just don't let it distract you, control you. You need to concentrate. Interpret the message . . . You'll receive another one soon.

Chapter Twenty-eight

—What happened this morning? Sam asks.

The question is the first thing out of her mouth when he walks into her office, and she can tell he's a little taken aback by it, but she's hurt and angry enough not to care.

—He called me again.

—We'll get to that. Tell me about this morning.

—Whatta you mean? Don't you want to know—

—You were one person last night—this warm, caring, sensitive guy—and a completely different person this morning. You couldn't get away from me fast enough.

—I just figured you had a lot to do.

He's not being honest with her. He's acting the same way he did when she asked about retiring and moving back here. Eventually he had leveled with her about that. Maybe if she pressed him enough he'd do the same now.

—Don't lie to me. At least don't do that.

—I'm not.

He looks around at her basement office with a quizzical expression.

—It's actually nice to be down here. Fewer interruptions.

He nods.

—You seemed like you were genuinely interested in me, she says, attracted to me like before, and then—boom, no interest at all. Are you trying to get back at me for what I did in Miami?

He looks sincerely shocked.

—No. Of course not.

—Is it the way I look now?

She reminds herself not to rub her hair. He comes over near her.

—You're so beautiful. I told you that. Come on. Don't do—

—Then what is it?

—Nothing.

—Was it because I didn't invite you into my room? Mad 'cause you didn't get some?

—No. It's not like that at all. *I'm* not like that.

—Is it your old girlfriend? What'd she do to you?

—There *is* nothing, but if there were, it wouldn't have anything to do with her.

—You were so honest with me for a while, why'd you stop?

—I didn't.

—What did Holly do to you?

—Nothing.

—You're lying.

—She didn't do anything to me. She just . . .

—What?

He hesitates a moment.

—When Graham died she told me she had secretly been in love with him and regretted not having acted on it before it was too late.

—What an awful thing to say. She doesn't deserve you.

—She doesn't want me. So it's not a problem.

—I'm sorry.

She knows how he feels—the insecurity and self-doubt, the rejection and humiliation.

—I just want the truth, then I'll leave you alone. You've got nothing to lose.

—I just felt silly. Stupid. Embarrassed.

Something has changed. She is breaking through. His defenses are coming down.

—Whatta you mean? she asks, her voice softening.

—Sitting outside your room like some kind of bodyguard when I couldn't stop an average man—let alone someone like Chabon or the guy we're after.

—That's it?

—I saw how absurd I was being. How ridiculous.

—It was kind, not ridiculous. It wasn't about stopping monsters, but letting me sleep soundly, which I did. And it was because you were out there. Why are you so hard on your—

—I had a panic attack. I'm supposed to be out there protecting you, and I'm flat on the floor, unable to move.

—I'm sorry, she says. I wish you would've woken me.

—I couldn't do anything.

—I meant afterwards. How long'd it last?

He shrugs.

—Ten minutes, maybe.

—You were out there ten hours, she says. So what if you were incapacitated for ten minutes?

—The other night at the tree stand when the killer dropped out of the branches and began to run, I froze. I was scared.

—I was too.

—But you didn't freeze, he says. You ran after him.

—If you froze, it was only for a split second. And you ran after him too.

—I ran after *you*, he says.

—Well, don't stop now.

He smiles.

—You're scared, she says. I'm scared too. And not just of what I feel for you, but of everything—including the guy burning people alive. I don't think I can stop him—and if I don't soon, I probably won't get the chance to even try anymore.

—I've got some more thoughts on that, he says.

It bothers her that he doesn't acknowledge her confession of having feelings for him, that he's willing to so quickly move off the topic at hand and back to the case, but the truth is, it's what she needs to be doing too.

—Let's have it, she says.

—I keep coming back to identity—the way he's robbing the victims of it and why he'd even want to.

—I've been thinking about that too. Who the victims are tells us so much about the killer.

—Which is why he's keeping it from us.

—Maybe it's not intentional. Just the result of the methodology he's using.

Daniel shakes his head.

—Even with the bodies burned beyond recognition, he could leave an identifier at the scene.

—That's true. I hadn't thought of—

Her phone buzzes and she looks down to see that it's Michelle.

—I've got to take this.

The altar is ready.

The All-Consuming Fire has spoken, and this is what he says: And thou shalt make an altar of acacia wood, five cubits long, and five cubits broad; the altar shall be foursquare: and the height thereof shall be three cubits. And thou shalt make the horns of it upon the four corners thereof: his horns shall be of the same: and thou shalt overlay it with brass. And thou shalt make his pans to receive his ashes, and his shovels, and his bowls, and his flesh hooks, and his fire pans: all the vessels thereof thou shalt make of brass.

He has carefully followed the instructions of the Eternal Flame, using only the very best materials, painstakingly handpicked and handcrafted every piece of wood, every sheet of brass. It has cost him a fortune, but it is as nothing to him.

The altar is built, the sacrifice chosen; tonight is the night—the beginning. Everything until now has been prelude, preparation.

Let the earth tremble, the seas roar, the heavens rejoice.

Chapter Twenty-nine

Wanda Jones wants nothing so much as owning her own business. If there's an entrepreneurial gene, Wanda has it, was born with it. From the time she was a little girl living in the Bayshore projects, she would offer goods and services to neighbors too poor to afford them, then give them free or barter just for the feel of the deal.

It's not an easy time to own your own business these days, corporate competition is too big and fights too unfair, and for a black woman in the Deep South, child, she might as well want to be president.

Still, she dreams and schemes, and occasionally starts a short-lived venture, all the while working odd jobs to make ends that refuse to meet at least get within waving distance of one another.

One of the more odd of her odd jobs allows her to read a lot, which is what she's doing right now, one-hundred and twenty feet in the air.

Wanda Jones is a part-time fire tower lookout for the Florida Division of Forestry, an OPS position, which means no benefits.

With the proliferation of cell phones, the need for fire towers had greatly decreased in recent years. The state legislature had made the positions part-time, and now the only time anyone is in the tower is on high fire-danger days—mostly in the spring and fall during dry spells, but on any day where the conditions of temperature, low relative humidity, long interval since previous rain, and high winds increase the risk of wildfires.

Wanda is in the tower on this late September afternoon because the summer rains are over, and the conditions are right for a quick spread. She is reading a new business book by a sister in Atlanta who got hers and is telling all her other girlfriends out there how to get theirs.

Looking up often, Wanda scans the pine and hardwood forests and open field farms around her for smoke. She has good sight and using binoculars actually throws off her estimates of distance.

She has scanned the entire area, straining in the dusky light of evening, making a three-sixty around the alidade, and is about to sit down again and return to her book when she sees it—smoke from a single, isolated fire coming from a field near Louisiana Lodge.

Using the alidade, she figures the approximate coordinates, and then, as she has been trained to do, she waits.

Back when she was a rookie, she would have radioed the dispatcher over in Bonifay and had transport haul a nearby crew, tractor, and fire plow to locations of unpermitted trash or leaf fires that were out long before the crew arrived. Now, she knows to watch and wait. If there's a change in color or spread, she'll radio dispatch right away, if there's not, she doesn't waste anybody's time.

As she watches, she observes no change. This is a controlled fire, she thinks. Still, it's a pretty intense one, and she's heard rumors about a guy burning bodies in the area. No need to radio dispatch, but should she call the police?

Seeing his sacrifice being consumed on his altar is far more satisfying than he could have ever imagined. It's perfection.

The Lord his God knew what he was doing when he instructed him to construct the altar—of course he did. He is the Eternal Flame. The sacrifice burns so much better this way, the fire hotter and bigger, the consumption so much quicker.

Accept my offering, oh Lord. Let its smoke be a sweet fragrance in your holy nostrils. I make it with clean hands and a pure heart. Purify me, your high priest, prepare me for the work you called me to, the mission for which you ignited my heart and fanned the flames of my love and devotion.

Chapter Thirty

Sam and Daniel reach the scene to find both the Division of Forestry and the Bayshore Volunteer Fire Department present, their large trucks parked on the side of the dirt road next to police, deputy, and highway patrol cars and two ambulances.

Things are moving, flying at her faster than she can process them. She had been on the phone with Michelle when she received the call.

—Agent Michaels, she had said, after putting Michelle on hold.

—We got another one, Tom Pippin, a Bayshore cop had told her. And Sheriff Gibson's missin'.

Passing between the vehicles, she bends beneath the crime scene tape wrapped around the trees at the edge of the property and enters the field, Daniel remaining behind until she sees what she has. She's not thinking clearly where he's concerned and is perhaps being overly careful, but she doesn't want to treat him differently than she would any other consultant.

A large crowd of mostly men in uniform stand roughly twenty feet back from the burned body, which looks to be on an altar of some kind, two TV news crews and a newspaper reporter beside them shooting video and taking pictures.

Everyone in the group is just waiting, unsure what to do in the absence of Preacher, Steve, or her. Clearly, they've been stunned into silence by the gruesome scene before them.

—What the hell's going on here? she says.

No one says anything.

The entire area smells of smoke, charred wood, and cooking meat, and she tries to breathe through her mouth and not think about what has produced the pungent odor.

She can't believe Preacher's missing. She feels vulnerable and alone, unequal to the task before her. She wants to cry—to just sit down right here and cry, but she can't. All she can do is pray Preacher is okay, and do her job. No time for anything else. This is her investigation. Emotional reactions will have to wait, tearful breakdowns saved for a more opportune time. One foot in front of the other. Take charge. Work the case. Nothing else to do for now.

—Who was first on the scene? she asks.

A midforties Bayshore patrolman lifts his hand.

—Everyone else behind the crime scene tape, she says. And if you're just here out of curiosity, go ahead and leave now. You and you, she adds, pointing to two Pine County deputies, keep everyone behind the line—including the media.

Slowly the crowd begins to move away, and Sam turns and walks toward the body, the young cop following behind her, trying to catch up.

—What can you tell me? she asks.

He starts to answer, but she stops him.

—You got a name?

—Adam Whitten, ma'am.

—What can you tell me, Adam?

—A fire tower lookout saw the smoke. Didn't think it was a wildfire. Had overheard rumors about bodies being burned. I responded to the call. Got here first.

Nearing the site, her shoes sloshing in the water left from the fire hoses, Sam can see that the scene is even more grisly than she imagined. The victim—please, God, don't let it be Preacher—has been filleted, his skin removed, his body cut into pieces and then nearly completely burned atop a brass box about four and a half feet squared and about two and a half feet high with what looks to be the horns of bulls pointing outward at each corner. A long pole extends through brass rings on each end of the box, as if it's designed to be carried by four people.

—We weren't sure if the water would destroy the evidence, he says, but we had to put the body out. Firemen used just enough.

The body parts are on top of a grate, wet, charred wood where the fire had been beneath it. Blood has been sprinkled around the sides of the brass box, and there are various tools—tongs, forks, pots, a small rake and shovel, all made of the same brass or bronze material—on the ground beside it. Every surface of every object and the ground surrounding them is speckled black by a wet, charred residue.

Sam says a quick prayer for Preacher again, then the victim on the altar in front of her, then one asking that they not be the same person.

—You call crime scene yet?

—Just you, he says.

She removes the phone from her belt and makes the call.

—Anything else you can tell me?

He shakes his head.

—Do me a favor, she says. Go get Dr. Davis and bring him to me. Maybe he can tell us what the fuck this is.

—Oh my God, Daniel says.

—What the hell *is* it? Sam asks.

—The brazen altar. I can't believe he built a brazen altar.

—What's a brazen altar?

—In the tabernacle of Moses. It was located in the outer court. It was used to make sacrifices. It looks like he built it to exact specifications. It must have taken weeks.

—What's the tabernacle of Moses?

—You didn't go to Sunday school?

—Must've missed that day.

—The tabernacle was the place of worship for the Hebrews. God gave Moses instructions on how to build it when he was atop Mount Sinai—you know, when he received the Ten Commandments.

—Oh yeah.

—It was essentially a huge tent so they could pack it up when it was time to go. They spent forty years wandering around the desert. It had an outer court with an altar like this one where sacrifices were made and a laver—

—A what?

—Like a giant brass basin where the priest would wash up after making the sacrifice, he continues. It's very messy work. Then there was an inner court with a golden lamp stand, a table of show bread, and an altar of incense. Beyond that, behind a veil was the holy of holies where the Ark of the Covenant was kept. Everyone was permitted in the outer court, only the priests were allowed in the inner court, and only the high priest was allowed in the holy of holies— and then only once a year.

—How would he know how to reconstruct this thing?

—It's in the Bible.

She shakes her head, turning to look at the altar again.

—He's making burnt offerings, he says.

—What?

—That's why he's burning them so completely, he says. Burnt offerings are supposed to be wholly consumed. Grab me a Bible.

—Where are we gonna get—

—We're in the Bible Belt, he says. Someone here will have one.

—I've got a New Testament in my pocket, Travis says.

—You walk around with a Bible in your pocket? Sam asks.

—I need the Hebrew Bible, Daniel says.

—The what? Travis asks.

—Old Testament.

—I've got a Bible in my truck, one of the volunteer firemen says.

—May I borrow it?

The Bible retrieved, Daniel opens it and reads.

—'The Lord called to Moses and spoke to him from the Tent of Meeting. He said, Speak to the Israelites and say to them: When any of you brings an offering to the Lord, bring as your offering an animal from either the herd or the flock. If the offering is a burnt offering from the herd, he is to offer a male without defect. He must present it at the entrance to the Tent of Meeting so that it will be acceptable to the Lord. He is to lay his hand on the head of the burnt offering, and it will be accepted on his behalf to make atonement for him. He is to slaughter the young bull before the Lord, and then Aaron's sons, the priests, shall bring the blood and sprinkle it against the altar on all sides at the entrance to the Tent of Meeting. He is to skin the burnt offering and cut it into pieces. The sons of Aaron, the priests, are to put fire on the altar and arrange wood on the fire. Then Aaron's sons, the priests, shall arrange the pieces, including the head and the fat, on the burning wood that is on the altar. He is to wash the inner parts and the legs with water, and the priest is to burn all of it on the altar. It is a burnt offering, an offering made by fire, an aroma pleasing to the Lord.'

—That's it, Sam says. You're right. That's what he's doing.

—It's why he took some of the victim up into the tree stand, he says. He sees himself as a priest making sacrifices. He's making burnt offerings to God. He's following ancient Israel's sacrificial system.

—What religion does that make him?

—It's hard to say exactly. It could be a group like Witnesses of Yahweh or Jehovah Nation—groups that follow the law of Moses, but are also anti-Semitic, believing themselves to replace the Jews in some way. I'll do some research and try to narrow it down for you.

—This one's not gonna tell us much more than the last one, Michelle Barnes is saying. The body's in even worse condition and the water has washed away any trace—if there was any. Our only hope is the skin. Maybe we'll get lucky. At least we'll have DNA if we ever have a possible identity on the victim to match it with.

Michelle's team is processing the scene. She stands a few feet away observing, Sam, Daniel, and Adam Whitten beside her.

Sam nods, willing herself to work the scene, deal with the evidence, block out completely the possibility it could be Preacher.

—But it will reveal things in other ways, she says. His use of the altar should tell us a lot about him and what he's doing—not to mention we might be able to trace the material he used back to him.

—His religious motivation, Daniel says. The fact that he's very specifically making his victims burnt offerings.

—The fact that he's connected to you in some way, Sam says.

They are quiet a moment, thinking about the implications.

—Can you think of anyone you know—no matter how casually—that might be capable of . . . this? A former student, a religious nut around here who's tried to talk to you or—

—No one. I've been thinking about it since we found the first body.

—I wonder if his fixation on you is personal or just a matter of your qualifications. Either way, he knows a lot about you. Your past profession, where you live, your friends, where you run.

It's a chilling thought, and she sees it register with him.

His *olah* has been made, his sacrifice accepted. He imagines the Great Pillar of Fire's pleasure. Like Abraham, Moses, David, Aaron, and all the great patriarchs and priests, he has done what Yahweh has asked of him. The world is less one more traitor and Yahweh is pleased and appeased.

Like those who had come before him, his act signifies his complete surrender to God. He is giving his all, his very best, being obedient to the commandments of the Most High. His sin, if he ever had any, had been transferred to the sinful sacrifice, then consumed, cleansed, purified.

He'd like to take a while and savor his sin offering, to bask in the glow of the flames that still shine on his skin, but he can't. He doesn't have time. There are too many more sacrifices to be made, too many sacred fires to light. This is just the beginning.

He wonders if Daniel gets his message now. Does he have any idea what I'm doing? I've given him everything he needs to understand my mission, my message, but can he read the signs? Does he understand the clues? Or does he know too much? That wouldn't be good. If he knows too much too soon, he'll ruin the plan, and he can't take that chance.

Better give him something else to worry about.

Chapter Thirty-one

She wakes out of a deep sleep to the sound of her phone ringing, heart racing, a bloom of dread spreading through her in anticipation of the bad news awaiting her connection to the call.

—Agent Michaels, she says.

—Did I wake you?

The chilling voice is computerized, causing the man (is he just a man?) to sound like the monster he is.

—It's okay, she says. I was just—

The image on the small screen catches her eye. Lifting her shoulder to hold the phone in place, she reaches for her weapon on the bedside table and turns on the lamp.

He's been in my room. Her eyes dart around to see if he's still here.

—Oh yeah. I left a little something for you. I hope you don't mind. I think you'll be happy to have it. I don't know why I feel compelled to keep helping you, but, well, there it is. By the way, you look so lovely when you sleep. I like your hair short. I really think Chabon was onto something.

After searching the room and confirming she's alone, she stands in front of the dresser, staring down at a small portable video player sitting on an open Gideon Bible.

The video playing on the screen is of a rustic public restroom. Shot at a high, odd angle, the footage shows an old, rusted faucet slowly dripping into a grime-smeared porcelain sink. In the mirror behind it, the restroom's reflection reveals Brian Katz strapped to a chair, the floor around him wet and littered with open and overturned gas cans. Beyond him, the door of a small storage closet is open. In it, a hot water heater, its bottom panel removed, stands upright against the bare cinderblock wall. Gathered around it, its tip touching the heater's exposed burner, is a slick white sheet, damp with fuel, open gas cans resting on it.

—I've left that ridiculous Gideon Bible open for you, and will only add this. You will seek and find if you seek the place of the very first sacrifice. Bye now.

—He was in my room, she says.

Hearing that makes Daniel feel the frustrating combination of rage and helplessness. He has come to her room to read the passage and try to discern where Brian might be.

—I'm so sorry, he says. I've got plenty of empty rooms. You're welcome to stay with me.

She is dressed and armed, jittery, seemingly unable to be still, unable to process the violation and her own vulnerability.

—Let me see the video before I read the passage, he says.

She plays it.

He watches.

—A lot of arsonists use this technique as a time-delay device so they can establish an alibi. Pop open the bottom of the hot water heater and put paper or cloth next to the burner. Looks like our guy's using a sheet soaked in gas. Leave the water running. When the tank empties to a certain level, it will refill, and the cold water will cause the thermostat to kick on the burner. When it does, it ignites the flammable material around it.

—How much time does Brian have?

—It's hard to say. It's a very slow drip, but we're still talking a matter of minutes, not hours. Depending on what the temperature is set for, the heater will kick on eventually just to keep the water warm—even if the tank is still full.

He nods.

—The bathroom reminds me of one at a high school football stadium. What exactly did he say?

—Something about seeking and finding at the place of the first sacrifice. At first I thought he meant out near the train depot, but we've covered the entire area. There aren't any other buildings out there.

—Unless they're underground, he says.

—You think they could be?

He shrugs.

—No idea. Where was the Bible open to?

She hands it to him. It's open to the book of Genesis, chapters twenty-two and twenty-three, but no verse is underlined, highlighted, or otherwise marked.

—When I realized he wasn't talking about *his* first sacrifice, but *the* first sacrifice, I read the pages he left open, she says. It's about when Abraham took his son, Isaac, up Mount Moriah to offer him as a burnt offering.

Daniel nods as he glances over the open pages.

—But I think it might be a trick, she continues. There's a note at the bottom of the page about other sacrifices, so obviously this isn't the first, right?

—Right.

—It says Abraham offered one earlier when he made a covenant with God. Noah did it too—and that was before him. But before any of them, Cain and Abel offered sacrifices. God accepted Abel's and rejected Cain's, and Cain killed Abel.

Daniel nods.

—It *is* a trick. According to the stories of Genesis, humans didn't make the first sacrifice. God did.

—*God?*

—When he killed animals to make coverings for Adam and Eve after they ate the forbidden fruit and realized they were naked.

—So what's the clue?

—Tell me what he said again?

—Seek and you will find if you seek where the first sacrifice was made, she says. So where would that be?

—The Garden of Eden, he says.

—*The Garden of Eden?* Where the hell is that?

He smiles.

—I just happen to know.

Elvy E. Callaway, a NAACP lawyer, Baptist minister, nephew of Confederate General John Bell Hood, and who unsuccessfully ran for governor in 1936, had been convinced that the original Garden of Eden was located near Bristol, Florida, near the Apalachicola River. He believed that he had not become governor because God had more important things for him to do, such as uncovering absolute proof of the Genesis account of purposeful creation.

His certainty that Bristol was the site of the Garden of Eden was based in part on the fact that, according to Genesis, every species of plant and tree grew in the garden, including gopher wood trees— which only grow one place in the world. Callaway claims that Noah built the arc out of gopher wood, then when the earth was flooded, he floated for five months and landed on Mount Ararat.

—You're kidding, right? Sam says.

—You can't make shit like this up, Daniel says.

They are racing down Highway 20 toward Bristol beneath a cloud-shrouded moon. The night is dark, the road empty, the illumination of the headlights absorbed by the fog.

—That's just . . . I don't even know how to respond to something like that.

—You'd be amazed how many North Floridians believe it.

She is driving, pushing the unmarked past ninety. The siren is off, but the bright blue flashers behind the grill cause deer grazing along the shoulders of the road to look up, alert, ears erect.

—I'd be shocked, but I don't know why. I shouldn't be. Why's he doing this? It's so different from the others. Don't you think?

He nods.

—Same with Ben. It's a game. He's just having fun with us, showing his superiority. Making us run around, keeping us busy, weary, distracted.

—You think he thinks we're getting too close?

—Probably just wants to make sure we don't.

—Is it possible we're closer than we think?

—Anything's possible, he says, but if we don't know it, it'd seem to negate it, wouldn't it?

She laughs.

—What?

—Every now and then you sound like a professor.

—Sorry, he says.

—No, I like it, she says. Makes me feel like I'm . . .

—What? You're what?

—Nothing.

—Tell me.

—It's silly. I don't know why I even . . . It's just one of those things that pop in your head.

—What was it?

—Nothing. Really.

—Please.

—I'd rather not.

—Okay.

—I was gonna say it makes me feel like I'm dating someone smart, she says. See. I told you it was silly.

—It's not silly, he says. You are.

—*I* am?

—No. I meant, you are dating someone smart.

—So we're dating?

—Dates that are atypical as fuck, but yeah, I'd say we're dating.

Chapter Thirty-two

—It's taking too long, she says. We're not going to make it.

She pictures the dripping faucet, hears the relentless wet tick, smells the gas fumes, feels Brian's fear, sees the water level dropping in the tank, the thermostat clicking on, the burner igniting the room.

—Maybe the deputies will find him, he says.

They are nearing Bristol, but it's been over thirty minutes since she was awakened to find the video in her room. Before leaving Bayshore, she called the Liberty County Sheriff's Office and had deputies dispatched to begin searching the area around the Garden of Eden.

—I wonder if we ever had time to save him, she says.

—I would think we do—or did, he says. I think he's manipulating us, controlling us, but I bet in his mind it's important to play fair, to give us a real chance, no matter how narrow the margin.

—I keep imagining it, she says. It's so vivid. I can actually smell him burning, see his flesh splitting, cooking.

—I'm so sorry. You've absorbed a lot of horror in the past few days.

He reaches over to pat her leg, but she reaches down and takes his hand.

Passing through Bristol, they turn onto State Road 12, and arrive in the area Callaway believed to be the Garden of Eden.

—Now what? she asks. There're so many houses and old buildings scattered about.

—Can you radio the deputies and find out where they've searched?

—We don't have time, she says, but lifts her radio off the seat and begins sending out the inquiry in ten-codes.

Up ahead he sees a sign for the Garden of Eden Botanical Garden.

—There, he says, pointing.

She drops the radio and guns the car, slinging it into the entrance, the rear end fishtailing on the dirt road. Without slowing, she crashes through the padlocked chain-link fence gates and drives as far as she can before stopping in front of the Visitor's Center.

Jumping out of the car, they run in different directions—Sam to the door of the center, Daniel to a map of the garden in a large plexiglass box beneath a lamp.

There are two possibilities—a restroom located about halfway through the walking tour and an employees-only greenhouse building in the back corner.

—Here, he shouts to Sam. One of—

An explosion sounds and an enormous ball of smoke and fire rolls up just above the trees, lighting up the night sky and the garden beneath.

—Fuck, Sam exclaims, and begins to run toward it.

Daniel follows.

They run down winding paths, between exotic bushes, beneath canopies of eclectic trees.

—I knew we didn't have enough time, she says. We couldn't have gotten here any faster.

As they near the building, they see an empty deputy's car parked behind a side gate, its lights flashing, door open, radio blaring.

In another moment, they see the deputy helping Brian up the path away from the burning building.

Sam lets out a huge sigh of relief and stops running.

—Thank God.

Unsteady on his feet, Brian holds a blood-soaked handkerchief to the back of his head.

—Did you see that? the deputy asks.

He's a soft, pale white man in a snug green uniform, obviously excited, his voice and the movements of his body betraying his jangling nerves.

They nod.

—I started to call to see if we could get the owners down here, but decided to just climb over the fence, and I'm sure glad I did. If I hadn't, he'd be a goner.

—Very nice work, Sam says.

He blushes.

Daniel looks at Brian.

—You okay?

He nods.

—My head hurts and I can't hear too well, but it's better than . . .

—His head's gonna need stitches, the deputy says. Ambulance is on the way.

Sam's phone rings and she steps away to answer it.

Hearing Stan's voice makes her nearly equal parts nervous, angry, hurt, and vulnerable, and she can feel herself stiffening, hardening, becoming defensive.

—What the hell did I put you in the middle of up there?

—Something.

—You okay? I heard what Chabon did.

—I'm fine. Just tired.

—You got a sheriff and a detective missing? Things are moving fast, aren't they?

And he doesn't even know about what's just happened.

—You need help with this thing, he says, I'll come myself.

She needs help. She told him that, but she doesn't want him here.

—Give me a couple more days and a few agents out of Tallahassee. We're getting somewhere.

—Who's *we?* he asks. I thought you didn't have any help.

—I'm using every resource I can find—cops, deputies, firemen. We're gonna get him. Probably get him faster if I had a few agents. I thought you were going to get me some?

—I'm working on it. It's your investigation. Run it however you like. I'll rush up the agents out of Tallahassee, but I may come up anyway. Just to see you. I miss you. I've been thinking a lot about us.

—I've got to go, she says. We'll talk later.

Leaning his recently stitched-up head gingerly atop the back seat of the unmarked, Brian recounts what happened to Sam and Daniel as they drive back to Pine Key.

—I was coming out of the post office. Just dropped off some promo packages that should've gone out yesterday. I was alone. Building and parking lot were empty. Walked to my car. I remember grabbing the door handle, but nothing after that until I came to in the bathroom at the gardens.

—Was he ever in the bathroom with you? Sam asks.

—When I woke up, he was taping me with a video camera. He was in all black—gloves, ski mask, boots—but I saw his eyes. They were . . . I don't know, I'm sure it was the bump on the head and the gas fumes, but they seemed to glow. I know it's crazy, but they were very dark and yet seemed to glow.

—How tall was he? What size?

—He was about my size, I'd say. At least as tall. May have been a little thinner. It was hard to tell with the outfit he was wearing.

—Can you think of anything else? The way he moved, smelled, something he said.

He shakes his head.

—You think he'll come back for me?

—I really don't, she says, but we'll keep an eye on you.

—Why'd he do this to *me*?

—We're not sure exactly, but he may have chosen you and Ben because of your relationship with Daniel.

—If that deputy hadn't gotten there when he did . . .

Daniel smiles.

—You'd've been a goner.

Chapter Thirty-three

Her task force is down to two Bayshore cops, two Pine County deputies, and a volunteer fireman who wants to be an arson investigator. It'd be comical if it weren't so pathetic.

She decides not to tell them about Brian's abduction and their adventure from the night before. It'd take too long and be too distracting.

Steve and Preacher are still missing, and most of the department is still searching for them.

She shakes her head. We're never gonna catch him.

Of course, Stan is supposed to be sending more help, but it's not here yet, and with or without additional help, she really wants to close the case—and soon.

—Okay. We don't have a lot of time. We don't have a lot of resources, but we can do this. Those of us in this room right now. We just have to be relentless.

The small group listens and nods, but she's not sure she's getting through. The drab, industrially dreary conference room doesn't look nearly as small as it did the last time the task force was in here.

—We've got several lines of inquiry that offer the best chances, and there are fewer of us. We're gonna split them up and work them hard, pursuing them as far as they take us. Remember, they're just leads, just long shots.

She hesitates a moment, but no one says anything so she continues.

—The first is the materials he used to construct the altar. He's getting sheets of brass and acacia wood, probably in fairly large quantities. Where? We need to do a local search, see if anyone in the area sells either of these two things, and we need to research online, see who ships the stuff and see if any of them have sent any here.

—What about checking with contractors? Travis asks. He's obviously good at building shit.

—That's good. Also, who in the area has a wood shop? Do any of them use acacia wood or work with brass?

—My brother's a contractor, he says. I'll take that one.

—Good, she says. Thanks. These are the kinds of ideas that bring about breakthroughs in cases.

—I'll do the online research for the materials, Jerry Douglas, the volunteer fireman says. I'm on the computer all the time anyway, and I'm pretty good at finding stuff.

—Great, she says. Thanks.

The conference room door opens and Julie, Gibson's secretary, her eyes red and face splotchy, motions for Sam.

News about Preacher, Sam thinks. Or Steve. And it's not good.

Sam holds up her finger to the woman.

—One minute. I'm almost finished.

The woman nods and closes the door.

—You think they found Preacher? a female deputy asks.

—I don't know, Sam says. But I need you to focus on these assignments. It's what Preacher would want you to do.

—You think he's dead? she asks.

—No, Sam says. I meant if he were here to tell you himself. Now, one more thing. We think our killer may have been part of a fringe religious group at one time. We're looking for a church or community or compound who believe in white supremacy. They'll probably also practice the law of Moses the way some Jewish people do. Probably see themselves as the real people of God.

—We'll take that, Adam Whitten says, nodding toward the other Bayshore cop seated beside him.

—Okay, Sam says. Remember, do your very best work. Concentrate, no matter what else is going on. There are innocent people's lives in your hands. This guy is not going to stop until we catch him.

The Bayshore cops leave the room and Julie comes back in.

Sam can tell the deputies and Douglas are slow to leave because they want to hear what she has to say. She starts to ask them to leave, but decides not to.

—Steve's dead, Julie says. Stabbed to death. Preacher was stabbed and lost a lot of blood. He's in a coma. He shot the guy that did it. He's dead. His name was Henry Marshall. His dad used to have a funeral home here. He's been living in the old, empty building like some sort of animal. He had mental problems.

—When did it happen? Sam asks, wondering if Marshall could be her UNSUB.

—Yesterday. Sometime around the middle of the day.

—So he's not our guy, Travis says.

—No, Sam says. He's not.

—Brian told me what happened last night, Ben says.

He's looking at Daniel, having turned his attention away from the editing monitor when he entered the room.

Daniel drops into a chair beside him, swiveling it to the opposite position so the two men are facing each other.

Joel, Brian, and Esther are at lunch, and the two men are alone in the building. The editing suite is dim except for the monitor and the men sitting directly in front of it. On the monitor, Rabbi Gold sits before a green screen in an expensive black suit and white shirt, lit to perfection by Brian the cinematographer perfectionist.

—Tell me about it, Ben says.

As Daniel describes what happened, he can tell that Ben is genuinely interested, his dark eyes intense, his small mouth twitching with amusement.

—You saved his life too.

Daniel shakes his head.

—We weren't in time. If the Liberty County deputy hadn't gotten there when he did . . .

—He only knew to look there because of you.

Daniel shrugs.

—Anyone could have figured it out. It was an insultingly easy clue. He was just having fun, playing games, keeping us distracted.

—This guy really scares me, Ben says.

—Me too.

Kennedy Todd Whitman, the legendary arson investigator, enters Sam's investigation as if he believes he has been sent directly from God to do so.

—Hey there little lady, he says as he steps up toward her and extends his enormous hand. I'm Kennedy Todd Whitman, and I'm the answer to your prayers.

His voice is deep and authoritative, which matches a thick-bodied man of over six and a half feet, but it's also raspy from years of fire breathing—crimes and cigarettes—and it growls forth as if out of a deep, smoky well inside him.

Beneath his giant ten-gallon cowboy hat, his crew cut is stiff and prickly and military-precise, and peeking out from his Western-style button down, his dark skin is fleshy and gleams from a hint of oiliness and sweat.

—If that's true then God has a wicked since of humor, she says.

—Spunky. I like it.

—Whew, I'm so relieved.

—Well, damnation, this filly ain't even green broke, fellas.

—I'm on my way to the hospital, she says. What can I do for you?

—It's what I can do for you. I've forgotten more about fire than this little weenie roaster you're after'll ever know. Stan sent me. Says he'll send a few more agents in a couple of days, but between you and me, that won't be necessary. I'll have the little fucker in custody long before then.

Stan is totally fuckin' with me.

—Murder book is in the conference room, she says. Get familiar with everything and we can talk when I get back.

—Will do, but don't be surprised if I solve it before you get back, missy, he says, then turns and walks away, his cowboy boots clicking on the tile floor as he does.

Chapter Thirty-four

He lays the hammer on the workbench and walks past the large power tools, out of his shop, what he thinks of as his staging area, and into his gallery.

The enormous space is convenient, but irrelevant, a shell. It's what's inside it, the work of his hands that is valuable, priceless.

He takes a few more steps, but only a few. He doesn't want to get so close that he can't see the scope, the enormity of what he's crafted.

The space is illuminated by burning torches and candlelight, which not only provides light and warmth, but brings the building and everything in it to life as their flames flicker and dance on every surface in the room.

Enjoy the work of your hands. Don't get so busy, so singularly focused on the mission that you don't take pleasure in this awesome thing the Lord is doing through you.

It is awesome. Inspiring. Full of meaning. But will anyone ever see it?

The thrill and joy of the moment is lessened by the thought that he may be the only one to see this awe-inspiring spectacle in all its glory. Sure, someone would stumble on it eventually, but he wants those so carefully studying his work to see it soon, to come at the appointed time.

He's given them all the clues they need. Why are they still so far away from uncovering the message? Daniel Davis is especially disappointing in this regard. He thought for sure he was a worthy decoder, but so far he seems as dense and deficient as the rest.

Sam thinks it strange that Frances Rainy is in Preacher Gibson's room. He's in a coma after all. What can she do for him?

She is standing on the far side of the bed, hovering over him. Sam walks over and stands opposite her.

—Any change? Sam whispers.

Frances Rainy shakes her head, but then speaks in a loud voice directed toward Preacher.

—He's just resting, building his strength back up. He'll wake up rested and feeling good soon.

She adjusts the top of the sheet at his chest, then touches his forehead with the back of her hand, letting it trail down his cheek.

She's not here as a counselor or a county employee. This is personal.

—He's truly a good man, Rainy says.

Sam nods.

—One of the rare ones.

—They're not so rare, she says.

They are silent a moment.

—It's probably gonna cost him the next election, she says, but I'm not leaving his side.

—How long have you two been together?

—Too long to still be sneaking around like he's a Montague and I'm a Capulet. Life's too short. We found each other too late to be wasting the little time we have. If he's not sheriff, it'll be the county's loss, and if I lose the county contract things will be tight, but life goes on—and ours will be together.

—You're right. And very brave. And who knows, maybe the voters will surprise you.

—Stranger things have happened. Who was it that said people are always better than we think they are?

—I don't know, but I'm sure that's true of most, just as the few monsters among us are far worse than any of the rest of us can imagine.

She nods, and they are quiet again for a few moments.

—Can I ask you something? Sam says.

—Sure.

—I was dating an older man in Miami, she says. My supervisor, actually.

Nodding, Frances Rainy shows no indication she finds the revelation surprising or distasteful.

—Unlike Preacher, he's a typical macho cop—big ego, not very sensitive, to me at least, and generally emotionally unavailable.

—That the kind of men you usually get involved with?

Sam thinks about it, then nods.

—More often than I should.

—Was that the kind of father you had?

—I guess, she says. Not the macho so much as the absent. We weren't very close, and he died when I was a junior in high school.

Frances Rainy nods, but doesn't say anything.

—The thing is, I've met someone here. Not at all like Stan or any of the other men I've been with.

—The retired religion professor?

—How'd you—

—Not much gets past ol' Preacher here.

—I'm really attracted to him, she says. And to what I might be able to have with a different sort of man. But sometimes it feels so strange—like it's all wrong. I know he has issues too and . . . I don't know. I guess . . . Can people change? I mean really change?

—I wouldn't do what I do if I wasn't convinced they could. Most don't, but most can. And the fact that you find him attractive is a very good sign. So's your awareness of your pattern. If you're willing to explore your relationship with your father, and if you realize that something this different is going to feel strange from time to time and just remember that it's just because it's unlike anything you've experienced—which is a good thing—you've got a real chance for a better relationship and a better life.

Sam has the urge to tell Frances about her scars, to reveal her secret, confess her fears and feeling that she is no longer attractive, but she just can't bring herself to do it. Instead, she continues to express her concerns about Stan.

—The other thing is, Stan just broke up with me a couple of weeks ago, she says. Isn't it too soon to be starting something with someone else?

—Probably, she says, but I'd still recommend it.

Sam smiles.

—Partly because I think you're looking for any excuse to run in the opposite direction, she says. Partly because people generally don't wait anyway. They can't. The force of love is way too strong. And partly because life is so fragile I'd say go in with eyes wide open, but don't waste another opportunity. Who knows if you'll get another?

Jerry Douglas sits inside the break room of the Bayshore Volunteer Fire Department working on his laptop, using Internet signal from city hall. He doesn't need to be here, he could just as easily do this at home, but he likes being close to the trucks, ready to roll should a call come in. He also likes being involved in the case, actually having responsibilities, contributing to catching the guy. At the moment, he's clicking around a couple of search engines, looking for the materials the killer used to build his altar.

Acacia wood comes from trees found mainly in the arid and semiarid regions of Africa. In these areas, they are the most ecologically important plants—often the only ones on an otherwise unforgiving terrain.

Several species of acacia also grow in the Sinai, the most common of which, *Acacia raddiana,* seems likely to be the acacia referred to in Scripture.

These slanted, fat-top trees have very small leaves, which helps them conserve water. During droughts, the trees can drop their leaves completely. Their flowers are white and grow in dense head-like clusters. The shape of the fruit is coiled and pod-like, and contains several very hard seeds.

Because the tree grows so slowly, the wood is hard and dense, its heart dark red-brown. Because the tree deposits many waste substances in the heartwood that act as preservatives, it resists decay, its density making it virtually impenetrable by insects and water.

No wonder the Bible people used the stuff.

If the killer built an altar exactly like the one in the Bible, then he wouldn't want acacia wood from Africa, but from Sinai.

Next search: Where can I buy Sinai acacia wood?

After several minutes, his search yields nothing promising. He can find acacia bowls and furniture easily enough, but no lumber, nothing large enough to enable him to make the altar—or, as Dr. Davis theorizes, several of them.

Maybe the guy bought furniture, took it apart, and built the altar from it. Maybe he didn't use acacia wood at all—but if all the other components were exact, why wouldn't he use the exact materials?

He knows everything is available for the right price. The wood is out there. He's just got to be patient. Make some phone calls. Track it down. Who knows? Maybe the process would help him track down the killer. Oh how he'd love to be the one to catch him.

He's about to take a break, clear his mind and come back to it, when another result of his search catches his eye. It's down at the bottom and doesn't appear to be relevant, but something about it causes him to click on it.

The page opens the official site of the Garden of Eden, a botanical garden featuring, among other things, biblical plants and trees.

He reads: 'In the garden's Middle Eastern area, one finds acacia trees, which God chose for the construction of the tabernacle.'

Less than thirty minutes away, the Garden of Eden is located in Bristol, Florida. It's perfect.

Snatching up the phone, he punches in the number on the screen.

—Hi, this is Jerry Douglas with the Pine County Sheriff's Office Task Force, he says. Have you guys had any acacia trees stolen recently?

—Did you find them? the lady on the other end says with a tinge of urgency and excitement.

Chapter Thirty-five

With the task force following up on other aspects of the investigation, Daniel turns his attention to finding a religious group that combines the seemingly contradictory systems of Nazism and Yahwehism.

He recalls certain sects of non-Jewish groups who follow the law of Moses—African denominations, such as Black Hebrew Israelites, who believe Moses and everyone else mentioned in the Hebrew Bible were black; and white faiths, such as House of Yahweh, that see themselves as the true Israelites and who attempt to keep all of the 613 laws or precepts found in the Five Books of Moses. Neither group has any form of Nazism in their belief systems and are not known for causing physical harm to others that he knows of, but new religious strains are breaking out all the time, mutating, often into militant, racist, fundamentalist, apocalyptic cults.

A colleague of his at the university specializes in new religious movements, particularly those shooting up in the rural South, and if anyone knows if a group like the one he's searching for even exists, it will be Dr. Morgan Haddon.

He calls Haddon from his cell phone as he's crossing the causeway from Pine Key to Bayshore. It's the first time he's called anyone from the department since he left, and wouldn't be doing so now if he felt he had a choice.

—Dan, that really you?

—'Tis.

—How are you? he asks, though the two weren't close even when they worked together, and his tone seems devoid of anything but mild curiosity.

—I'm good, actually, thanks.

—We were all affected by what happened to Graham, and then to find out that he and Holly were—

—They weren't, he says. She just cared very deeply for him.

—Did I hear you're working on a non-academic book?

—Didn't know there were such things, did you?

He laughs.

—Someone said it was some sort of self-help title.

Not that he needed one, but his brief exchange is a reminder of how petty and self-important the closed, insulated society of academia could be.

—You think you'll come back? Haddon asks.

—Can't imagine any circumstances under which I would.

Wanting the conversation to end as soon as possible, Daniel explains why he's called and what he's looking for.

—This for your book? he asks, his tone amused.

—No, I've been looking for a new church to join.

It's a joke and Haddon knows it, but he responds as if he doesn't.

—You started going to church again?

Daniel laughs.

Not a church attender, and not knowing a single religion professor in the department who is, Daniel is not nearly as dismissive of organized religion as his colleagues. Haddon has meant the remark as an insult, but Daniel finds that he is past caring what the hollow, gossipy little man thinks.

—Know of any groups that might fit the criteria? Daniel asks.

—As a matter of fact, I do, Haddon says. And they're both right over there in your neck of the woods, so to speak. I've got a graduate student doing research on them. Shall I have him give you a call?

—Got any religious nuts working for you? Travis asks.

—Just a couple of your kinfolk, Bernie Clark says.

He doesn't smile, and Travis isn't sure if he's kidding or not. Travis is born-again and not ashamed of the gospel and everyone knows where he stands, but he didn't think anyone considered him a Jesus freak or anything.

Bernie Clark is an older man, probably pushing seventy, and the deeply tanned face beneath the thick white hair is veined with a dense web of wrinkles.

—Seriously, Travis says.

The two men are standing at the entrance to a new subdivision, Whispering Pines Estates, next to Clark's oversized pickup truck, a door with Bernie Clark Construction painted on it open, revealing the clutter of building plans, material catalogs, empty Pepsi bottles, and tools inside.

The truck is parked on a newly paved asphalt road that leads past the brick-faced, furnished, and landscaped model home to a dozen others that are in various stages of completion.

—You'll have to be a little more specific, Clark says.

No contractor in Pine County employs more builders than Bernie Clark. He has more new houses going up in Bayshore than all the other construction companies combined, and unlike them, he has several mansions going up out on Pine Key, as well. Anybody could build the little cookie-cutter starter homes on quarter-acre lots in the multitude of subdivisions being put in all over Bayshore, but to build mansions on Pine Key that make the Jews happy takes a real craftsman. Clark's numerous crews fit into two categories—those who work in and around Bayshore, and there were a lot of them, and those who work in Pine Key, and there were only a few of them.

Travis thinks, The few, the proud, the Jew house builders, and smiles.

—Something amusing? Clark asks.

—No, sir.

The cheap-looking homes going up here, made all the more ridiculous by having a brick-front facade, would never have been permitted on Pine Key. The Jews had taste—he had to give 'em that.

—Travis, I don't have a lot of time, Clark says.

—Do you have anybody with his own shop, like at his house or some place?

—I'm sure a lot of my men have their own shops, he says. But I wouldn't know which ones.

—What about bronze or brass?

—What about them?

Clark's phone rings, and he takes it off his belt, looks at the display, but doesn't answer it.

—Got anybody who's good with it?

—I've got a few men.

—What about a guy who's in a strange religion, good with bronze, and has his own shop?

—This about the murders?

—Yes sir, it is.

—What do all these things have to do with them? You think one of my men's the killer?

—I can't say anything else about it.

—Well, give me a day or so and I'll see what I can find out. I'll give you a call.

Chapter Thirty-six

—Preacher is a compassionate man, Frances Rainy is saying.

Sam nods.

—Whenever possible his philosophy is to help instead of punish people, she continues. We've got way too many people wanting just to lock up troubled people and throw away the key. He's not like that. You aren't either. I can tell.

—I'm probably a little more like that than Preacher.

—But you probably deal with a different kind of criminal too.

—That's true.

—You familiar with the Samaritan Law? Frances says. They should have one of those for law enforcement officers. Try to help somebody and if it doesn't work out, you're not held responsible.

—Who did Preacher try to help? Sam asks.

—Boy named River Scott. We both did. In fact, it was probably me who talked him into it.

—Who is River Scott?

—Try your best not to let this hurt this dear, sweet man or his reputation.

—I'll do what I can. I promise you that.

—River is a troubled young man from an abusive home who was caught, more than once, setting fires.

—Oh my God, Sam says. Where is he now?

—We don't know.

No wonder Preacher had turned over the investigation so quickly. Usually, local law enforcement only calls in FDLE when they have to, when they take a case as far as they can, but it had been the first thing Preacher had done. He suspected this kid from the very beginning.

—Tell me everything you can about him.

She does.

—And the first time he missed an appointment was the day we found the first body?

—He'd missed appointments before, she says. Difference is this time he hasn't come back.

—And he's a track star?

—Was, yeah.

—Tell me about the abuse he suffered.

—I can't, she says. It's—

—We're way past that, Sam says. You're asking for my help. Well, I need yours. You've already violated the law and virtually all ethical standards. Now's not the time to get—

—Okay, she says. We were just getting into a lot of the specifics, but there was the typical verbal and physical abuse.

—What about sexual?

—I don't think there was, she says. Not in the usual sense. If anything, just the opposite. His parents had some strange, strict religion.

This could be it. He might just be the one.

—He's got a lot of issues around sex, she says. A lot of guilt and shame. If his parents ever caught him masturbating, they'd punish him severely.

—How?

—With fire, she says. They'd burn him.

—There's some strange shit goes on out in these woods, Nathan Crace, Dr. Haddon's grad student says. I'm from here and had no idea.

—You're from Bayshore? Daniel asks.

—No, I meant North Florida, he says. Grew up in Wewahitchka.

He has long, straight dirty-blond hair that he has to flip out of his face by shaking his head back or brushing it with his hands—both of which he does often.

—Just out in the woods? Daniel asks.

They are sitting in the window of the little bakery a block off Main Street, sipping coffee and eating glazed doughnuts.

—Actually, I was talking about the entire area, dude, he says. You know, the sticks.

He's tall and so thin he looks emaciated, his long, pale face dotted with tiny red bumps. He is young, and he looks even younger, which makes his deep voice all the more incongruous with his persona.

—Got ya, Daniel says. Dr. Haddon tell you what I was looking for?

—He did, he says, licking glaze from his fingertips.

—Any religions in the area qualify?

—Two. One's here in town trying to fit in, seem mainstream. The other, which is far more fringe and radical, has a compound out near Louisiana Lodge. You know where that is?

—Yeah, Daniel says with a smile. I've heard of it.

—I'm making headway with the Witnesses of Yahweh—the group in town, but not really getting anywhere with Jehovah Nation. I know there are some genuinely religious guys in the Nation, but its incarnation here is more a biker gang or outlaw militia than anything else.

—Tell me about the Witnesses.

—Their racism is pretty subtle, but it's there, he says. They're white supremacist, they're just not militant about it. They see themselves as being the true Hebrews, a lost tribe of Israel. Most of their doctrine and teachings come from the Hebrew Bible, not the New

Testament. Women aren't allowed to lead or have any kind of authority. And soon God's fiery wrath is going to be poured out on all the
godless—including mongrels, homosexuals and other perverts, and
generally people who are not them.

—Where are they located?

—In a storefront just a few blocks from here, he says. They have
a very small congregation.

—Who's their leader? Daniel asks. Think he'd talk to me?

—Calls himself High Priest Aaron Ben Aaron, though I doubt
it's the name his mother gave him. And he loves to talk.

Chapter Thirty-seven

By the time Jerry Douglas reaches the Garden of Eden Botanical Garden, it's getting dark. The garden is closed for the day, but a middle-aged woman named Maggie has waited to show him around.

As he parks his car and walks toward the entrance, he smells smoke in the air—not enough for there to be a fire, but perhaps the smoldering remnants of one.

Maggie comes out of the visitor center and meets him at the warped front gates.

After introductions, she leads him through the gates, which she locks behind them with what looks to be a brand new chain and lock, and tells him about the garden as they walk toward the Middle Eastern area.

Even in the dim light, Jerry can see the enormity and elegance of the garden. Built around two lakes, the thick, verdant garden has canopied paths that wind around bushes, flowers, and trees in perfectly manicured beds and landscaped scenes of natural beauty.

Originally a 30-acre private estate belonging to Mr. and Mrs. William Broderick, a couple who had no children, it was donated to the Florida Conservancy for use as a botanical garden.

The garden's mission is to actively participate in the conservation of rare, threatened, and endangered plant species, to serve the botanical and horticultural needs of Liberty County, to offer a place of meditation, and to nurture biblical plants for better understanding of the Bible.

The tranquil garden is the perfect place for prayer and meditation, and pilgrims from many faith professions travel to the Garden of Eden for just such purposes, moved by the fact that the species of trees and plants surrounding them also surrounded Abraham, Moses, David, and Jesus.

—The acacia trees are just up on the left, Maggie says.

She's wearing a light blue denim jumper that extends down to her ankles with white tennis shoes peeking out beneath it. Not particularly unattractive, she wears no makeup whatsoever, has no hair style to speak of, and slumps her shoulders slightly.

—Do you know much about them? she asks.

—Not really, Jerry says.

—The acacia, or *shitim* in Hebrew, is the wood God chose for the tabernacle. Exodus twenty-six fifteen says, 'You shall make planks of the tabernacle of acacia wood, standing erect. Ten cubits the length of each plank, and a cubit and a half the width of each plank.' According to Jewish tradition, the reason there are so many of these trees in the Sinai region is the Patriarch Jacob anticipated the need for having lumber in the desert—divine inspiration, no doubt.

—No doubt, Jerry says.

—He planted them in Egypt and instructed the Hebrews to take the wood with them when the Exodus occurred. Here we are.

Growing at an angle as if on the side of a mountain, the small trees look like something from the Bible.

—These things ever catch on fire but not burn? Jerry says.

She hesitates a moment, then smiles.

Just twelve feet tall, the base of the trees have a diameter of only ten inches.

—They're smaller than I thought they'd be, he says.

—They took our larger ones, she says. Up here.

She leads him farther up the cement path and shows him the stumps of the stolen trees.

—They took eight, she says. Backed a truck up to the service entrance gate right down there, sawed the trees down, loaded them, and got out of here—all in one night between the time we closed and the time we reopened the next morning.

He took enough to build a lot more than one altar.

—He leave anything behind?

—Sheriff's department came out and looked around, made a few molds of shoe prints and tire tracks, but nothing ever came of it.

—Before it happened, you notice anyone hanging around this area, paying extra attention to the trees or the service entrance?

—Not really. Unless we're giving a tour, we're not out here much when our visitors are.

—What about an employee or volunteer who quit or was fired—maybe wasn't here very long.

She shakes her head.

—No, no one, she says. Why would someone do this?

—How'd he saw down the trees without anyone hearing?

—No one's out here at night, she says. None of us live anywhere close. We wouldn't have known about the explosion last night if y'all hadn't called us.

—The explosion?

—You think they're connected?

Aaron Ben Aaron, a white man in his fifties, is bald and has a long, square white beard and icy blue eyes behind small, round glasses. He's dressed in a white priestly robe, a purple cord around the girth of his large, round midsection, and worn brown sandals that reveal toenails in need of trimming.

With the hat, he could be the priest in the carving.

—Why are you interested in our faith, Dr. Davis?

—Several reasons, Daniel says. Like Nathan, I'm a student of religion, and I'm always on the lookout for new revelation. Partly it's curiosity, but it's also that at heart I'm a seeker, always looking for the truth.

—Well, look no further, Aaron says. You've found it. Yeshua said he did not come to destroy the law but to fulfill it.

Daniel nods.

The Witnesses of Yahweh's church is a small storefront with folding chairs set up theater style facing the back and the podium, communion table, and ark holding the Torah that are arranged there. Homemade banners line the walls and blinds cover the plate glass windows in the front.

—False prophets try to say that we as Christians are exempt from the law, Aaron continues, but this is not what Yeshua taught. The master, our great high priest, never told us to violate the law of Moses, just elaborated on how to better fulfill it. 'You have heard it said of old love your neighbor and hate your enemy, but I say to you love your enemies.' This is not an abolishing, but a broadening, a clarifying of the law of Moses.

—What about sacrifices? Do they still have a role in the new covenant?

—Certainly so. Just because Yeshua as our great high priest offered himself as our sacrifice doesn't do away with the sacrificial system. We continue to sin, to break the law, so there must be a price paid. Without the shedding of blood there can be no remission of sin.

The three men sit on the front row in folding chairs, having to turn awkwardly in their seats to see one another. After having made the introductions, Nathan has remained silent, seeming to have zoned out, unaware of what is being said.

—Do you actually offer animal sacrifices?

—We offer sacrifices. I cannot be more specific than that for obvious reasons. We live under an oppressive secular regime. The godless government is looking for any reason it can find to close my doors, to shut up Eden from the world.

—Who are the people of God spoken of in scripture?

—We are. I can trace my family all the way back to Moses.

—And the Jews?

—Many people, perhaps yourself included, have wrongly assumed Semites are spoken of in scripture, but Yahweh's covenant is with the white man. Why else would he rule the world? We are superior in every way to every other race, more advanced, more wealthy. If it weren't for us, the others would still be sniffing each other in the jungle.

Daniel nods. He's heard it all before. Xenophobia whitewashed by religion and taken to an extreme. It sickens him but he does his best not to let it show.

—One of the things I've been studying lately is the role of fire in religion. Can you share with me how fire fits into your faith?

—Yahweh is the all-consuming fire, he says. He purges and refines us, burning off all that is unclean and impure. As a prophet, I have his fire shut up in my bones. I must speak. I cannot hold it back.

Daniel recognizes the allusion to the Hebrew prophet Jeremiah.

Though much of what Aaron Ben Aaron is saying fits with what Daniel believes to be the killer's view, he doesn't think the man is the killer. In addition to being far older than the profile suggests, he's also far too fat to have outrun him on the tracks Sunday night. He may not be the killer, but he certainly could have inspired him.

—One of the reasons I've been so interested in fire's role in religion lately is because I'm helping the police with their investigation into the recent rash of deaths by fire in the area. We have reason to believe that whoever's doing them has a religious motivation, that he's offering sacrifices by fire.

—Ah, I see, Aaron says, his demeanor changing instantly. The real reason for your interest. He sits up, straightening his robe, pushing his glasses up on his nose.

—I'm honestly interested in your religion, Daniel says, but I'm also looking for the young man who is burning people alive as human sacrifices—which is something Yahweh never asked for, wouldn't you agree?

—Actually, there is the instance of Isaac, he says. And there is the Holocaust, which, if it happened, was allowed by Yahweh.

—It wouldn't be good for the spread of your religion if the murderer was a member of your congregation and you didn't help us stop him.

—I assure you he is not. I have a small congregation and know each member of my flock intimately.

Daniel stands, realizing what a waste of time this is.

—However, Aaron says, I might just know who you are looking for.

Chapter Thirty-eight

Evening.

Diffused light. Golden glow.

The corrugated tin fence surrounding the compound is warped, rusted, graffiti-covered. In many places, the trees, bushes, and weeds are so thick, it can't be seen.

Off of Highway 371 on the very edge of Pine County, it's out of the jurisdiction of the Bayshore Police Department.

—But we're on the task force, Adam Whitten is saying. That extends our goddam jurisdiction.

A white man in his midforties, Whitten, who tries to conceal the fact that he is short by wearing cowboy boots and a ten-gallon hat, is also thick-bodied and a little soft, and has yet to find a way to conceal that.

—You better radio Agent Michaels, his partner Colin Dyson says.

Too pretty and intelligent to be a patrol cop, Dyson could do anything he wanted if he weren't a black man in Pine County—something that has made him cautious.

—I don't need some woman state cop to tell me what I can and can't do, he says. Long after she's gone back to Miami, I'll still be here in America protecting and serving.

—What's your plan exactly? Dyson asks. Just roll up on 'em and ask if any of 'em been burnin' bitches?

—Something like that, yeah.

—Okay, Dyson says, feeling the Kevlar vest beneath his uniform shirt.

—You scared of a few rednecks with rifles?

—Obviously not. Who you think I work with every damn day?

Adam pulls the car off the highway onto the recently graded dirt road and down to the entrance of the compound of the religious redneck militia that calls itself Jehovah Nation.

The entrance of the compound is comprised of two large chain-link fence gates with razor wire looped around the top of them. Behind the chain-link, sheets of tin have been bolted into place, and beside it, signs warning of bad dogs, worse owners, and serious bodily harm for anyone with enough of a death wish to even try to enter.

The moment they park and get out, a smaller gate in the tin fence swings open.

—Got a warrant?

The question comes from a large, muscle-bound man wearing a too-small wife beater and jeans tucked into leather motorcycle boots.

Through the small gate opening, Adam sees at least two men with outstanding warrants and enough illegal weapons to start a small war.

—We just have—

—Come back when you do.

Before either man can say anything, the gate closes and the man disappears.

—Did you see all those weapons? Dyson asks. And wasn't that Paul Cox and Gary Peterson?

—I did, Adam says. And it was.

—That gives us the right to go in, he says.

—Absolutely, but I think you're right, Dyce. Best to let the lady cop handle this one.

Open.

Empty.

Breathe.

In.

Out.

Breathe.   •

Daniel prepares himself to start over. To clear his mind of everything and, with fresh eyes and a new perspective, look at, think about, and meditate on all the evidence again.

Louisiana Lodge is quiet, dim in the diminishing day.

Concentrate. Still your mind. Right now. This is all that matters.

Running with Ben.

Train depot.

Belt, shoes.

Tree stand.

Carving.

Something there . . . Something scratching at the edge of his subconscious.

Let it come.

Surfacing. Floating up. Making itself known.

The cross. The symbol. Tree stand. Something . . . bothering him.

Stumbling over to the old, large, scarred wooden kitchen table, he drops into an uncomfortable wooden chair and begins to study the photos of the carvings he printed out on Ben's computer.

Scattered among the crime scene photos are open books displaying a variety of crosses with additional bars.

Looking back and forth between the photos and the images in the books, he tries to determine which cross the unfinished symbol is by process of elimination.

Of course, it might not be a cross at all, but from what is present, some form or variation of a cross seems likely.

Since the extra bars are not on the main bar but extend off the cross bars, the symbol is not the papal or patriarchal cross. The cross potent seems possible, but the angle is wrong. It's possible it's the Jerusalem or crusader's cross, but only if he was carving the four smaller crosses to touch the large center one, and if he were doing that, it would cease to be the Jerusalem cross.

Leaning back in his chair, he reaches for a pad of paper and a pen on the counter near the phone. Drawing the symbol as it is on his pad, he begins to attempt to complete it, extending to the cross bars that are present, adding additional ones.

And then he sees it.

Shaking his head, frustrated with himself that he didn't see it before, he stares at a bent cross. It's all in the angle. Because of the angle there's no other type of cross it could be. The symbol is that of an equilateral cross with its arms bent at right angles. A holy symbol in Hinduism, Jainism, and Buddhism, the bent cross is better known in the West as a swastika, the emblem of anti-Semitism, of Nazism, and unimaginable atrocities.

In the euphoric rush of his discovery, he snatches up the phone and calls Sam.

—I've got something. Fits with what we know of the victims so far.

—Lay it on me.

He does.

—So we're looking for a neo-Nazi?

—Which explains why he took Ben and Brian. Wasn't just because of our friendship, but because they're Jewish.

—You think our victims are Jewish?

—There's a good chance.

—Does this fit with the brazen altar thingy?

—Completely. A lot of Fundamentalist, white supremacist, anti-Semitic Christian religions, ironically enough, attempt to keep all the laws of Moses.

—What's that mean?

—They could hold the altar, the Scriptures, *and* the swastika sacred.

—Could it be a group?

—I don't think so. But our guy may have been a part of one in the past. I think we're right to check with local radical religions, Fundamentalists, anti-Semitic militias for an angry young man who left their group because they weren't extreme enough for him. And we need to check Pine Key for members of the Jewish community who are missing.

She's about to say something when he lets out a loud gasp of exasperation.

—What?

—I should've thought of this before.

—Thought of what?

—You know what the word *holocaust* means?

—No. What?

—It comes from a Greek word meaning fire sacrifice or burnt offering.

When they end the call, he punches in Ben's number and gets his machine.

—Ben, it's Daniel. Pick up. There's a madman killing Jews and I need your help to stop him. Ben? Are you home?

Chapter Thirty-nine

Stetson Knee's Friday night party following the Bayshore football game is something the kids who like to drink and smoke pot look forward to all week. He calls it the Fifth Quarter and charges five bucks to enter, though what the kids are entering is an empty field not far from the river.

Out of school for a couple of years now and not making much progress at the community college in Panama City, Stetson knows it's pathetic to still be partying with high school kids, but he enjoys making the fliers, booking the bands, and getting wasted with everyone else.

Tonight's game went into overtime, so the party was late getting started, but it's picking up steam now, carloads of kids pulling into the field, paying, and parking. He'll make out like a bandit tonight, his only overhead, the cost of producing the fliers and beer for the band. The dumbass kids pay five bucks to come to a field he doesn't even own and bring their own bottles and baggies.

He had gotten word that his parties were getting too big, too infamous for underage drinking, the passing around of big blunts, and sixteen- and seventeen-year-old girls waking up pregnant. Word was the sheriff planned to shut him down.

And maybe that was his plan, though probably not while he's in a coma.

But Stetson is wrong once again. He watches as the deputy cars pull up, lights flashing, sirens blurting, which leads to kids scattering. Most jumping into their cars and racing away, some running into the woods.

Apparently here only to break up the party, scare the kids, and send them home before they're too drunk to drive, deputies allow those leaving to do so, just signaling for them to slow down as they do.

But not everyone realizes this, and Stetson guesses more than a couple of kids are going to spend the night lost in the woods.

He is preparing to make his final offering of the day when he hears all the commotion coming through the woods. So far, things have gone according to plan. He's been disappointed in Daniel and the lady agent. He had such high hopes for them—especially Daniel, but he's just not proving to be a worthy interpreter, Aaron to his Moses, Paul to his Jesus.

And now this interruption. It's too much. It makes him angry, fills him with a righteous indignation that someone would dare to trample on holy ground, halt the work of the Lord. Well, he can't let that happen. He won't.

Jess and Mandy are sharing a joint when five-o rolls up.

Dropping the joint, Mandy heads for the woods. Jess, hesitating a moment, grabs the joint and follows her.

She's got a head start and she's running as fast as she can, but Jess catches her before she's much more than a mile in.

—Wait up, he says. What're you doin'?

—Do you know how much weed and moonshine are in my car?

A lot, he realizes. Not so much grass, but a hell of a lot of hooch. A friend of theirs steals it from his dad's stash, and tonight he gave them enough to share with the whole group.

—Shit, he says. What're we gonna do?

—Run home. Tell my parents my car was stolen.

—You know how far it is?

—I can do it. Can you?

—Well, yeah, but I'm tired from the game and a little high.

—You got any other—

They hear a noise, stop running and talking, and turn to see a figure not far from them.

Another kid from the party?

As the figure begins to run in their direction, Jess thinks, He don't run like no kid. Seems older. Something's wrong. He swings around toward Mandy.

—Run, he says.

She does.

When he turns back around, the man is almost on him. Crouching down in a defensive position like he had so many times during the game tonight, he gets ready, and when the man is close enough, he lowers his shoulder and tackles him.

Not sure what to do now, Jess just lies on the man, trying to give Mandy as much of a head start as he can. It's not much of a plan, but in his condition, it's the best he can come up with. So he doesn't move. Just lies there.

At first, he's surprised the man doesn't do anything—doesn't make any sounds except breathing and doesn't try to move. Then he realizes he probably knocked the breath out of him.

He lies there for a few more minutes without moving, then, deciding to get up, discovers he can't. Evidently, him not moving had been the other man's plan, as well.

Rolling the limp body off of him, he stands, the rage in him rising. Not only has his work been interrupted, but now he's had to waste his syringe of succinyl choline on this smelly, intoxicated hayseed.

He had discovered succinyl choline while conducting his extensive research for his work, his mission. It's a neuromuscular paralytic that leaves a person wide awake, though completely paralyzed. By using it, he can concentrate on what he's doing and not have to worry about his sacrifices jumping up and running away. He can also enjoy the expressions on their faces when they realize they're actually on fire and can do nothing about it. They deserve to suffer, to experience just a taste of the pain and death they have inflicted, feeling just a foretaste of hellfires awaiting them.

Of course, it took him a while to figure out the dosages. Too much and the sacrifice will die before the fire is burning good. Too little and they scream. The stuff works fast, so he has to start the fire as soon as he administers the injection, but it's not a problem. He's always been an eager boy.

Now with his sacrifice still waiting, his frustration at the interruption, and the waste of his succinyl choline, he still has to find the girl.

Chapter Forty

Unable to sleep, Daniel drives into Bayshore and runs along the beach, telling himself it's not because it takes him right in front of the Driftwood.

He could say that he's too afraid to run on the train tracks or anywhere near his house, and he wouldn't be lying, but these reasons, though good, aren't his primary motivation. The truth is, if he really wanted to be truthful, he's not too tired to sleep. In fact, the only thing he wants to do more than sleep is see Sam.

A half-moon partially shrouded by thin shreds of clouds illuminates the beach and reflects, as if on glass, on the smooth surface of the Gulf. The night is warm, but not hot, and the sand feels cool on his bare feet.

The waves are gentle, rolling ashore with little sound or splash, bringing with them the soft whisper of a Gulf breeze.

After warming up, he's got a good pace going, his long stride leaving little divots in the sand, but as he nears the Driftwood, he slows down.

Wrapped in a sheet from the extra bed in her room, Sam lies in a plastic lounge chair on her balcony, enjoying the tender roll of the gentle tide.

She can't believe she's not asleep. It's what she needs more than anything right now. How will she have any chance of catching this guy if she's not at her very best, and how can she be when she's so sleep deprived she finds it difficult to form a thought, to sustain any kind of internal dialog?

She had come in earlier, taken a shower, toweled off just enough not to be soaking wet, and had fallen into bed. Then, an hour later, she had awakened and was unable to fall back asleep. After nearly another hour of trying to drift back off, she wrapped her naked body in the crisp white sheet from the double bed opposite the one she had been sleeping on and stumbled out onto the balcony. Instantly soothed by the sounds of the sea, she wondered why she hadn't tried this before.

After a long while, her eyelids become heavy again, signaling the approach of sleep. Fighting it for a couple of moments, she is just about to give in, to close her eyes and dream she is drifting on the smooth surface of the Gulf, when she sees him.

There, in the distance, as if a figment of her imagination, Daniel Davis is running down the beach toward her.

When he looks up and sees her, he has a choice to make. He can keep running, hoping she'll invite him up, letting her make the first move since she had been the one to rebuff his previous advances, or he can take a chance, overcome his fear and just run up to her room, and beat her door down if he has to.

It's more than just a choice between connection and solitude, love and fear. It's a choice between life and death, between moving on with the rest of his life or remaining frozen in fear.

Making his choice, he turns and runs up toward the hotel, through the door to the stairwell, up the stairs, and to her door, which he finds open.

She is there waiting for him, her bare, pale shoulders showing above the white sheet wrapped around her.

Without saying a word, he takes her face in his hands and kisses her passionately on the mouth, kicking the door shut behind him with his foot.

She kisses back and he continues.

When he moves his hands from her face to explore the rest of her body, he finds, to his immense joy, that she is naked beneath the sheet. With hands that are tender, but eager, he caresses her taut body, lingering at various places along the way.

Participating every bit as much as he, her mouth and hands match his hunger and intensity as if mirror images of his.

—Wait, she says, stepping back.

—What is it?

She reaches over and turns on the lamp near the television.

—I've got to tell you something first.

Here we go. Test time. Will he pass? Oh dear God, please let him.

—Okay.

—About me, she says. My body.

Chapter Forty-one

—As long as you're not a dude, he says, it won't be a problem.

She tries to smile, but can't.

—My grandmother and mother both died of breast cancer, she says. It's one of the reasons I'm taking Frances Rainy's advice and giving in to what I feel for you.

—I don't follow.

—Life is short. Can't let fear keep us from living.

He nods, and she can tell he understands.

—From birth to age thirty-nine, she says, one in two-hundred and thirty-one women get breast cancer. From forty to fifty-nine that changes to one in twenty-five.

He nods, listening intently.

—I'll be forty in a few months, she says. With my family history, I'd be the one in twenty-five, so I recently underwent a double mastectomy. Not only do I have no breasts, I have no feeling in my chest whatsoever. I'm scarred—I think it's the real reason why Stan broke up with me.

She searches his face.

—You can leave now, she says, and I'll understand. I really will.
Hell, I see myself in the mirror every day and I'm just starting to
get used to it. I won't think less of you. I really won't. I plan to have
reconstructive surgery, but I haven't yet, so—

—Leave the light on, he says.

He steps toward her, takes the sheet in his hands, and gently pulls
at it. She lets go and it falls to the floor.

He studies her scars, tracing the tumescent tissue with the tip of
his finger.

She searches his face again, this time for even the slightest sign of
revulsion, but smiles and lets out a relieved sigh when she finds only
desire.

—You are so beautiful I can barely breathe, he says.

Tears sting her eyes.

—It doesn't bother you?

Stan wouldn't touch her after the surgery, saying she needed
to heal first, but breaking up with her before she had. Actually, he
couldn't even bring himself to look at her.

—Just the opposite, he says. These wounds speak of your brav-
ery, your strength, your commitment to fight for your life. They make
me love you even more.

Love? Did he just say love?

He finds her more attractive than any woman he's ever seen. Her
body is a ballad of beauty and pain, of strength and fragility, and he
wants to spend the rest of his life exploring it. He feels nothing but
desire. He's got to convince her of that.

—You are your scars, he says, as I am mine. Of all the bodies in
all the world, yours is the one I want to make love to.

Pulling her to him, he presses her chest to his, kissing her mouth,
as his fingers caress her body.

—Oh God, she says, when his fingers find the moistness between
her legs.

He lingers there.

—This could still be a mistake for other reasons, she whispers.

—I know.

She pulls his running shorts down and takes him in her hand.

It's been so long, he's nearly forgotten how good it feels, how much he needs the touch of a woman—no longer just any woman. *This* woman.

—It's too soon. I just broke up with my boyfriend.

—I know.

Stepping out of his shorts that are now on the floor, he lifts her in his arms and carries her to the bed.

—We should wait, she says.

—We really should, he says, and slides inside her.

The next morning, they wake beside each other on the balcony to the sounds of seagulls, their naked bodies wrapped in the same sheet she had been the night before.

On their sides, spooning, her in front, his arms around her, he pulls her to him.

As she wiggles against him, she can feel his body's immediate response.

—Good morning, he says.

—Morning.

—Is it too soon for me to ask you to marry me?

She smiles, a warmth spreading inside her she can't ever remember experiencing before.

—Little bit, yeah.

It's completely ridiculous, of course, but it's sweet and it makes her feel good.

—Would you let me know when enough time has passed?

—Sure, she says, but I doubt you'll still want to by then.

Chapter Forty-two

When Sam walks into Mandy's hospital room, she is surprised to find her alone.

—Where are your parents?

She shrugs.

—Probably out getting some food or something.

She's raising herself, and doing a bad job.

Sam is filled with anger as she remembers the stifling small-town despair she witnessed growing up not far from here, in a town not unlike this one.

Drinking and drugging have become small-town substitutes for family, purpose, and ambition. The idea of a good time for many young people like Mandy is gettin' wasted on the weekend. Gather at the river, someone's house, or at the local bog-in and drink beer, whiskey, or moonshine, pop pills pilfered from their parents' medicine cabinets, and smoke grass.

And for those for whom this is not enough, there is crack and meth.

And where are their parents? Doing the same things, still living like they're in high school, moving from relationship to relationship, numbing themselves against the shallowness and emptiness, barely more responsible than their teenagers, and in many instances not as.

If she didn't remember before, Sam is reminded again now why she fled from the small town she grew up in and never looked back.

—How do you feel? Sam asks.

—Not too bad.

That's the pain meds. She has a broken leg, a fractured wrist, and several abrasions. She had been hit by a car when she ran out of the woods screaming for help.

—Have you found Jess yet? she asks, her voice small, airy, a little girl's.

Sam shakes her head.

—Where were you and Jess when you saw the man in the woods?

—I don't know. We just ran in and kept on running.

—How long had you been running before you saw him?

She shrugs.

—Look, I was so messed up, I have no clue. Maybe ten minutes, maybe more.

—And you were running hard the whole time?

—Yeah, I think, she says. I'm just not sure. I stopped to puke one time, but I think that was after we saw him.

—You told Officer Stewart there was something odd about the man.

Mandy nods.

—He was wearing a robe, she says. And carrying a torch.

—You're sure?

—Positive. I didn't really see it until I turned back to see what was happening. Jess was on top of the guy, but then the guy just kinda rolled him off and stood up. When he did, I saw his robe and torch.

Sam's phone vibrates and she pulls it off her belt, flips it open, and answers it.

—Agent Michaels, it's Colin Dyson. We found the boy.

The tall grass, bahia shoots, and weeds of the small field are bent from car and truck tires and littered with beer cans, whiskey bottles, potato chip bags, condom wrappers, and drug paraphernalia. In a few spots, the blackened logs of bonfires remain in pits dug in the earth.

Now, where the trucks and cars of young people had been, cop cars, emergency vehicles, and the FDLE crime scene van are parked. The only vehicle remaining from the previous night is Mandy's old gray SUV.

Sam passes through the field, sickened by the waste and aimlessness it represents, and into the woods beyond it, bowing beneath crime scene tape, watching for cottonmouths and rattlesnakes.

No path to speak of, she is treading on damp swamp bed, dead leaves and pine straw, over fallen cypress trees, and around the thick bases of water oaks. About fifty feet in, she is joined by Colin Dyson and Adam Whitten.

—This gonna affect our raid on the Jehovah militia? Whitten asks.

She shakes her head.

—You still get to break their front door down.

She doubts he'd be nearly so eager if he didn't have a dozen specially trained FDLE agents going in with him.

—Whatta we got? she asks.

—We think the killer murdered the boy, though how we're not exactly sure, then went after the girl, Dyson says. She comes out on the road and gets hit before he can get her, and by the time he gets back here, there are deputies searching the woods for kids.

—That sounds right.

They arrive at the body, stopping short so as not to disturb the techs. Michelle Barnes steps over to her.

Jess is lying face up, eyes shut, the whiskers on his pale chin long and scraggly. Except for his unnatural stillness and lack of color, he looks to be hung over, sleeping it off.

—I take it cause of death is not apparent, Sam says.

—No sign whatsoever, she says, except a tiny puncture wound, which may actually be the break we need.

—How's that?

—We know he's drugging his victims, we just don't know what he's using because of the condition of the bodies, but if he used the same agent here, we'll know what it is.

—As soon as you can.

—Will do. And it looks like I could have an ID on the train depot victim as early as this afternoon.

On her way back to her car, Sam calls Daniel.

—Hey, he says, his voice groggy.

—You asleep? she asks.

—Someone kept me up most of the night.

—The same someone who managed to climb out of bed and get out here to fight crime this morning? You awake now?

—Wide.

—You know how we've been patrolling around your plantation?

—It's not a plantation, but yes, I know.

—Well, he's not over there. He's over here.

—Where's here?

—A river swamp out in the middle of nowhere . . . I don't know.

—You found another body?

—No, well, yeah, she says, but it's different. We think a kid interrupted him.

—Oh, no.

—He didn't burn him, just killed him. We're not even sure how he did it, but he didn't use fire.

—He wasn't part of his plan.

—Exactly, she says.

—I've got people searching this area, but can you think of why he'd be here?

—I'd have to know where 'here' is.

—If I send you a map with a big X marking this spot, would you see if you can come up with why he's changed locations?

—Sure, he says. You gonna bring it over?

—I get to go raid the compound of a redneck militia.

—Be careful.

—I will.

—We gonna talk about last night? he asks.

—I would think this morning would be the more pressing issue.

—This morning?

—You proposed.

—You sure?

—I was wearing a wire at the time.

—Where exactly was it hidden?

—I knew it was just the sex talking.

—It wasn't. But there's one way to find out.

—I've got to go.

—So we'll talk later?

—We'll talk sooner if you figure out what this guy's up to, where he is, and how I find him.

—I'm having serious doubts about you, Daniel.

Daniel has just stepped out of the shower to answer his phone, water dripping off him, pooling on the cool tile around his feet.

It's the same eerie electronic voice as before.

—Are you really trying? Can you see what wondrous works are being wrought right before your very eyes?

—I'm sorry. I'm trying. I really am.

—What about poor Brian? What would you have told his parents if that cop hadn't stumbled upon him?

—I'm not sure.

—Now is the appointed time.

—Tell me what I'm missing. Teach me how to see.

—The fire will fall, the sacrifices be consumed. The iron, clay, brass, silver, and gold will be broken to pieces together and become like chaff of the summer threshing floors. The wind will carry them away so that no place is found for them.

—What does that mean? Daniel asks, but the line is dead before he finishes.

Chapter Forty-three

—I only got three guys who work with brass and have their own shop, Bernie Clark says, his voice sounding distant and tiny on the car speakerphone. And none of 'em's religious.

—Hold on, Travis says. Let me get something to write on.

He pulls his patrol car over to the side of the road.

—You want me to write it? Jerry Douglas asks.

The two men are on their way to meet with the Liberty County detective in charge of the Garden of Eden robbery.

—I got it.

Travis withdraws a small spiral-bound notebook out of his pocket, flips it open, then pulls out a tiny pencil with no eraser like the ones in church pews or putt-putt golf places. Except for old TV detectives, Jerry's never seen anyone actually use them before.

—Shoot, he says, his pencil poised over his pad.

Travis then writes down the three names.

—You got addresses?

—Son, I feel bad as hell about doing this, Clark says. These are my guys. They're no more killers than I am. Will you make sure and tell them I told you that?

—Will do, Travis says.

Clark gives him the addresses, then the two men end the call.

—If you need to follow up on that, Jerry says, I can meet with the Liberty guy alone.

—Neither should take very long, Travis says, and I'll be dang surprised if either of 'em help us catch the guy.

It's a sacred place, meant to be quiet, hushed. He wishes she'd stop whimpering. Doesn't she realize what this is, what she's a part of? He's not sure any of them have—maybe when they felt the fire, maybe then, but even if they didn't, even if they were clueless as to their part in the awesome work of the All-Consuming Fire, they didn't whimper and whine like this little bitch.

She wants me to kill her. To do it quickly, but I won't.

In an attempt to block out her blithering, he recites from memory what the Lord commanded him to do, what he has done, beholding it with his eyes as the holy words issue forth from his mouth.

—'Make the tabernacle with ten curtains of finely twisted linen and blue, purple and scarlet yarn, with cherubim worked into them by a skilled craftsman. All the curtains are to be the same size—twenty-eight cubits long and four cubits wide. The curtain will separate the Holy Place from the Most Holy Place. Put the atonement cover on the ark of the Testimony in the Most Holy Place. Place the table outside the curtain on the north side of the tabernacle and put the lampstand opposite it on the south side.'

All this he has done—done well, and it is good. Now if he can just get the little bitch to shut her dirty little mouth.

—I'm not going to kill you, he says. But I *will* cut out your tongue.

When Preacher blinks a few times and opens his eyes, Frances Rainy's
heart feels like it flips inside her chest. A broad smile spreads across
her face as tears stream down to meet it.

—Oh, thank you God, I thought I had lost you.

Preacher looks up at her and smiles.

—You're in Bayshore Memorial, she says. You've been in a coma.
Do you remember what happened?

He thinks about it for a moment and nods.

—Who?

—The Marshall boy. He went crazy. Been living there for a long
time.

—Is he dead?

She nods.

—Steve?

Nods again.

—Marshall killed him long before you got there.

His dry mouth turns down and his eyes glisten.

—How do you feel?

—Good, he says. Very rested.

—He managed to miss all your vital organs when he stabbed you,
but you lost a lot of blood. The doctors repaired the damage, gave
you blood, and sewed you up.

—And you've been here . . .

—The entire time, she says. Do I smell?

—So . . .

—The cat's out of the bag, she says. Nigga's out of the wood-
shed, moving out of the slave quarters and into the big house.

—Will you marry me? he asks.

—If you still want me to after you're out of here and feeling back
to normal, she says. I sure as hell will.

Cup of coffee in hand, Daniel paces about the morning- sun-dappled rooms of Louisiana Lodge, refreshing his memory about the brazen altar and burnt offerings.

When the ancient Israelites entered the courtyard of the taber-nacle, the brazen altar or altar of burnt offerings was the first thing they would see. To its left, there was an ash heap, where the ashes from the altar were placed. Between the brazen altar and the doorway to the inner court stood the brazen laver where the priests cleansed themselves.

From the Hebrew word *olah*, meaning ascending, burnt offerings were ones that were consumed by fire, ascending to God while being consumed.

Part of every offering was burned in the sacred fire, but burnt offerings were wholly burned.

One of the consecratory offerings, burnt offerings emphasize the offerer's complete surrender and submission to God. Bringing the sacrificial animal to the brazen altar, the offerer laid his hands on the head of the sacrifice to transmit his sins and killed it on the north side of the altar, and the priest collected the blood and sprinkled it around the altar, then dissected the sacrifice, washing the unclean parts and carefully laying them on the fire of the altar of burnt offer-ings.

He's the offerer *and* the priest. As the offerer, he chooses his sacrifice, brings it to the site, and kills it. As the priest, he removes the skin, sprinkles the blood, cuts up the body, and places it on the altar. As the priest, he's also responsible for the care and maintenance of the fire.

Since the sacrifice is completely consumed on the altar, the of-ferer and the priest are surrendering not in part, as with other sacri-fices, but completely. Like many of their contemporaries, the patri-archs and priests of ancient Israel offered burnt offerings. Abraham, the father of Judaism, Islam, and Christianity, had even been willing to make a holocaust of his son. Burnt offerings are meant to bring cleansing, purification, and atonement—a life taken, a life spared.

Daniel shudders when he reads that burnt offerings were the most frequent form of sacrifices made. They actually had the continual burnt offering—one every morning and evening—in addition to one every Sabbath, the beginning of each month, and special ones on every holy day.

Then it hits him. The first sacrifice was made on Rosh Hashanah. The Day of Atonement is only days away, and it calls for no less than nine burnt offerings in a single day.

Casting the book aside, he finds his phone and calls Sam.

—It's Rosh Hashanah, he says.

—Well, happy new year. But I thought it was last week.

—No. It was. That's when he killed his first victim.

—I was just about to call you. Dentist on Pine Key was able to give us an ID on the depot victim.

—Was she Jewish?

—She was. Naomi Abramson. She was supposed to be on a cruise. No one missed her.

—Where are you?

—On my way to kick in a door, but I can drop by for a minute.

—So he's killing according to Jewish holy days?

They're in his kitchen. Neither of them has eaten today, and he has cinnamon rolls in the oven. She is seated at the table. It's covered with printouts of the carvings and open books displaying crosses, along with books about the tabernacle of Moses and Jewish holy days.

—I think so, he says. The first victim was killed on Rosh Hashanah.

—That's when we found her. Not when she was killed. She was killed the night before.

—Yeah, he says. Jewish holy days always begin at sundown and end at sundown. The night he killed his first victim, Rosh Hashanah began at sundown. When we found the body, Rosh Hashanah was still taking place and ended at sundown that night.

—And we now know she was Jewish.

—So it fits.

He turns his attention away from the window in the oven door and looks at her. Tossing the oven mitt on the counter, he steps over in front of her.

They are quiet a moment, gazing into one another's tired eyes, something undeniable passing between them.

Eventually, she looks away.

—If this was about Rosh Hashanah, why keep—

—I don't think it was. I mean, yes, that started everything, but it was just the beginning. I think what he's doing will culminate in Yom Kippur, the Day of Atonement. Rosh Hashanah and Yom Kippur are extremely important, a time of reflection and reassessment. It's the beginning of a new year, a time when some believe God is deciding who will live and who will die in the coming year. All the activities around this time, all the prayers, rites, and rituals are meant to influence God's decision. It's a time of repenting for past sins, atoning, consecrating yourself to God, pledging love and future service.

He steps over to the oven and looks through the window again.

—He atoning for his sins or judging his victims for theirs? she asks.

—Maybe both, though I'd imagine he sees himself as sinless and godlike. Thinks he's on a mission from God.

—But why is he using Jewish holy days to kill Jews?

—He could see himself as the true servant of God and them as false, so he's mocking their holy days, he says. Or he could believe that he is following the law of Moses and is punishing them because they are not, or because as he sees it, they rejected the messiah, or any number of less logical reasons.

She shakes her head.

—Religion, man.

—I know.

—How'd you get involved in it? You don't seem very religious.

—When my parents died, I felt a spiritual presence so palpable I couldn't deny it. It sustained me. It was mysterious and subtle and I dedicated my life to understanding it. I became a student and eventually a teacher of religion, but all that's done is obscure the presence I felt back then.

—So are you religious or not?

He shrugs.

—Not in a way most people would recognize, but in my own way—at least somewhat. I try to practice the best of what I've learned from all religions. It's a way of living, of being in the world—not dogma or something outward others can see. I try to live in harmony with the way, to flow, to breathe, to be.

She nods.

—I know what you're saying—that you're inward directed and not like the ignorant loudmouth assholes—

—The Tao Te Ching says those that say, don't know, he says.

—Exactly, and those that know, don't say, but you're wrong about people not being able to tell. You have this . . . I don't know, aura. It's so . . . It's hard to explain, but it's obvious you're different—I don't know, deeper, more . . . something. I guess it's spiritual. I just don't like the word.

He is genuinely touched, obviously uncomfortable, his eyes moist as he looks away.

—Thank you, he says, and they are quiet for a long moment.

—So Rosh Hashanah was when? she asks.

—September twenty-third, he says. Actually, it began at sundown on Friday, the twenty-second.

—And Yom Kippur?

—Begins at sundown on Sunday, October first.

—We've only got a few days. No wonder things are moving so fast. Feels like we've been working this for weeks.

He switches the oven off and withdraws the pan, a sweet, cinnamony aroma filling the room.

—So what day did we find the brazen altar?

—Days of Awe, he says. They begin with Rosh Hashanah and end with Yom Kippur.

—Oh great, she says. The Days of fuckin' Awe?

—I think he'll make two burnt offerings a day during the Days of Awe. And nine on Yom Kippur.

—*Nine. Fuck.* God, it sucks to be me about now.

—Pretty bad for his victims too, he says with a smile.

She laughs.

—There you go, she says. You're getting the hang of it. So where are all the victims?

—I don't know, he says. I must be missing something. And I could be wrong about all of it. If your lab finds more than one type of blood on the altar, we'll know.

—But if you're right, why aren't we getting any missing persons reports?

—We need to talk to Ben, he says. If the guy is killing Jews, then they're coming from Pine Key.

Chapter Forty-four

—Why is he doing this?

—I'm not sure exactly, but I think I finally know *what* he's doing—or at least part of it.

—Tell me.

Daniel tells him the conclusions he's reached and why.

—Will it never end? Ben says. Will we just keep being subjected to horror and pain and death until the end of time? How much more can we take?

—I'm so, so sorry.

—It's just so raw, he says, nodding toward the monitor. Working on this project has all my nerves exposed.

Though intended to be an inspirational project about the survival of the Jews, many of the stories featured in the documentary are far more depressing than they are uplifting. Many of the people interviewed seem almost guilty and ashamed of what their parents and grandparents had to do just to make it possible for them to be alive today. In the case of Rabbi Gold, his father had been a kapo or trustee during the Holocaust just to make it out alive.

Daniel nods.

—So you think I'm right? Based on what we know of what he's doing.

—Yeah. Sadly, I do. God, human history is just an account of the persecution of the Jews.

—I know it feels that way.

—It *is* that way, Ben says. And you know it.

—Well, here's your chance to do something about it. Help me figure out who it is.

—How?

—Find out if anyone is missing from the island. If I'm right, there are more victims. Where are they? Who are they? Why is he choosing them? Why aren't they being reported missing?

—It's a small island, Ben says. Closed community—we've had to be, as you can see. There's no way one of us is missing and the others don't notice.

Sam stands in the woods across the dirt road from the entry to the Jehovah Nation compound with men specially trained for flashbang entries. Members of the elite FDLE SWAT team, they are dressed in riot gear including fire-resistant Nomex flightsuits, body armor with level three bullet-proof vests, gloves, helmets, and balaclava or protective face covering. In addition to their special military-type training and rigorous demands beyond that of ordinary agents, they each receive two days every month of ongoing training in special weapons and tactics, which includes hostage situations and counter-terrorism.

Originally known as the Special Weapons Assault Team, SWAT, now Special Weapons and Tactics, began in 1967 in the Los Angeles Police Department for the purpose of performing dangerous operations such as high risk entries like the one today, riot control, making dangerous arrests, serving high-risk warrants, and general CQB or close quarters battle.

If you're going through a door, these are the guys you want with you.

She had considered calling in DEA because of the suspected drugs inside the compound or ATF because of the weapons, and though both are great agencies and have well-trained teams, there's no SWAT team she trusts more than that of her own agency.

Since, like most small counties, the Pine County Sheriff's Department doesn't have a SWAT team, they routinely call in teams from other agencies, including and most often FDLE. However, because anyone arrested by the FDLE team will be placed in the local jail, smaller counties use ATF and DEA when they can so that those arrested will be placed in federal detention centers like the one in Tallahassee. This prevents a small area like Pine County from having to incur the extra costs of housing inmates in their jails. Mindful of this, once the arrests are made, Sam intends to call in ATF on the weapons charges and DEA on the drug charges, remanding the detainees over to them. Preacher doesn't need the additional stress of going over budget because his jail is overrun with Jehovah Nationers.

—We're ready, ma'am, the team leader says. We'll go on your word.

Sam takes a deep breath and lets it out.

—No time to waste, she says. Go.

Taking a few steps back, she puts in her earpiece, lifts her binoculars, and waits for the balloon to go up.

And in a moment it does.

Bam.

The door is rammed open.

Flash.

Bang.

Agents file through the opening, tossing flashbang grenades, shouting, weapons drawn.

Producing a blinding flash equal to one million Candela flash and a deafening blast between 170-180 decibels, the flashbang grenade incapacitates without causing serious injury.

Originally designed for the British Special Air Service, flashbangs or stun grenades are used to confuse, disorient, or momentarily distract potential threats for up to five seconds, seriously degrading the effectiveness of adversaries for up to a minute.

—Police, someone yells. Hands up.

Shots are fired.

Sam can't tell if they are from her team or members of the Nation, but she suspects the latter.

Boards break. Crack. Splinter.

More explosions.

More shouts.

More of both for a few minutes.

—Clear, someone yells.

—Clear, someone else yells.

For the next few moments there is radio silence and few noises coming from over the fence, then a volley of shots, and an explosion.

—Fire, someone yells. Fire. Fire.

Daniel spreads out the large map on the long wooden table in Ben's creative suite.

Also known as the war room, the small conference area is where Ben and his staff hold production meetings and meet with talent and clients. Like the rest of the offices, the room is dim except for spots on the table and the walls that track lights illuminate. Black leather chairs surround the dark wood table, a round speakerphone device in the center of it.

At one end of the table is Ben's large leather executive chair, at the other, there is no chair, but a flat screen monitor on the wall. One of the long walls of the room has windows with closed blinds, the other covered with storyboards and artwork for various projects the company has produced.

—Your theory may be flawed, Ben says.

This statement comes without preamble as he walks in on Daniel studying the map.

—Why's that?

—No one's missing over here. I told you. It's a small island. We'd know.

—Thanks for checking.

—You don't sound too surprised.

—It's not the only theory of mine that's been wrong. This cop shit is harder than it looks.

—What else you been wrong about?

—I thought he'd be making burnt offerings twice a day during the Days of Awe. Morning and evening, like in the tabernacle, but nothing.

—Just because they haven't found any yet doesn't mean there aren't any.

—That's true, but his others were so flashy, so . . . I think he'd want us to find them.

Ben nods.

—You're right. You really do suck at this. What're you doin'?

—Studying the area where the killer was seen.

—Why here?

—I figured you'd want to help. After all, it's your people who are being killed.

—Actually, I thought we just disproved that.

—Now's not the time to get hung up on details.

The hunting and fishing map, provided by a local bait and tackle shop, looks to be hand-drawn sketches of land veined by rivers, streams, and tributaries. The scale of the map is off and it shows such a small section of Pine County that it's difficult to follow. Daniel finds it disorienting and confusing, but eventually believes he has a handle on it.

The map shows the Dead River running through Indian Swamp on one side and Ford's Hell on the other. The very tip of the dense, unforgiving river swamp known as Ford's Hell is inside the North Florida Wildlife Preserve where the first body had been found inside the old depot next to the train tracks. Across the Dead, at the edge of Indian Swamp, the body of the young boy was found. Though separated by the wide body of water, the two locations are only a few miles apart.

The body on the brazen altar found near his lodge is some ten miles away.

Ben slides his finger across the map from Louisiana Lodge over to Ford's Hell.

—Look how large this is, he says. It's thousands and thousands of acres. He could be anywhere.

Chapter Forty-five

—I'll make this brief, Sam says.

The task force, what's left of it, plus Tobias Myers and Kennedy Todd Whitman, is gathered once again in the conference room. The various lines of inquiry seem to be yielding nothing.

Exhaustion.

Frustration.

Anger.

Everyone is on edge—it shows in body language, it can be heard in tone and word choice.

—I know it's been a long week, Sam continues, but we're gaining momentum and our best chance of catching the UNSUB we're after is by sharing information and coordinating efforts.

She's not sure about the momentum, but everything else she's said is true.

Sitting around the table are Travis Brogdon, Margaret Glass, Adam Whitten, Colin Dyson, Jerry Douglas, Tobias Myers, Kennedy Todd Whitman, and Daniel. Sam is standing at the far end of the table opposite the door.

Jerry snickers when she says 'sharing information,' but she lets it go. Whatever's on his mind will come out eventually.

Taking a deep breath, she begins her brief review, which includes a sketch of the bodies that had been found, how they were killed, the crime scenes, and the little forensics they have. She finishes with the current lines of inquiry that have kept the team busy the past few days.

—Everything is moving extremely fast. This is just the sixth day of the investigation. We've all just got to suck it up and keep going. Something we're doing is going to lead to a break in the case, but we don't know what it is, so we've all just got to keep knocking on doors, following up leads.

—Sharing information, Jerry adds.

Though she detects a hint of sarcasm in his voice, she just nods.

—Right.

Her review complete, it's Daniel's turn.

—Based on the carving found in the tree stand at the first crime scene, especially what I believe to be a Nazi symbol, the manner of death, particularly the use of the brazen altar from the tabernacle of Moses, and the time frame of the murders, we believe it's possible these killings are religiously motivated. We found the first body on Rosh Hashanah, the Jewish New Year, and given the use of the brazen altar, I think it's possible he's an extremist, white supremacist Christian who follows the law of Moses and is making burnt offerings of Jewish people. We're in the midst of the Days of Awe now, and I think he may be making sacrifices daily, perhaps twice a day, working his way up to Yom Kippur or the Day of Atonement, when he will attempt to make no fewer than nine.

He pauses a moment, giving the officers time to digest the information.

—There're a couple of problems with this theory, he continues. As best we can tell, no one else is missing from Pine Key, and we haven't found any other sacrifices, even though we are patrolling the areas close to the old depot and Louisiana Landing every night.

—If we're right, Sam says, we don't have long to stop him. The Day of Atonement begins sundown on Sunday night. That doesn't give us much time, so we can't slow down. We can do this, but it's going to take all of us. Okay, what else do we have?

—I've talked to several contractors, Travis says. I should have a list of builders who are religious, who work with brass, and who have their own shops by tomorrow.

—Good work, Sam says. But I wouldn't limit it to guys who seem religious, because our guy may not appear to be. His motivation is so internalized it may not show up in his day-to-day activities. The same is true of him seeming crazy. Chances are he's going to seem to coworkers, family, and friends like the most normal, nice, charming man they ever met. Everyone remember the mask of sanity. Chances are our guy's wearing one.

Jerry Douglas clears his throat.

—Since we're sharing information now, I know where he got the acacia wood to build his altar—and he got enough to build several.

They listen intently as he tells them about his Internet research and his trip to the Garden of Eden. He gives more detail than they need, but he's done good work and is proud of it, and Sam allows it.

—The Garden of Eden? Daniel asks.

—Yeah, Douglas says. Heard of it? Care to share with us about the abduction and explosion?

—The what? Adam Whitten asks.

All her work at building unity and encouraging her troops has been for nothing.

—The killer has been playing games with Dr. Davis, she says.

—*What?* Travis says.

—Twice now, he's abducted someone and given clues as to how to save them.

—And you didn't tell us? Margaret Glass says. Why?

—I'm sorry, she says. I should have. I just didn't want to distract you. I know how busy you all are, how much stress you're under.

And with what happened to Steve, and Preacher being out . . . I just thought—

Douglas starts to say something, but Daniel cuts him off.

—Listen, he says. We don't have time to get distracted. Agent Michaels made the right call. We all need to focus on our part of the investigation. As much as we all might like to, only Agent Michaels needs to see the whole.

The room is quiet a moment, then Douglas nods.

—Sorry, he says. I'm meeting with the Liberty County deputy who conducted the investigation in the morning. Maybe something'll come out of it.

—Very nice, Jerry, Sam says. Good work. Obviously, we need to take a closer look at the garden. Stealing the trees and playing one of his games there may mean he's got a direct connection to it we can uncover. Of course, it's possible he just spotted the restroom when he stole the trees and remembered it when he wanted to play one of his little games, but either way we've got to find out.

Jerry nods.

—I'm on it.

—Anything else? Sam asks.

Daniel nods.

—I did some checking to see if there were any white supremacist groups around here that have as part of their religion keeping the law of Moses, and I found two.

—We've got to put this guy on the payroll, Colin says.

Adam Whitten snickers.

—Oh, he's gettin' paid.

—You say paid or laid? Margaret Glass asks.

Yet to make a single contribution to the investigation, Sam suspects Margaret Glass is a lazy busybody just here out of curiosity.

Ignoring them, Sam clears her throat and the room goes quiet.

—What'd you find out? she asks.

—There are at least two groups who qualify, he says. The Witnesses of Yahweh and Jehovah Nation.

Someone stifles a yawn, which is followed by others in the room. Her team, such as it is, is weary—exhausted in mind and body—and she's aware how much they need rest. Unsure if this review is doing any good at all, she decides to wrap it up quickly and send them home for the night.

—I actually got to talk to the leader of the other group, Daniel says. The one whose door Sam didn't knock on. Aaron Ben Aaron who leads the Witnesses of Yahweh. They have a little storefront on Second Street not far from the post office. He actually looks like the priest figure from the carving, but I think he's too old and too fat to be the killer or to have outrun us on the tracks Sunday night.

—How old is he? Sam asks.

—Fifties.

She nods.

—Too old to be our guy.

—But I think he could be the inspiration for the figure in the carving, Daniel says. When I suggested it, he said no one in his congregation would be involved in anything like this, but that there was a young man who they had to kick out of the church because they caught him on more than one occasion trying to set fire to their sanctuary. His name is River Scott.

Sam nods.

—I put out an APB on him earlier this afternoon.

Chapter Forty-six

—I want a lawyer, Kel Klavan says.

—You like playing with fire, do you, Kel? Sam asks.

When the SWAT team thought everyone was subdued, Klavan, hidden in a back room full of guns and ammunition, had turned over a fifty-gallon drum of gasoline and tossed a match onto it.

—Like roastin' pig, he says, yeah.

She smiles.

None of her guys had been harmed, but Klavan managed to roast a few of his own.

A pale white man with a big bald head, he has intense green eyes, piercings in both ears and eyebrows, a bushy blond Vandyke, and large, straight white teeth.

—I want a lawyer.

They are seated in the Pine County Sheriff's Department interview room, a small, empty room except for a table and four chairs. One wall is nearly completely covered by a framed two-way mirror, behind which are an assortment of detectives and deputies.

He slowly looks down from her eyes to her chest, leering at what he thinks are her breasts.

She smiles. The joke's on him. For a long while she didn't even feel like a woman. Now, thanks in part to Daniel, she feels beautiful, desirable, and powerful—not really missing her missing breasts at all.

—What about sacrifices? she asks. Burnt offerings? Like making those?

He shakes his head and laughs.

—I ain't down with that Jehovah shit. I's just crashin' with a brother of mine for a few days. He ain't part of the Nation neither, but the freaks think he is.

She nods.

Within a few minutes of being with Klavan, she knows he's not the killer.

—That's all I'm sayin', Klavan says. I want a lawyer.

—You're not under arrest, she says. I haven't charged you with anything. Why do you keep throwing lawyers at me?

—'Sume you're running my prints, he says.

—I'm sure we are, she says.

—I want a lawyer.

—I have no idea what your rap sheet says, but you can help your-self by answering a few questions.

—I want—

—I know what you want, she says. But listen, if you're not a member of the Nation and you don't owe them anything, why not help yourself out a little.

—'Cause, I don't squeal, pig, he says. That's the difference be-tween us.

—One question, she says. No squealing. Any of the Nation guys like fire as much as you?

He hesitates a moment.

—There was a kid stayin' there a while, he says, but he left not long after I got there. Messed-up little fucker. He liked burning shit more than anyone I ever met.

—Kid have a name?

—Everybody called him Torch, he says, then looks up and squints. His real name had something to do with water, but I can't—

—River? she asks.

—Yeah, he says. River. Now, I—

—Want a lawyer, she says. I know.

—Every single man in the compound was violating a condition of his parole, Colin Dyson says. So we got 'em.

—That's good, Sam says, but I want them on federal drugs and weapons charges.

They're standing in the hallway outside the interview and recording rooms. Over the course of the investigation, as her task force has continued to shrink, she has increasingly counted on Colin. Unlike his partner, he is smart and insightful, eager to help, willing to work hard. When Daniel's not around, he is the one she tosses ideas around with.

—Won't be a problem, he says. We found enough of both to make the feds love us, but why?

—Jail's too small. So's the budget, and with Preacher out, it's just better. Turn them over to the feds and Uncle Sam picks up the tab. Besides, federal charges carry a higher minimum mandatory.

—Sweet, he says, nodding appreciatively.

—Hey. I'm not just another pretty face.

He smiles.

—How many we talkin'?

—Seventeen, countin' the two in the hospital.

—Whatta you think? she says. Is River our guy?

—Don't know enough about him to say for sure, but he seems a little young to have pulled all this off.

She nods.

—Still be good to get him off the street, he says.

—So we thinking our guy's not part of either group?

—I think Dr. Davis was right to suspect that he's been inspired by or even part of one of these types of groups in the past, he says, but I doubt he is now.

—That describes what River Scott did. He was involved in both groups, but also left both.

—I'm not saying it's *not* him.

She nods.

—I know. But you're right. Someone as confident, organized, and patient as our guy is probably older, but maybe River is criminally mature past his years.

The door opens again and Whitten steps out.

—Would you guys go ahead and process Klavan and find him a nice cell?

Whitten hesitates, but Dyson nods.

—Sure, he says.

From the squad room down the hall, Sam hears Julie, Preacher's secretary, calling her.

—Down here, she says.

—Glad I caught you. I thought you were gone.

—What is it?

—Panama City Police just called. A man fitting the description of the APB you put out has been staying at the rescue mission downtown.

Chapter Forty-seven

A group of men in soiled, mismatched, and ill-fitting clothes are gathered beneath a security lamp like moths in front of the rescue mission in downtown Panama City. Various ages, most of the men look older than they are.

There're normal years, then there're street years.

Beyond the tall buildings on Harrison Avenue and the boats bobbing on St. Andrew Bay, the sun seems to be sinking behind Mexico, the dim evening air left in its wake cooler, less humid.

The moment Sam and Colin step out of the car, a young man matching River Scott's description takes off running.

Jumping back in the car, they race after him, radioing PCPD to notify them of their pursuit and to request backup.

Ducking behind buildings, cutting through alleyways, River passes in back of businesses lining Harrison, down the small slope and into McKenzie Park, emerging on the other side without slowing. Turning on Beach Drive, he crosses over Massalina Bayou on the little drawbridge, and ducks into an abandoned warehouse on the other side.

Screeching to a stop outside the warehouse, Sam and Colin jump out of the car, guns drawn, and run toward the loose piece of tin where River has just entered.

—He's probably just running through and will come out on the other side, she says. I'll check. You stay here and make sure he doesn't come back out the front. If he stays inside, we'll go in together.

She runs around the side of the building, her body beginning to feel the effects of the adrenaline spike.

—If he comes out, don't shoot him. Remember, he's just a kid.

Perhaps having something to do with the building, repair, or storage of boats, the rusted tin warehouse sits next to the water and smells of brine and 2-stroke premix boat motor fuel.

Coming around the back, Sam jumps up on a loading dock and pulls on the old metal handle of a sliding cargo door. It doesn't budge.

Stepping back, she searches for another entry, a busted out window or a loose sheet of tin, but all the windows are boarded up and there are no other entry points.

Jumping off the loading dock, she steps back away from the building and looks up. Unlike the windows on the first floor, those of the second story are missing, their frames splintered. Too high for her to climb up to, she thinks it's possible River could leap from one of them into the bayou.

She waits for a moment, then decides to go back around and enter through the front.

As she reaches the corner of the building, she hears a shout from inside. Running full out, she doesn't hesitate when she makes it to the loose piece of tin, dashing in.

Momentarily blinded by the dark, she pauses a minute, and by the time her eyes have adjusted she hears sirens in the distance.

—Please don't, Colin is saying. Please.

The acrid odor of fuel fumes assaults her olfactory senses, the air so permeated she feels the ethereal substance soaking into her skin, even as she tastes it in her mouth.

—Don't come any closer, River yells.

She turns to the back corner where the voices are coming from to see River and Colin standing in a pool of fuel, the oily substance still sloshing out of an overturned barrel nearby. Colin's clothes and skin appear to be wet and he is no longer holding his gun, though she can't see where it is.

—Please, Colin says. We're not here to hurt you. We want to help you.

River is holding an old-fashioned lighter in his right hand, the top flipped back, the flame rising out of it, flickering as he moves it about.

—Boy, you been playing with your little pecker again? River says, his voice mimicking that of an older country man with a heavy Southern accent. I'a burn it off.

—Please.

—River? Sam calls.

—Mama? he asks, turning as if having forgotten she is there. I'm tryin' to be good, Mama. Blood-bought. Spirit-filled. Refined by fire. The tongue is a fire, a world of iniquity. See how great a forest a little flame kindles.

Sam lowers and holsters her weapon.

Get him away from Colin. Away from the gas.

—River, I want you to come over to me.

Be his mama. Soften your voice. Speak with more of an accent. Just get him away from Colin. Get him out of this building.

—Whatcha gonna do to me, Mama?

—Nothing, baby. Come on. Come to Mama.

With River's attention on Sam, Colin takes off running, but slips on the slick surface and trips.

Get up. Get up. Hurry.

Sirens sound right outside the opening.

Doors slam.

River dives on top of Colin, dropping the lighter as he does.

—Don't try to run away from me, boy, he says in the other voice.

When the lighter hits the floor and bounces, it ignites the substance and a bright blue flame spreads out in all directions, engulfing the two men.

Colin screams.

Sam runs toward them, but is knocked back when the fire reaches the overturned barrel and explodes.

Outside, shouts.

—Fire. Fire. Call a fire truck and ambulance.

Inside, Colin continues to scream, joined now by River, a sound unlike any she's ever heard.

Arms wrap around her. Hands grab her, big, powerful hands, and she is being pulled from the building, away from the running flames, away from the horrific screams, only to discover once outside that the screams are now inside her—and just might always be.

—She's still not answering, Daniel says.

—What is it?

—The Nazi symbol, Daniel says. The burnt offering. The priest.

—Yeah?

—Think about what he made his victim take off.

Ben nods.

—Shoes and jewelry and stuff?

—Why?

—She wouldn't need them where she was going? Ben asks.

—Yeah, Daniel says. In a manner of speaking. Think about it. Train depot. Train tracks. Leaving any valuables behind.

Ben's eyes widen.

—He's recreating the most horrible, infamous burnt offering in human history.

Chapter Forty-eight

'It was a denial of God. It was a denial of man. It was the destruction of the world in miniature form.'

This quote from Auschwitz survivor Hugo Gryn haunts Daniel, but not as much as the pictures of mass graves, piles and piles of bodies, of once vital human beings with dreams. Images are seared into his brain—partly from teaching about the Holocaust in one of his religion courses, partly because he's always been fascinated with it and still can't truly understand how it happened, and partly and most recently from conducting research for his work on Ben's Passover Project—images of naked, vulnerable women, publicly humiliated, walking to their nameless deaths in mass graves, a Nazi soldier with a rifle pointed at their heads.

When he closes his eyes, he sees shaved heads, emaciated bodies, open sores, and the lifeless eyes of the living, eyes that have seen more horror and inhumanity than a human being can process. He sees the Gypsy boys, their bones showing beneath their skin, their penises and testicles missing, selected for experimentations in sterilization, lined up, being photographed, cataloged by Auschwitz cameras.

He sees horrors he can't comprehend, and he can't fathom that it all happened so recently.

Less horrific, though no less an emblem of human waste and tragedy, are the pictures of stacks and stacks of suitcases, mounds of shoes, piles of belts, boxes of jewelry—the Jewish valuables robbed from them before they boarded cattle cars for their journey to hell. The items removed from the victim in the old train depot remind him of this.

—There's still a hole in your theory, Ben says.

—Just one? Daniel asks.

—No, several, but one big one. If this guy is creating a new Holocaust, where are the Jews he's using for offerings coming from?

—I'm not sure, Daniel says, but—

Stopping abruptly, his eyes widen as his mouth drops open.

—What is it? Ben asks, turning to look at the storyboards behind him.

—The Passover Project. What if he's killing the people coming into town to shoot segments for it?

—But wouldn't we know if they didn't make it home?

—Would you? Daniel asks. Do you have a list of those featured and contact information? Let's call and find out.

Deborah Schoen had always thought of herself, partially as a joke, partially not, as the last Jewish-American Princess. Not exactly a diva or a prima donna, though her dad had often called her prima Deborah, she's had an easy, indulged life, but even had she not, nothing could have prepared her for this. Nothing.

She is naked, lying on the hard, dirty floor of a dark trailer of some sort, perhaps the back of a truck or a train car, three dead bodies in various stages of decay surrounding her. She is starving to death—a phrase she's often used to refer to being mildly hungry is now literally true. She is dehydrated, delirious from the heat, and she can smell the odor of burning flesh nearby.

I'm not gonna die like this. I refuse to give the sick prick the satisfaction.

Like everyone else who takes in even a modicum of news, current affairs, and popular culture, Deborah has seen reports of serial killers, seen movies portraying murderous psychopaths, but it never occurred to her to be afraid of them. They were too far removed from her world. Poor white trash and hookers are the victims of such monsters—and probably their kin. Not her, not the people she knows.

But here she is, the victim of a human being missing the part that makes him human.

I may die, but not in the way he wants me to.

Eventually he'll come back, sliding the door open to toss another body inside, and when he does she'll be ready.

Stay alive, and when he opens that door, run. Run like your life depends on it.

Furious, Sam punches in Stan's number, anger shooting out of her with every tap of her finger.

Where's my help? she wants to scream at him. Where are the goddam agents you promised me?

Calm yourself. Don't want to lose your job.

Right now, I do.

Take a breath. Don't let this fucker ruin your future.

After several rings, a recording of his now hateful-to-her voice comes on and asks her to leave a message.

Slowly, calmly, very cooly, she gives him an update, tells him what has just happened, thanks him, sarcastically, for Kennedy Todd Whitman, and asks where the promised agents from Tallahassee are.

In the editing suite, the monitor before them plays the Passover Project, the computer screen beside it displaying the names, addresses, and phone numbers of the Jewish people featured because they, their parents, or their grandparents had survived in a miraculous way.

The gray-haired woman on the screen, shriveled and hunched over, is recounting how her wealthy grandfather paid a lot of money to send his son, her father, and his new wife from Poland to America in August of 1939, just days before the German invasion.

—Call her, Daniel says.

—She lives in New York, Ben says. It's an hour later there. She's old. Probably sound asleep with her teeth in a glass beside her bed.

—Wake her up.

Ben shakes his head, sighs, then picks up the phone and taps in the number.

A long time passes as Ben listens into the phone pressed to the side of his head and doesn't say anything.

—See, Daniel says.

—Mrs. Hirshel? It's Benjamin Greene . . . from the Passover Project . . . Yes, ma'am, I know. I'm sorry. I didn't realize. Yes, ma'am. I'll call you back tomorrow.

—Shit, Daniel says. I was sure that was it.

—It's a good theory. We should probably try a few others.

—Really?

—But this time you get to wake up the old people.

Daniel tries just two numbers. On the first, he reaches an answering machine. On the second, he reaches a lonely old man all too happy for the call who tells Daniel half his life story before he's able to get off the line.

—Got any other theories? Ben asks. Anybody else we can hassle tonight?

Chapter Forty-nine

Daniel opens his front door and smiles when he sees Sam standing there, but his happiness quickly fades as he sees the weary, distressed expression on her face.

—You okay?

—Tell me the whole world's not a horrible place filled with monsters.

—Come in, he says, and let me show you.

—Colin died today.

—*What?*

—It seems like the whole world's on fire.

—Oh, Sam, I'm so sorry.

She tells him about the day she's had, and he listens intently, wishing he could have been there for her, able to protect her, keep her from such things.

When she is finished with her horrific story, he holds her, trying to absorb some of the pain and distress. Though they are silent, he feels something passing between them, an intimacy born out of crisis and concern. Perhaps it's far too soon to tell, and maybe most of what he feels is infatuation intensified by the circumstances of the investigation, but he can't help himself. He is in love with her—irrationally, insanely, inescapably in love.

Eventually, as he holds her, his body begins to respond to the feel of hers.

—I can't make love tonight, she says.

He nods.

—I didn't imagine you could. I just can't stop the response. It's automatic.

—And wonderful, she adds. And flattering. I'm just so fucked up right now.

—Of course.

—Can I still stay here?

—Stay forever.

Deborah Schoen, the one-time Jewish-American princess, can hear movement outside the door. She has no way of knowing, but believes it to be night. Of course, she's deranged and delusional, so she can't trust her feelings.

He thinks we're all dead. That's why he's opening the door.

She lies perfectly still right in front of the door, trying to quiet her breathing.

The door slides open, and while the monster lifts a body onto the platform, she rolls, falling out of the—what is it? A boxcar?—and onto the ground. She crawls away until she can get to her feet, and then she runs.

Disoriented, she's not sure where to run, so she just runs.

It's night. She sees piles of sand and gravel overgrown with weeds, rusting machinery, a dilapidated warehouse in the distance.

She's weak and hungry. Every part of her is in pain, but she's running for her life and she knows it.

Tripping.

Falling.

Gashing.

Hands and knees.

Cuts.

Scrapes.

Tears.

Gravel.

Sand.

Rock.

Made it. In the woods now.

Limbs slap at her naked body, stinging her skin, rocks and sticks stab her feet, cutting the soft flesh, and she begins to cry.

Don't stop, she tells herself. Don't let him catch you. You're tougher than you think. You can do this. Think about Mom and Dad, about George. Think about—

She hears something.

Whipping her head around, she sees that nothing is there. Relieved, she sighs and turns back.

He's there in front of her, pale moonlight on a long steel blade, and she can't think of anything.

Death comes as relief, an end to all the pain and the hunger gnawing away at her, and, as she falls into his arms in what appears to be an intimate embrace, she manages one more thought.

At least I didn't starve to death.

—Can't sleep? Sam asks.

Daniel sits at the kitchen table, studying crime scene photographs and other evidence in the flicker of candlelight and a small desk lamp. Sam has just stumbled in from the bedroom wearing one of his button-downs, looking unbearably sexy in that sleepy-vulnerable way.

It's late or early, the world outside the window is dark, the light above the table turning the glass to mirror, their weary, disheveled reflections staring back at them.

—I woke up with something, he says. A piece of the puzzle, but lost it by the time I was fully conscious.

—That's your body's way of telling you it needs more rest.

—What about you? I figured you'd sleep until—

—I'll sleep on Monday when they take this case away from me. When I have time to think about what I could've done differently, when I'm confronted with the fact that my failures cost lives and I'm too depressed to do anything else.

—And you're certain it's not River Scott?

She nods.

—As certain as I can be. The truth is he was too crazy.

—That's a scary thought.

—He couldn't drive, didn't even have a place of his own, and has an alibi for the time of the train depot murder.

He nods.

—I think we're getting close.

She laughs.

—Seriously.

—The closest we'll ever get was in the tree that night, she says, and that was by accident. I should've never taken this case—not after I saw what this guy was doing and how he was doing it. I was no match for him and I knew it, but my goddam pride got the better of me and now all I've done is delay his capture and get people killed.

—I disagree, but I understand how you feel, and I still think we're getting close. Look.

He shows her the map.

—We think he's working over here, he says, pointing to the area where the train tracks cross the river.

—It makes sense, but we've had cops combing the woods around there since we found the body of the boy. They haven't found anything. It's like the theory of the victims being Jews. It seems right, but we can't find any that are missing.

—We haven't found missing persons of any kind, so it doesn't mean they're not Jews. Look at this.

He shows her the crime scene photo of the train depot victim's belongings, then a picture of a train depot in Germany during the Holocaust that shows piles of shoes, belts, watches, jewelry.

Her eyes widen.

—He's recreating the Holocaust, he says. On a smaller scale.

He tells her about his theory that the victims are people who come to Pine Key to film their stories of survival and how it had been disproven with a few phone calls.

—That's a good theory. That should've been it.

—See, he says. We're getting somewhere.

—Maybe, she says, her demeanor changing, lifting, lightening. Did you think of what woke you up yet?

He lets out a noise of frustration.

—It was almost there, but it's gone again.

—It'll come to you.

—I know I'm not supposed to be, but I'm enjoying this.

She nods.

—It's one of our dirty little secrets. Even the darkest, most dangerous cases are such a rush. I feel guilty sometimes for enjoying what I do so much.

—I love working with you, he says, reaching over and brushing the hair back from her face, then running his finger along her cheek.

—Same here, she says. You're really good at this—and that's not just the infatuation talking.

—I can't even think of what it was that woke me up.

—Think of something else and it'll come to you. Here.

She unbuttons the shirt she's wearing and opens it, exposing the scars he finds sacred and erotic, and he realizes what a gift it is she is giving him.

—You sure?

—You sense any hesitation?

Stepping toward him, she drops the shirt and is completely naked now. He starts to stand, but she stops him.

He pushes his chair back and she kneels before him. Pulling down his shorts, she smiles at just how aroused he is by her wounded body, and she feels beautiful and desirable.

—God, you're so hard, she says, her breathless words carrying on their soft currents admiration and appreciation.

—God, you're so gorgeous, he says.

She takes him in her mouth and passionately and enthusiastically expresses her own arousal.

After a few moments, she stands and straddles him, then taking him in her hand, lowers herself onto him.

Slowly.

Rhythmically.

Her athletic body moves atop him in an intense and intimate interconnected dance, hands caressing, mouths open, tongues searching, two souls melting into one.

The wave of the small candle flames catches his eye and he glances over at them.

Warmth.

Tangerine-like light.

Soft glow.

How beautiful, spiritual, transcendent. How can something so magical be used as a weapon by a madman?

Faster now.

Riding.

Writhing.

Building.

Rising.

Wanting to . . .

—Don't wait, she tells him.

—You sure?

—You sense any hesitation?

He laughs and then comes, his climax causing his nerves to jangle, his body to rock, then unclench, then shudder.

He stays inside her as long as he can, as they hold each other and kiss and whisper and laugh.

After a long while, she climbs off him and they stand and dress, continuing to touch each other often and tenderly.

Eventually, she picks up the crime scene photos and begins to flip through them, and he remembers what he woke up thinking about.

—I really like your methods, he says. I just *thought* I liked working with you before.

—My pleasure. Did it—

—That's it.

—What is it?

—The symbol, he says. In the carving.

—Yeah?

He grabs the photo of the carving and holds it up.

—Look.

—You don't think it's a swastika?

—No, I think it is. That's about all it can be. But look where it is. She looks.

—See how it's drawn down near the body on the flame?

—Yeah?

—What if I had it backwards? What if the symbol is meant for the sacrifice, not the priest?

—Someone killing Nazis? she asks.

—Or Neo-Nazis. We better check with the Witnesses of Yahweh and Jehovah Nation to see if they're missing any members.

Chapter Fifty

—Sir, I told you, we're a small group, Aaron Ben Aaron says. If someone was missing, I'd know.

It's early Sunday morning. Sam and Daniel have interrupted the priest from preparing for his worship service, actually found him prostrate on the floor before the makeshift altar of his makeshift church, praying in Hebrew.

An anti-Semite who prays in Hebrew and follows the law of Moses. Human beings are nothing if not interesting and ironic.

Though Sam had asked the question, Aaron addressed his answer to Daniel, and has yet to make eye contact with her.

—Girls make you nervous, Aaron? she asks.

—Please tell your associate that it is forbidden for me to talk to a woman who is not my wife, he says to Daniel.

Far more formal than the first time they had spoken, Aaron's care over his language makes him seem guilty—or at least afraid.

She shakes her head.

—Religion, she says as if it's a dirty word.

—Don't look at *me*, Daniel says.

—It's your thing.

Her manner is playful, even slightly flirtatious, and Daniel can't help but smile.

—It's not my thing, he says. I happen to—

—Is there anything else you need? Aaron asks.

Daniel looks back at Sam.

—Can he think of anyone who wishes ill toward his group? she says.

—Can you think of anyone who wishes ill toward your group? Daniel asks.

—No.

—No, Daniel says, looking at Sam with a straight face.

—I mean not specifically, he says. Not locally. Not really. But if you mean in a general sense, all the filthy, greedy Zionists of the world. Like Ishmael hated Isaac, they hate us, the true sons of Yahweh.

—Do I have to repeat that? Daniel asks.

—I got it, she says.

—Anybody left lately? she asks. Moved or quit coming?

He shakes his head, though continues looking at Daniel.

—We haven't lost a member in two years.

Probably haven't added any either, Daniel thinks, but doesn't say anything.

—Anyone who shares your views or is sympathetic to your cause missing?

—Not that I know of, he says. Yahweh takes care of his own.

—I really thought that might be it, Daniel says.

—Still might be, she says. I'll check with the Jehovah Nation guys sitting in the Pine County jail. They love me. I'm sure they'd be happy to help.

Back in her car, parked on the curb in front of the Witnesses' storefront, discouraged over the lack of progress, Sam feels hollow inside, defeated. For a moment, in her excitement about the possibility of a break in the case, she had forgotten about Colin and Preacher and Steve and what Chabon had done to her, but now the weight of it all rests squarely on her.

—Is that what you're about to do now? he asks.

She shakes her head.

—First I've got to call Colin Dyson's widow, then my boss again. Then, if I still have a job—or if I'm still on the case—I'll talk to them. I was hoping to have something to offer for all my failures.

—You haven't—

—You're sweet, she says. But I'm serious. I may not just be off the case. I may be out of the agency.

—What can I do?

—Nothing, she says. Well, there is one thing.

—Name it.

—Tell me why there's so much anti-Semitism in the world?

—That's a long and complex story, he says.

—Just give me the short, simple version.

—Well, it doesn't just come from one place or for one reason, but much of it in the last two-thousand years comes from the Passion narratives in the Gospels—the accounts of the trial and execution of Jesus.

—I don't understand.

—The way they're written conveys that a Roman governor proclaims Jesus innocent and wants to release him, but a Jewish mob proclaims him guilty and cries for his blood.

—That's not how it happened?

—Most scholars don't think so. Rome, who executed Jesus as a political prisoner, later became the center of Christianity, a former Jewish sect, and has downplayed its part in the murder and blamed the Jewish people. They have the crowd of Jews cry out for his blood, even saying let his blood be on our heads and that of our children.

—I never thought of it that way, she says.

—Christianity began as a movement in Judaism, he says. It was one sect among many, such as the Essenes, the Pharisees, the Sadducees, trying to win the battle for the future of the Jewish religion. That conflict was among brothers and friends until Christianity became a Gentile religion, then it became truly dangerous. It's much more complicated and involved than that, but in part Christian anti-Judaism evolved into European anti-Semitism, which led to the Holocaust—and that's just in the West. The conflicts in the East are a whole other matter.

She nods.

—Hard to fathom, but at least I have some historical framework for the sickness.

—What about on the case, he says. What else is there I can do?

—I honestly can't think of anything. If I do, I'll call you.

It sounds dismissive, but she can't help it. She just can't give him anything else at the moment.

—Okay, he says, opening the door and getting out. I'll get a ride home.

—I don't mind—

—It's no problem, he says. Go ahead and do what you need to. Who knows? I may attend a Witnesses of Yahweh service.

When Sam pulls away, Daniel, not sure what to do, walks up to Main Street, around the corner, and down to the café.

What am I missing? My theories seem to fit the evidence. What am I doing wrong? What am I not seeing?

Inside the Bayshore Café he orders coffee, orange juice, and bacon.

The waitress, who is friendly and chipper but seems sensitive to his preoccupation, says little else after her initial greeting.

He sits for a long time, thinking, drinking several cups of coffee, leaving his bacon and juice untouched. Frustrated, he stands up, still unsure of what he's going to do next, and decides to leave.

He sees Esther at the counter paying for what looks to be several carry-out breakfasts.

—Hey, she says.

—Hey.

—You here alone?

—Yeah. You?

—Just picking up breakfast, she says. I don't cook. Sunday morning Ethan and I sleep in, then one of us picks up breakfast while the other vacuums and dusts the house.

—You headed back over to the island?

—Yeah.

—Can I catch a ride?

Chapter Fifty-one

Just as Esther is pulling onto Main Street, Daniel's phone rings.

—Where are you? Ben asks.

—Downtown Bayshore, he says. I'm with Esther. She's giving me a ride over to the island. You home?

—At the office, he says.

—I'll be there in twenty minutes or so.

—You were right, he says.

—About?

—I just got a call from Miami. Rabbi Gold never made it home. Daniel sits up.

—Why are we just now hearing about it?

—When he left here, he was supposed to spend the Sabbath with a rabbi friend of his in Tallahassee and speak at the synagogue, then fly back last night. He lives alone. He missed a meeting this morning. When they called Rabbi Kushner in Tallahassee, he said he never showed up. He called and left a message on his machine, but didn't think much of it. Said he figured something came up and that he wound up not coming up for the taping. Figured he'd hear from him after Yom Kippur.

Ben pauses, but Daniel doesn't say anything.

—You there?

—Just thinking, he says. So if it's him, he's taking some and not others. We've got to call them all.

—I'm just about to start.

—Wonder why he's picking the ones he is?

—We narrow down who it is and I bet we'll know, he says. I just can't get over how you figured out it was people coming in to shoot segments for the Passover. We're gonna get this guy.

As Sam is about to enter her basement office, her phone rings. Expecting a call from Stan Winston after he's talked with the commissioner, she doesn't look at the display, just answers.

—Agent Michaels.

—Sam, it's Michelle. I rushed toxicology and have something for you.

—Bless you. Your timing couldn't be better.

—The puncture we found in the young man's leg was from a syringe, she says. The killer used succinyl choline on him. It's a neuromuscular paralytic that leaves the victim wide awake, but completely paralyzed.

—So he can burn them alive, Sam says.

—I'm assuming that's what was in the other bodies, but I can't say definitively.

—He doesn't have to worry about them screaming or running, Sam says. He can just carry out his ritual and watch them suffer.

—He'd have to do it quickly, Michelle says. Eventually, the drug will paralyze everything, including the lungs and heart. Depending on the dosage and just how immobile he wants them, he would only have a few minutes.

—How hard would it be for him to get?

—Not very, she says. He could obtain it from a pharmaceutical supply firm or steal it from a hospital.

Instead of dropping Daniel off at Pine Key Productions, Esther joins him, excited by the possibility of catching the killer, horrified that his victims might actually be the precious people featured in their documentary. She parks her small, champagne-colored Honda by Ben's BMW Roadster, and they jump out.

Upon entering the building, they go directly to the editing suite.

The Passover Project is playing on the screen. Beside it, the list of participants is displayed on the computer monitor, but the room is empty.

—Ben? Daniel yells.

There's no answer.

—I'll check around, Esther says. He's probably in his office.

Pausing the documentary, Daniel pulls out his cell phone and calls Sam to give her the news about Rabbi Gold.

—Were you not ready for this assignment? Stan Winston asks.

—I think I was, Sam says. That I am. It's only been a week and this is an unusual and unusually difficult case.

Sam is at her desk in her dungeon office, shoes off, elbow on the chair arm, head propped in her hand.

—Of course, we really didn't know what kind of case it was when we first got the call, he says. So I was dependent on you to tell me you needed help.

—I did, she says. From the very beginning.

He's enjoying this. The only thing he has over me is power.

During their relationship, Stan had often felt insecure, vulnerable, concerned he was too old, too unattractive, too lacking libido. He never said so explicitly, but it was there implicit in his words and actions, and in those times he would attempt to compensate with his power, his position, his political prowess within the department.

—We really are getting close now, she says.

—Who's we? Who's left?

—The task force.

—The commissioner said he had heard rumors that you and I were involved and wanted to know if that had influenced my decision.

—What'd you tell him?

—You're a good cop, we're not seeing each other—but I'm not sure he believed me. I may lose my job over this.

—But it's early, she says. We're making good progress.

—Don't you see? he says. It looks like I was trying to fast track your career.

—I don't understand.

—I called in a favor to get you assigned to the case, he says. It should have gone to the Tallahassee region, but the director there owed me one, so I cashed in the marker.

—Why?

He starts to stay something, but stops.

—Why? she asks again.

—To keep you away longer, he says. To give you more time to heal. I was afraid you might make a scene, cause trouble for me.

His words cut her. How can he think she's that petty, childish, or hung up on him? He doesn't even know me. Never did. Now, never will.

—You really don't know me at all, she says.

—So it looks like I pulled strings to help you.

—But—

—A couple of experienced officers from the Tallahassee office will be there in the morning. Brief them. Make sure they have everything they need, then get back down here and report to my office.

—Send me some help like I've asked for, but don't take me off the case. I've worked too hard. I'm too close. I—

—It's out of my hands, he says.

—But don't you see? We have a better chance of catching him if I'm here.

—I gave you an order.

—But—

—Sam, he says. Two cops are dead.

She is quiet a long moment, thinking, wondering. Why hadn't he gotten her the help she'd asked for? Why had he been so adamant about not involving the FBI?

—You set me up, she says.

—What?

—To fail. You put me in the middle of this thing and then refused to give me the resources I needed.

—I only said don't turn the case over to the feds. I happen to believe our agency can actually clear cases.

—I could've really used *our* agency. What happened to the agents you were going to send?

—They'll be there tomorrow.

—They should've been here days ago. And Kennedy Todd Whitman? Was that a fuckin' joke?

—Don't be—

—You wanted me to fail. Set it up so I would.

—Don't be ridiculous—and don't you dare make irresponsible accusations. If you try to take me down, I assure you I'll take you with me.

—He's not here, Esther says. I've looked everywhere, including the bathroom.

—Where would he have gone without his car? Daniel asks, trying not to panic. Home? Somewhere to get breakfast?

—I'll check, she says, pulling out her phone. I'm sure he just dashed out for a second to get something, but with the murders and Rabbi Gold missing . . . it's got me freakin'.

Deciding to let Esther find Ben, Daniel tries to figure out how the killer is choosing his victims. He thinks of the method of murder, the making of burnt offerings, its connection to the Holocaust. He thinks about the crime scenes, the photos and images now burned into his brain. He thinks of the carving and the symbol, its place-ment, its significance. He recalls what he knows of Rabbi Gold, of his background, of his personality and politics. He thinks about it all, allowing his mind to make random connections and associations.

Esther says something, but he's not sure what.

—I'm sorry, what?

—He's not at home, she says. There's nowhere else he would walk. It's too far.

—Call his cell phone, he says.

—Sorry, she says. I'm just so afraid.

—It's okay, he says. I'm a little afraid myself.

—That's not what I wanted to hear, she says.

With shaky hands and trembling fingers, she presses a couple of buttons, waits a moment, then from somewhere in the building, Ben's phone begins to ring.

Chapter Fifty-two

—I can't look, Esther says. You'll have to.

Daniel stands and follows the sound of the ringing phone, stepping out of the editing room, down the hallway, and into the small foyer of the entrance.

Ben is obviously not in the small tiled area.

The sound of the phone continues another moment, then stops, its ring replaced by a periodic beep.

Daniel pulls out the ceramic pot from the corner, the fake tree it holds shaking as he does, but the phone is not there. He then looks at the small sofa not far away and sees the tip of the phone on the floor poking out from beneath the side of it.

—Is it . . . Esther says from the hallway.

—It's his phone, he says, standing up and walking back over to her.

—It could have slipped out of his pocket when he was sitting on the couch, she says.

—It could have, but we both know it didn't.

Ben's phone rings again and Esther jumps.

Daniel steps a few feet away as he answers it.

—The fire is going to fall, Daniel, the deranged voice says. Benjamin will be judged. Will you be there?

—Where?

—I've told you everything you need to know. You have until sundown.

—I've got people searching for Ben, Sam says, nodding toward the monitor. You just concentrate on this.

She has just walked in and found Daniel and Esther sitting at the editing desk.

Daniel nods.

—Brian and Joel are headed in, Esther says. I had called them earlier to see if they'd heard from Ben, and they both want to help.

—I'm sure we can find something for them to do, Sam says.

Daniel, though staring straight ahead, is not really looking at the image on the monitor.

—What is it? Sam asks.

—I was just going over everything and . . . I almost had something, but it's gone.

—That's happening a lot lately, she says with a smile. Mind must be out of practice.

—It's that kind of encouragement that's so valuable in times like these.

She smiles.

—Talk it through with me. We can figure it out.

—I was thinking about the Nazi symbol in the carving. At first I thought it represented the priest, but later because it's drawn next to the victim, I thought it represented him.

—But none of the Witnesses or the Nation are missing, she says.

—I know.

—And Rabbi Gold is.

—I—that's it, he says. It's still meant to be connected with the sacrifice, not the priest.

—But the victims are Jewish.

—Rabbi Gold's father was a kapo during the Holocaust.

—A what?

—Oh my God, Esther says.

—A what? Sam says again. What's a kapo?

—The inmate captain of a work party in the concentration camps during the Holocaust, Daniel says. A Jew who worked for the Nazis. They were seen as betrayers and were often cruel, abusive, and occasionally murderous. Some of them were actually put on trial after the war.

—So he's—

—Making holocausts of the descendants of betrayers, Daniel says. Of those he thinks should have died, but didn't.

—And had they died, their descendants, the people he's offering, wouldn't be alive, right? Sam asks.

Esther nods.

—He's killing people he thinks should never have been born.

—Do you remember which people interviewed for the project had parents or grandparents who were Nazi trustees? he asks.

—Not all the people we interviewed are survivors of the Holocaust, she says. A lot are, but the project covers any story of miraculous survival. Rabbi Gold's the only one who mentioned a family member being a kapo, and he was hesitant. You could tell it embarrassed him.

—Other similar positions were block orderlies, block seniors, block clerks, and *arbeitsdienstes*, Daniel says. Were any of those mentioned?

—Yeah, they were, Esther says. A few different ones, but just a quick reference in passing.

—Can you find their numbers and call them? Sam asks.

—Yeah, they're right here, she says, snatching up the phone and punching in a number from the computer.

—You're a genius, Sam says.

—We'd have smart kids, he says.

They are standing out in the hallway, waiting as Esther makes the calls.

Sam smiles.

—Yes we would. Of course, they might not be if they take after their mother.

—You know that's not—

—I'm off the case. Two agents from Tallahassee will take over in the morning.

—This'll be over by then. We only have until sundown.

—Is it possible Ben's not a victim, but the perp? she asks. He could have set this whole thing up just to find these people and punish them. I mean, who else knows all this—

He shakes his head.

—It's not Ben. I should be more shocked that you would even think it could be him, but you thought it was me, originally.

—If not Ben, then who?

—Somebody involved with or aware of the project, he says.

—Who all is that?

—Me, Ben, Esther, Brian, and Joel, he says. The people interviewed, the sponsors. You'd have to ask Esther who else.

—How have these people not been reported missing?

—They're all old, he says. Probably live alone like Rabbi Gold. It hasn't been that long either. They're spread out all over the country and are probably just now being reported missing. Doesn't it have to be over forty-eight hours or something?

—Yeah, but this has been over a period of at least a couple of weeks if you count the victims he experimented with, she says. I find it difficult to believe that no one—

Esther appears in the doorway.

—Of the ones with a family member who worked as a Nazi trustee, two are not answering their phones and five have been reported missing.

—So we're talking seven people total? Sam asks.

—Rabbi Gold makes eight, she says.

Ben makes nine, Daniel thinks.

—Do you know if any of Ben's family were—

Esther shakes her head.

—He's never mentioned it.

—But his interest in this subject had to come from somewhere,
Sam says.

Esther nods.

—Why haven't any of the family or friends of the missing people
called here to see what happened? Sam asks.

—Several of them have, she says. Said a young man here assured
them they had gotten on the plane, left here just fine, but that he'd
notify the authorities.

—So who is it? Sam asks. Joel or Brian?

—Neither, Esther says. There's no way—

—Let's see which one doesn't show up, Daniel says.

—Call Joel again, Sam says.

—What's going on? Brian asks.

Esther shakes her head as she punches Joel's number into her
phone.

Brian's arrival has them suspecting Joel of being the killer—especially since he lives so much closer than Brian and should have
arrived before him.

—Joel lives right there, Brian says, pointing to a condo unit
through the window.

—He's not answering, Sam says.

Daniel turns to Esther.

—Where was he when you talked to him?

—Said he was home and would be right here.

—Is he missing too? Brian asks.

—Let's go see, Sam says. Esther, you keep trying him. We'll walk over there.

—You okay? Brian asks.

Daniel nods.

—Any more attacks?

He shakes his head.

The two men are a few steps behind Sam, walking toward Joel's condo. Brian's voice is very low, difficult to hear over the wind and the waves, but Daniel wouldn't want him to be any louder. Evidently aware they need some privacy, Sam has neither slowed her pace nor tried to get them to catch up.

—Have you decided if you're going to see a therapist? Brian asks.

—Not sure yet. Things have been so busy with the case—and now with Ben missing . . .

—There are always reasons not to seek help, he says. I understand it's an insane time right now, but it'll slow down eventually. Just be careful—we can always find an excuse not to deal with things we need to.

Chapter Fifty-three

—I'm going in, Sam says.

She's been knocking for several moments.

—I don't know, Brian says. It's—

—Ben's running out of time, Daniel says.

—Help me force the lock.

—What? No, Brian says. Wait. I have a key. I show it for him sometimes if he's not around.

Sam and Daniel both look confused.

—He's got to rent it out a certain number of days a year to be able to afford it.

—Where does he stay then?

Brian shrugs.

—I'm not sure.

—His workshop?

Sam nods.

—Probably so.

Brian looks confused.

—What workshop? Oh. You're wrong. If he's anything, Joel's a victim.

Joel's condo is immaculate, its white tile floors, carpet, and countertops spotless.

—Joel? Sam yells. Police.

—It looks like a set, Daniel says.

Sam nods.

Brian shakes his head and lets out a sigh.

—I told you, he rents it out. Has to keep it perfect all the time.

—Spread out, Sam says. Look around. Try not to disturb anything. If you find anything suspicious, yell for me.

It doesn't take long.

In less than ten minutes, they've searched the entire condominium and found nothing remotely suspicious except for a large locked trunk beneath blankets in the back of his closet.

With a hammer, a screwdriver, and a pair of pliers found in a small toolbox beneath the sink, Sam and Daniel break into the trunk, Brian telling them how embarrassed they're going to be when they find Joel's porn.

—I'm telling you, it's not him, Brian says. I can't—

He stops mid-sentence as the trunk is opened and the souvenirs of a compulsive killer are revealed.

Sam withdraws a pair of latex gloves from a small pouch on her belt, puts them on, kneels down in front of the trunk, and begins to look through its contents.

Beneath the layer of belts, shoes, watches, and jewelry—all in individual plastic bags—are books and Internet printouts on fire, accelerants, the law of Moses, the tabernacle, the Holocaust, religious textbooks and manuals on arson and homicide investigation, and journals where the monster had cataloged his work, recorded his reasons.

—Uncle Tom son of a bitch, Brian says, shaking his head.

—What? Sam asks, looking up in shock.

—I can't believe he's one of those.

—You think he's a self-hating Jew? Daniel asks.

—A what? Sam asks.

—When an individual internalizes the negative stereotypes about his ethnic identity, Daniel says. Some people refer to it as the silent Holocaust. It's an inferiority complex that results from anti-Semitism. Same can be applied to any oppressed or terrorized people. Native-Americans. African-Americans.

—Why'd you call him a—

Though she's looking at Brian, Daniel answers.

—All ethnic groups who've been subjected to this form of mental and psychological abuse and brainwashing have examples of it. In the African-American community they are known as Uncle Toms or Oreos or—

—Oreos?

—Black on the outside, white on the inside, Daniel explains.

Looking back down at the materials, Sam opens one of the journals and reads, 'Like Elijah, I place the offering on the altar, but the fire only falls if it be his will.' She looks back up to Daniel.

—Elijah?

—A prophet in ancient Israel, Daniel says. He had a battle of the bands with some other prophets. Yahweh versus Baal.

—You lost me.

—They wanted to see which God was real, so they took turns offering sacrifices. The prophets of Baal went first. They placed their sacrifice on the altar but didn't light the fire. Then they prayed for hours trying to get Baal to send down fire to consume the sacrifice. He never did. When it was Elijah's turn, he had the people pour water on the altar, the wood, and the sacrifice. He then prayed to Yahweh and fire came down and consumed the holocaust, wood, stones, and even lapped up the water in the trench.

Brian nods appreciatively.

—You really know your stuff.

—What does that mean? Sam asks.

—Though he's starting the fires, he sees them as the work of Yahweh, Daniel says. Judging these people. Keep on reading.

Sam finds her place and reads.

—'If their forefathers hadn't betrayed our people, hadn't murdered them to save their own skin, they wouldn't be here today. They shouldn't be here. This is not what was meant to be. All I'm doing is letting Yahweh judge, letting the fire decide. I'm just the priest, Yahweh is the fire. He alone can judge.'

—That's his way of not taking responsibility for what he's doing, Daniel says.

—I just can't believe it, Brian says. There's no way it's Joel. No way.

—I've got to get crime scene out here to process this.

—Ben's running out of time, Daniel says. Sure you don't want to go through it ourselves? Does it say anything about where he's doing them?

She skims several pages, trailing her gloved finger over the words.

—Just a lot of talk about the tabernacle, ovens, camps, and train tracks that end in hell.

—The tracks are the key, Daniel says, but I just can't figure out—

—With the mill gone, the tracks end in the bay, Brian says. Could he be dumping the bodies in there?

Daniel shakes his head.

—I don't think so, he says. As far as religious symbols go, water is the opposite of fire. Though there is a Catholic ritual during Easter vigil where a candle is plunged into the baptismal water, but . . .

—Could that be it? Sam asks.

—Everything he's doing is Jewish, not Catholic.

—Is there not a Jewish equivalent?

Daniel thinks for a moment, then shakes his head slowly.

—Not that I know of. The priest would wash himself in the laver after making the sacrifice on the brazen altar, but—

—Wasn't one of the passages you read to us about washing some of the parts of the sacrifice in the laver? Sam asks.

—Yeah, but before they were burned, not after, he says. And I don't see how the bay could fit with that anyway.

—Still, we should have some officers at the old mill site, she says. And a boat patrolling the bay. Where are you going?

—To run the tracks, he says. Ben's running out of time. It'll be sundown soon. I can't just sit out here on the island waiting for some cop to pull his body out of the bay.

Chapter Fifty-four

Kapos at Auschwitz were given special privileges for decreasing the men in their work squads, and the murderous little bastards did it in a variety of ways—all cruel, all arbitrary, all as random as everything else in the chaotic, upside-down world.

He recalls a story he read about a Sunday morning on the yard in one of the blocks of Auschwitz where some five hundred men had lined up to enjoy the sun—the only time such things were permitted at the camp.

The brief peace and rest was interrupted by the call of a caps-off drill by a particularly nasty kapo. The simple drill required each prisoner to remove the flat caps from their shaven heads and slap them against their right thighs with the flat of their hands. What appeared like any other military-style exercise was actually an excuse to thin the ranks, to put men to death for their inability to follow the simple orders.

The first man to be executed had a disfigured right hand and was unable to carry out the order with exact precision. The second victim was deaf, unable to hear the command.

Shot in the head simply because they couldn't take off their cap in the exact manner they were ordered to. Killed by their own. Abused, beaten, murdered, by their very own people. The Nazis he could understand. They were evil German bastards, animals really, but his own people, damning their own souls by betraying their brothers, this he could not understand—or abide.

He can't just sit by and let the offspring of such weak and wicked men enjoy easy, indulged lives. No. God forbid!

It's too bad Ben's still unconscious. He could be witnessing something extraordinary. Instead, he's asleep having what he's sure are ordinary dreams.

Ben isn't the last of the kapo survivors' descendants he's going to punish. There's one more, but he's also had to use other less worthy sacrifices to complete his plan—those who won't be missed for a while, like homeless from Tallahassee and Panama City.

He wishes he could limit his holocausts to the descendants of kapos and block seniors, but he needs too many, so he's forced to use other methods of selection, being just as arbitrary in his approach as the Nazis and their kapos had been in theirs.

He needs them for the altars, for the train, for the mass grave out back, for the ovens, his precious handmade ovens. He doesn't have many, but it's enough to approximate the death camp on a miniature scale. He now wishes he would've held on to the half-burned bodies he did his first experiments on, but he didn't realize he'd need them, and in those early days he hadn't been able to see the full scope of what Yahweh had called him to do.

He places the bound Ben not far from one of the crematories he built, and puts on his gloves.

The ovens, fashioned after those used in the Nazi death camps, are made of brick with steel bars on which the body lies that extend into the ovens.

Gripping the bars with his gloved hands, he lifts them up like a weightlifter doing a clean jerk. The body on the bars, now at a ninety-degree angle, slides into the large, square oven, sparks and flames shooting up around it as it does.

—You knew I wouldn't let you come alone, didn't you? Sam asks.

—I hoped you wouldn't, Daniel says.

They are in her car parked near the train tracks in the North Florida Wildlife Preserve, the afternoon sun seeming to descend more rapidly since they arrived.

—And you knew if I came I wouldn't be stupid enough not to bring backup.

—I know you're not stupid.

Not far from them, Travis Brogdan and Adam Whitten are unloading ATVs off a trailer hooked to Travis's truck.

—I don't know, she says. Even with backup, this is a stupid thing to do.

—Why?

—Look at our backup, she says.

He looks over at Travis and Adam.

—We got Barney Fife and Goober.

—Call the SWAT team, he says.

—They wouldn't get here in time. Besides, I'm off the case. I can't call anybody. And what if you're wrong? What if we spend all our time out here in the woods instead of working the evidence, and he's somewhere else?

—Why don't you go work the evidence and let me, Travis, and Adam conduct the search out here?

—What if you have another attack?

With the space between the two sets of tracks only wide enough for one ATV, they drive single file down the bumpy terrain, Adam in front, then Sam, Daniel, and Travis.

Adam and Travis ride camouflage ATVs, Sam and Daniel matching red ones.

Unable to talk above the loud roar of the engines, they race along in silence, their eyes searching the area around them as they do.

Adam speeds along faster than Daniel thinks is safe, but everyone keeps up. At the depot, Adam holds his fist up and comes to a stop. All four riders turn off their ATVs and take off their helmets.

—We're not exactly mounting a sneak attack, are we? Travis says.

—No, but if we actually happen to find him, we might have the strength to capture him, Adam says. If we tried to run it, we'd be too tired to do anything once we found him.

—We wanna look around here or keep goin'? Travis asks.

—How much farther is it from here to the old mill site? Sam asks.

—I'd say it's another three or four miles to the river then another seven miles or so to the bay.

—We need to keep going, Daniel says.

Sam nods.

—Is there anything between the river and the mill site?

—Hell of a lot of pine trees, Adam says.

—Anything like this old depot?

—No ma'am, I don't think there is, Travis says, but once we get to the river we should have cell service for a little while. We could call somebody and find out for sure. My grandaddy used to work on the train. I could ask him.

Putting their helmets back on, they crank their vehicles and continue their journey.

As they ride, they continue to scan the woods on either side for signs of Joel or Ben, but see no evidence of human beings having been back here recently. Eventually, Daniel begins to get motion sickness from looking at the blurred trees passing by, his head begins to ache and his eyes feel strained, and he wonders if the others are experiencing the same thing.

Thinking of the others reminds him that he's the only one out here not armed.

After what seems like a very long time, during which the sun continues its descent toward the Day of Atonement, the rusting top of the old train trellis that crosses the Dead River can be seen in the distance.

Before reaching the river, Adam stops and removes his helmet, the others doing likewise.

—Should have signal now, he says, pulling out his cell phone.

The others pull out their phones. Sam's is ringing. A moment later, all four people are taking or making calls.

—Sam, it's Michelle. Not sure if it'll help or not, but the lab found traces of sodium sulfate on the base of the bronze altar.

—What would that come from?

—That's the strange thing, Michelle says. If the paper mill were still there, I'd say *it*.

—Okay, Sam says. Thanks.

—Brian, it's Daniel. Any word from Ben?

—No. Esther's still calling around, but . . . How are things out there?

—Nothing so far, he says.

—Thanks for what you're doing for him, man.

—Do you know of anything near the tracks out here? Between the river and the bay?

—Seems like there's something, he says. Hold on, let me check. I've got an old map and I'm looking online at a historical site that features the area. Na, nothing close to the tracks.

—Okay, thanks for looking.

—Wait, here's something, he says. I'm gonna send you a picture. Looks like the only thing anywhere even remotely close is an abandoned materials plant near where the old chemical company used to be, though I doubt there's anything left of either one of them.

—Where are they?

—If they're still there, he says, they're about two miles past the river. The tracks separate. One continues toward the old mill site, the other breaks off toward the old chemical company, passing through the materials plant on the way.

—The lab found traces of sodium sulfate, Sam says, a chemical used in making paper, on the altar Joel used in Daniel's field. Since there's not a paper mill anymore, we've got to figure out where it might have come from.

—I know, Travis says. My granddaddy said a few miles the other side of the river, the tracks split up. One goes straight to the mill site, the other to where the chemical plant used to be.

—That's got to be it, she says.

—Can't be, he says. They tore it down when they demolished the mill.

—There's a materials plant near it that might still be standing, Daniel says. I should have a picture of it in a minute.

His phone makes an alert noise and he opens it.

Clicking on the icon to view the image, he gasps.

—Oh my God.

—What is it? Sam asks, the others leaning in, studying Daniel.

He holds up the image of the three train tracks intersecting at the factory, the opening in its center large enough for a train to pass through, above it a small square tower with a triangular roof rising to a point.

—That's it, Sam says.

—What is it? Travis asks.

—The entrance to the materials plant, Daniel says, has an eerie resemblance to that of Auschwitz.

A symbol the world over of the Holocaust, the Nazi extermination camp known as Auschwitz was the largest of the death camps, with three main camps and some fifty sub-camps. Located in southern Poland about forty miles from Krakow, the camp witnessed the murder of over 1.1 million people, ninety percent of whom were Jews.

The entrance to the materials yard and warehouse resembles that of the camp known as Auschwitz II or Birkenau, the largest of the camps and the one that became synonymous with Auschwitz.

Established in April of 1940 under the direction of Heinrich Himmler, chief of two Nazi organizations—the Nazi guards known as the SS and the secret police known as the Gestapo—Auschwitz originally housed political prisoners from occupied Poland and from concentration camps within Germany. Auschwitz II, built in 1941, had four gas chambers, designed to resemble showers, and four crematoria.

Prisoners were transported from all over Nazi-occupied Europe by train, arriving at Auschwitz II in daily convoys. When inmates reached the camp, about three-quarters of them went directly to the gas chambers of Auschwitz II, including women, children, the elderly, and the feeble. Auschwitz II had the capability of gassing and cremating over twenty thousand people each day.

Chapter Fifty-five

As she puts on her helmet and cranks her ATV, Sam feels energy humming through her, the excitement pumping through her with each beat of her pounding heart.

This is it. We've got him. We're really going to get him.

She follows Adam as he pulls up on the track and out onto the trellis, the tires of her ATV bouncing on the railroad ties.

The rush of excitement is tempered by the fast approach of nightfall, her heart sinking with the sun, and she worries that they won't be in time.

Beneath the railroad ties, she can see the dark waters of the Dead River rippling as if in the wake of an unseen boat, the tips of its small waves lapping at the cement pilings of the trellis.

When she looks up, Adam is right in front of her, his ATV stopped on the tracks. She grabs the brakes and skids to a stop, but not without bumping the back of his vehicle.

Adam pulls his helmet off and the others do the same.

—Bridge is open, he says. We can't cross.

They all look up ahead.

At the end of three sections of trellis, there's an open space equaling the length of one trellis or about a hundred feet. Beyond it, a large, motorized swinging section of the bridge equaling the length of two trellises stands open, perpendicular to them. On the other side of the open bridge, there's another open space equaling a length of trellis, then two more trellises to land.

The rusted metal frame of the swinging bridge section of the trellis balances on a large metal base in the center that rises out of the river. The top of the structure holds various outdated antennas and signal lights that appear to no longer work. On one side of the bridge, attached to two large steel supports, is a small tin shed control room.

—I thought this wasn't in use any longer, Sam says.

—It's not, Travis says. They must just leave it open so boats can pass now.

Sam searches the small corrugated tin booth in the center of the bridge for signs that an operator might be inside, but there are none. The windows are broken and boarded up, and there is no boat tied to the base of the bridge, which means unless he swam out to it, there is no one aboard the rusting old rig.

—What're we gonna do? Daniel asks.

—Nothin' we can do, Adam says. Ride back to our vehicles and drive around.

—That'll take too long. It'll be way after dark.

—Well, Travis says, unless you can walk on water . . .

—Even if you could, it's still four miles to the materials plant.

—I can run *that*, Daniel says, climbing off his ATV.

—What're you doin'? Sam asks.

—Gonna swim over and run from there.

—What? No. I'll call the others.

—They're at the bay, he says. They'd never make it in time.

—But—

—You know I'm right, he says. Call them. Call everybody and get them coming, but we've got to go from here. We don't have time to go back and drive around.

—How can they even get there from the other side? Travis asks.

—What? Sam says.

—There're no trails or roads, he says. The only road that goes to the old chemical plant is closed. Bridge was taken out last year during Hurricane Diane. They're gonna have to follow the tracks in from the other direction.

—Which'll take even longer, Daniel says. We've got to go. Come on. Ben's alive until sundown.

Sam looks at the others.

—I can't swim, Travis says.

—I can swim, Adam says, but I can't run no four miles.

—Looks like it's just us, Sam says.

—This isn't a good idea, Travis says. They call it the Dead River for a reason. Chances are you'll land on a cypress stump if you jump off this thing, and even if you don't, the current's so strong, it'll probably pull you a mile downstream. Then there's the cottonmouths and gators.

—He's right, Sam says.

—One of y'all gonna lend me a gun? Daniel asks.

—Didn't you hear him?

—It'd get so wet it probably wouldn't fire anyway, Adam says.

—Tell the group coming in from the other way not to shoot me, Daniel says.

—What?

He then climbs over the barricade and jumps from the trellis.

The cold water is deep and dark. The drop from twenty feet propels Daniel down into liquid blackness for what seems like a minute or more, yet he never touches the bottom.

When he finally stops his downward momentum and can begin
to swim toward the surface, he kicks with his feet and pulls with his
cupped hands, but fears he will run out of breath before he reaches
the top. When he eventually breaks the surface, the current has already carried him fifteen feet downstream.

—You crazy son of a bitch, Adam yells. When'd you grow such a
big pair of balls?

He swims with all his strength, kicking though his shoes hinder
the process, clawing the water with his hands, yet making very little
progress toward reaching the other side, his movement taking him
down instead of across the river.

Several times, his arms and legs graze objects in the water. He's
not sure what he's coming in contact with, but he hopes it's fish and
tree limbs instead of snakes and gators.

—Here comes another lunatic, Adam yells. I guess her balls're big
as yours.

Daniel turns to see Sam torpedoing into the water.

He waits until her head breaks the surface before returning to his
futile attempts at crossing, turning periodically to make sure she's still
above water.

After several more minutes and a minuscule amount of forward
motion, Daniel hears gunshots and turns toward them.

He's got water in his eyes and ears, but he can see that Adam and
Travis are firing their weapons from the trellis, yelling and waving
their arms in the air. Daniel turns in the direction of their motions
and sees a small boat headed in his direction. He begins to wave his
hands while treading water. Sam does likewise.

When the boat slows, the noise of its engine dying down enough
for the redheaded man in camouflage overalls to hear, Adam points
out Daniel and Sam and asks the man to give them a ride to the other
side.

—Him too, while you're at it, he says, and pushes Travis into the
water.

When Travis resurfaces, he flails about, panicking, but the large man in the boat manages to pull him in. He then picks up Sam and drives over to Daniel.

—What the hell're y'all doin'? the man asks.

—Trying to get to the other side, Daniel says.

—Must be pretty damn and hellfire important.

After he delivers them to the other side Sam explains the situation, and he lets Daniel borrow his shotgun. They climb the embankment up to the tracks and begin to run down them.

—Thanks for coming along, Travis, Sam says.

He smiles.

—Couldn't let you guys have *all* the fun.

Chapter Fifty-six

Wet clothes clinging to their bodies, soaked feet sloshing in squeaking shoes, they run at a steady, fast pace down the tracks toward an uncertain destiny.

Daniel, out in front, holds the shotgun with both hands, barrel down.

—You know how to shoot that thing?

—It's a shotgun, Daniel says. Point and shoot and anything in a block of what you're aiming at's gonna get some buckshot.

—Just make sure we're not in that block.

—Better let us do the shooting unless there's just no other option, Sam says.

—Like if we're dead, Travis says. And you're certain we're dead. And the guy's still coming for you.

—And you're certain that you're certain, Sam adds.

—Guys, I've—

—Reading a book about it isn't the same as doing it, she says with a smile.

—I grew up here, remember? I used to hunt with my uncle when I was a kid.

—Been a long time since you was a kid, Travis says.

—Are you two talking so much because you're nervous? Daniel asks. I'm not gonna shoot you.

They run for what seems like a lot longer, their pace slowing, their breaths labored, their expressions pain-filled.

—You're not gonna get the chance to shoot me, Travis says. My heart's gonna explode first.

—My side feels like it's gonna split open, Sam says. Shouldn't we have reached the turnoff by now?

—Still two tracks, Travis says. So, guess not.

—Pain makes you more of a smartass?

—I'm in pain. I'm bein' a smartass. So, guess so.

Sam looks at Daniel.

—Shoot him, she says. I'll say it was an accident.

Daniel doesn't say anything.

—What is it? she asks.

Just ahead of them, beneath a rusting old fire tower reaching high into the indifferent sky, the set of tracks to the right veer off in that direction.

Like most of the Division of Forestry lookout towers in the area, the abandoned fire tower consists of a small room or cab located atop a large steel frame some two-hundred feet in the air. A series of platforms, each with a flight of stairs, leads to the tin box high above the tall pines surrounding it.

—Shouldn't be far now, Sam says.

Daniel picks up the pace a bit, and the others stay right with him.

Less than a mile down the track, they reach the entrance to the materials plant, a splintered wooden sign, faded and pocked, listing the plant rules.

—All visitors must check in at office, Travis reads. I'll do that while you two go shoot the monster.

Another two-hundred feet from where they are, the tracks join others and all disappear beneath the factory tower.

Remarkably like the entrance to Auschwitz, the materials plant tower is centered between two long factories extending out from it lengthwise. The tower and the factories are missing windows and sheets of tin, and those that remain show signs that soon nature will rule over the ground it stands on once again.

Daniel continues running.

—Wait, Sam says. We need a plan.

—Without stopping, Daniel says, I'll get Ben, you two get the monster.

—Everybody be careful, Sam says. Shoot Joel if you have to. Don't hesitate.

They run beneath the tower and find a materials yard filled with rusted equipment and piles of sand, rock, limestone, and pulp by-products, weeds and vines covering it all.

The final glow of the sun fades and full darkness falls.

To the left, beyond an old graffiti-covered boxcar, a tall two-tier factory stands, the glass of its windows broken, rust showing beneath the faded white paint of the corrugated tin.

From the instant Daniel steps into the yard, he smells smoke, char, and burning flesh.

Please not Ben. Please.

Since it's closest, he runs over to the boxcar, sets his shotgun on the ground, and slides its door open, gagging as the first gust of the foul air slaps him in the face.

The boxcar holds what looks to be at least four bodies in various stages of decomposition. They are not burned, just rotting, the emaciated bodies being eaten by maggots.

He didn't have a cattle car, Daniel thinks, so he's improvising.

Sam runs up.

—What is it?

—He recreated the cattle car experience of the Holocaust, letting them die inside, as many Jews did on their journey to the ovens.

From across the yard, Travis makes a sound like a bird, and they turn to see him.

He points to the factory, motioning them to enter from the opposite end.

Going around the boxcar, they walk toward the smaller of the two tiers, hurrying when they see the faint, intermittent glow of a flame through the small windows near the roof.

Crouching in a shooter's stance, Sam enters the building first, her drawn gun dripping. Daniel follows close behind, glancing over his shoulder occasionally as he does.

The room they have entered sits in one corner of the shorter factory building. It's dark inside, but Daniel can just make out the tools and material used in constructing the brazen altar when Sam clicks on a penlight, shakes it, and shines it around, its weak beam turning on and off, illuminating small spots of the room and its contents.

—His workshop, Sam says.

He nods.

—You okay?

—Yeah. Come on. We're close.

They proceed to the back of the room and into the vast, open three-story factory.

And there it is.

In the dim, warm glow of torches scattered throughout the factory, the elaborate wooden and fabric structure looks like an illusion.

—What is it? she asks.

—The tabernacle. He's built the entire tabernacle of Moses.

Daniel begins to run toward the large piecemeal tent, Sam following, scanning the building for Joel.

—We've got to get to the altar of burnt offerings, he says.

As they near the tabernacle, they smell the fumes. Everything is slick with accelerant, the factory floor slippery with it.

—All he has to do is drop a match, Sam says, and this whole place will go up in an instant.

Daniel nods, trying not to think about it. His fear is back, flashes of fire in his mind, his childhood home burning, the smell of burning flesh. As he thinks about his mom, her kind, warm eyes and the way she had always smelled of Dove soap, his stomach turns and he has to swallow back the bile rising in his throat.

—Let's get Ben and get out of here, he says, his voice small and shaky. Wait for backup.

They enter the tabernacle, the fumes so strong now they're intoxicating, and enter the courtyard. In an instant, he can see that the tabernacle and all its furnishings have been built to the exact specifications mentioned in the Hebrew Bible.

Bound, gagged, and unconscious, Ben lies on the altar, his hair and clothes slick with the same accelerant pooled on the factory floor.

A pile of ashes and charred remains on the floor next to the altar confirms Ben is not the first sacrifice to be laid here.

There is no fire in or on the altar, but the golden candle stand has been brought out of the holy place and stands in the middle of the brazen laver, which instead of water holds a pool of fuel. One of the candles on the stand has been removed and stands on the ledge of the laver directly in the accelerant, its flame moments away from igniting a blaze that will consume them all.

—Get the candle, he says. I'll get Ben.

Daniel works on Ben's restraints, but he is cuffed and chained to an eye bolt that's been welded to the altar, and it's not budging.

—It's rigged, she says. Booby-trapped to knock over the candle stand if you get near it. It'd take too long to dismantle it. We've just got to get him, warn Travis, and get out of here.

—He's chained to the altar, he says. I can't free him.

Sam glances back at the candle.

—There's not enough time to get a tool from the workshop, she says.

—Whatta we do?

—TRAVIS, she yells.

—YEAH? he replies from what sounds like the other side of the factory.

—GET OUT NOW, she yells. THE WHOLE PLACE IS ABOUT TO BLOW.

—OKAY.

Sam points her weapon at the eye bolt.

—Hold his legs up, she says.

—The spark, he says, fear gripping him so tightly he can't breathe.

—I know, she says, but it's going up one way or the other. This way we get him and get out.

He nods and pulls Ben's legs back away from the eye bolt, the chain snapping taut as he does.

Before she can squeeze off a round, they hear a loud poof, see giant flames running toward them, and hear Travis begin to scream.

Chapter Fifty-seven

Sam fires three quick shots, the bullets ricocheting off the altar, the sparks igniting another fire, much closer.

Travis continues to scream as the fire continues to spread. From the sound of his screams, Daniel guesses he's on fire and is running through the tabernacle spreading the flames.

Frozen in fear, he can no longer move no matter how hard he tries. His breath is coming so quickly now, his heart beating so fast that he's lightheaded and about to hyperventilate.

—Daniel, Sam yells.

He can't even turn toward her.

—Daniel, she yells again. Pull the chain. Pick up Ben.

Superimposed over the spreading fire of the tabernacle, he sees the thin, light-colored paneling of his parents' hallway burning as if walls of fire, framed photographs of the happy family, food for hungry flames.

—Daniel, Sam yells again.

Unlike Travis, his parents didn't scream, didn't cry or whimper. He realizes now they must have been dead from smoke inhalation long before the beast turned their flesh to ash.

—Daniel, please, Sam yells. We've got to get out of here.

An old red brick church they'd never attended, two coffins side by side surrounded by flowers from friends he didn't know, and the dreamlike feeling of unreality, but then something else—a presence, an undeniable, palpable presence, enfolding, engulfing him the way the fire had his parents and all they owned in the world, and he was okay.

—Daniel, please, Sam yells again. We're gonna die.

He pulls on the chain and it gives.

Lifting Ben, he turns to see fire arching all around them.

They're surrounded, waves of flames lapping at them from every direction.

—Whatta we do? Sam asks.

Daniel looks around.

—Look, he says. Grab that.

He points to one of the long acacia poles extending through the rings on the altar.

Sam pulls it free and they run to the side of the tabernacle, the floor beneath them on fire. Coughing from the smoke, sweating from the heat, they reach the side of the tent.

—We've got to do this quickly, he says. We're gonna get burned no matter what, but maybe we can get out of here alive. I'm gonna lift the side of the tent with the pole and you'll roll out beneath it. Then from the other side, you lift on it and do the same for us. I'll push Ben through and then follow him.

They do as Daniel described, their clothes catching on fire as they roll through the accelerant on the floor.

—Come on, he says, lifting Ben over his shoulder. When you get outside, drop to the ground and just keep rolling.

By the time they are outside and have their clothes and hair out, the entire building is engulfed in flames.

Sam jumps up and draws her weapon, searching the area around them for Joel, but there is no sign of him.

—You think he's inside? she asks.

—I don't know, he says. I'm just glad we're not.

—Poor Travis, she says. Maybe he was running because he was chasing Joel. Maybe he's the reason Joel's not out here trying to finish us off.

Ben begins to cough, his bloodshot eyes blinking open.

—What's— he begins, but starts to cough again.

—We saved your life, Daniel says. And this is all your fault.

—*My* fault?

—Your employee. Your project.

—Sure, Ben says, blame the Jews. We're what's wrong with the world.

Just then, an explosion blows a large, jagged hole out the side of the warehouse. Daniel and Sam stand and run toward it.

—Wait for me, Ben says. I wanna see. And I don't wanna be alone.

Daniel helps him up and they walk around the side of the building, Ben cuffed and shackled, doing the inmate shuffle.

The hole is enormous and shows the sea of fire raging in the building. Through the opening, the back wall is visible, and they can see the row of small oven-like crematories like the ones the Nazis used.

—Auschwitz, Daniel says. He recreated virtually the whole camp from the train to the crematories, adding to it the tabernacle and tying in the original holocausts or burnt offerings.

Nearly all of the tabernacle fabric is gone, the wooden posts of its frame little more than charred poles. They watch as the last of the holy place tent burns away, revealing Joel in full priestly regalia standing before the holy of holies, his robe and miter garments of fire.

—Why isn't he running? Sam asks.

—He may have been planning to offer himself as a priestly burnt offering all along, Daniel says. Maybe it's why he wanted us here.

—Who is it? Ben asks.

Sam and Daniel turn to him in shock.

—You don't know? he asks.

—Joel, she says.

—*My Joel?* I wondered what you meant by my employee.

—You never saw him?

—The last thing I remember was being in my office and hearing someone come in the building, he says. I thought it was you. He shakes his head. Joel did all this?

Daniel explains everything to him.

—But his grandfather was a kapo, Ben says.

—Which is probably why he's making himself a burnt offering, Daniel says.

—The one decent thing he's done, Sam says.

Chapter Fifty-eight

—You don't have to hang around here, Sam says. This is going to take a while.

Cops and crime scene techs are beginning to arrive, waiting for the fire to die down so they can move through the site, snap pictures, take measurements, catalog the catastrophe, chronicle the holocaust.

Sam, Daniel, and Ben have been treated for the minor burns they sustained. The bodies of Joel and Travis have been pulled from the building, along with three other as yet unidentified bodies, all only partially consumed by the fire.

—Sam, someone yells.

They turn to see Stan Winston in a suit getting out of the hi-rail truck and heading toward them.

—You okay? he asks as he grabs and hugs her.

She doesn't really hug back, just pats him a little.

—I'm fine, sir, she says. Thanks.

—Good work, he says. Hell of a job. I'm so glad you're safe. This was no small thing you did. You'll probably make special agent off this.

—I couldn't have done it without Daniel, she says. He's really the one who figured everything out and saved Ben's life.

—Actually, we all played an important part, Kennedy Todd Whitman says, peeking around from behind Stan.

Ignoring him, Stan turns to Daniel and extends his hand.

—We really appreciate all your help. It's nice to have you back.

—Thanks.

—I'm gonna walk them over to the truck, Sam says. I'll be right back.

They pass beneath the entrance, lit now by huge banks of halogen lights, looking like an apparition of Auschwitz.

—You thank him for saving your life? Sam asks Ben.

Ben nods.

—The first time.

They reach the hi-rail truck and Ben climbs in, Daniel lingering behind a moment to be with Sam.

—I'll call you later, Sam says.

—Okay.

—Or come by when I finish up here.

—Even better.

They kiss and she heads back to the others.

Pausing a moment before getting in the cab of the truck, Daniel turns to take one last look at Sheol.

And as he does . . .

Something about it bothers him.

—It wasn't an old picture, he says.

—What? Ben asks, leaning out of the truck.

—Is there any signal out here?

—I got two bars, Ben says. Why? What is it?

—The picture Brian sent me.

—The what?

—It wasn't old, he says. It was recent. I thought he took it from a book, but he was here. It's him. He's the killer. He set Joel up. Killed him like all the others. All that shit about Joel being a self-hating Jew . . . He's the one who fielded the calls about those who were missing. He's the one who's been one step ahead of us all the way. I knew that one trunk inside an otherwise immaculate condo wasn't right. I bet if we have it tested, the handwriting in the journals will be his, not Joel's. He has a key to Joel's place. He hit you over the head from behind and never let you see him because he was setting up Joel. That's the reason Joel didn't move, just stood there and burned to death inside the priestly garments. Brian had drugged him like the others.

—Oh my God, Ben says. Are you sure?

—I should've seen it sooner, but he set up that fake abduction— actually that should have tipped me off. The video of you was handheld, the camera moving around showing everything. The one of him was on a tripod and it was framed by a professional cinematographer, composed artistically to show everything. And the killer called me right after we found you, but he had to wait a while after we found him because he was in the car with us. Daniel shakes his head. He rode home with us. He knew everything. I can't believe how much I told him about myself—all I've been going through. He had to love that.

—Sorry about that, Ben says. If I'd've known he was the killer, I wouldn't have recommended you let him shrink your head.

Daniel pulls out his cell phone and calls the number Brian sent him the picture from.

—Hello.

—Brian, it's Daniel. Did I wake you?

—It's okay, he says. I was waiting to hear news about Ben and I must've dosed off.

—Where are you?

—How's Ben? he asks. Did you find him?

—We did, Daniel says. He wants to see you. Where are you?

—I'm still at the office, he says.

—Let me call you back on the office line, Daniel says.

Brian doesn't say anything.

—Is there a reason I can't call you back on the office line?

—You know, don't you?

—Know what?

—You're trying to trip me up, Brian says, his voice different, cold, with more of an edge.

—Where are you really? Daniel asks.

—Far, far away, he says.

—Couldn't be that far yet.

—You'd be surprised. I've been planning this a long time. The whole project worked out to perfection. Don't you think?

—Except for Ben.

—That was part of the plan, he says. Who else could make the movie?

Daniel can't think of anything to say.

—Sorry about all the fire, Brian says. I know that had to bring up some unpleasant memories. Perhaps we could talk about them sometime.

Daniel still doesn't say anything.

—You played your part rather well, I thought, Brian says. A little slow, but . . . Oh, and I know they'll have to do all their pathetic little tests, but I haven't left a single thing behind I didn't mean to.

—I'm going to find you, Daniel says.

Brian begins to laugh, and the line goes dead.

Chapter Fifty-nine

—He's watching us right now, Daniel says.

—What? Ben asks, leaning up in the seat and looking around.

They are in the cab of the hi-rail truck, heading down the track back toward Bayshore.

—The killer? the driver asks. I thought he was dead.

He's a thin young black man in his early twenties.

—Whatta we do? he asks, tapping the breaks, beginning to panic.

—Don't stop, Daniel says. Just keep driving.

He begins to accelerate.

—Don't speed up either. Just drive normally—or even a little slow.

—Are you sure? Ben asks.

—Remember what he did the night he made his first sacrifice at the train depot? Daniel says. He climbed up in the tree stand to watch.

—Yeah? Why'd he do that?

—To feel like God—the smoke of the sacrifice rising up to him. He's doing the same thing right now.

—Where is he?

—The fire tower, he says. Has to be. Call Sam and tell her, he says. Tell her everything. Let her know he's watching. Tell her to send just a few men and tell them not to be obvious.

—Whatta you gonna do?

—Go on up, he says. Make sure he's still there. I'm afraid my phone call may have made him run.

He leans up past Ben and asks the driver for a lighter.

—All I got's a box of matches, he says.

—Good enough. When you reach the curve up there where this track joins the other, slow down enough for me to jump out, but don't stop.

He then reaches up and turns the cab light to the off position so it won't come on when he opens the door.

—What's gotten into you? Ben asks.

—It's what's gotten out, he says, opening the door slightly and stepping out.

Rushing up the rusting metal steps toward the cab at the top, Daniel searches the tower for signs that Brian had ascended these same stairs earlier tonight.

In the faint light of the moon, he can make out traces of the sand and soil-tinged residue he's looking for, confirming Brian's shoes have the same accelerant on them his do.

It's two-hundred feet to the top and will take him a few minutes to reach—time to think about what he's doing.

His racing heart is one part adrenaline, two parts fear, the trembling in his body increasing with every step, and he can feel the threat of panic gnawing at the edges.

I'm not gonna stop. No matter what. I refuse to live in fear, to be controlled by terror any longer.

He realizes this is something he absolutely must do, the next step—a hell of a lot of them, actually—in his recovery, in his reawakening.

I'd rather die doing this than live a long life in fear.

As he continues to climb, he can see the entire horrific scene at the materials plant below. This is the perfect place for him to observe his offerings, behold his devastating masterwork. Nearing the top, he sees that the fire continues to devour, the smoke of the burnt offerings rising up into the night, above the treetops, into the heavens, eerily backlit by moonlight.

Daniel stops one flight down from the top and withdraws the small box of matches from his pocket.

The access hatch in the bottom of the lookout booth is open, but it's dark inside, no movement, no noise.

As he steps from the small platform onto the first stair of the last flight, Brian rushes out of the darkness from the corner behind him and jabs a needle into the base of his neck.

Hurling himself backwards, Daniel knocks Brian down, and he strikes the steel beam in the corner, knocking the syringe out of his neck, the small object falling down to the ground below.

Searching for the dropped box of matches, Daniel takes two steps toward the final flight of stairs and collapses.

The partial dose of succinyl choline renders Daniel defenseless, though not completely paralyzed, and as Brian drags him up the stairs to the lookout station, he manages to snag the tiny box of matches with the awkward tips of his barely functional fingers.

Next to the open door in the floor, Daniel lies in the small station, unable to move anything but the ends of his extremities.

—Feels like a panic attack, doesn't it? Brian asks. Wonder how much got in you. Can't believe you broke my last syringe. I ought to go ahead and kill you just for that, but I think it's more poetic if you die like you lived, paralyzed, gripped by fear, don't you?

Daniel tries to nod, but a slight jerk of his head is all he can manage.

On the floor of the cab, not far from where he lies, sits a charred chunk of flesh, black and bloody. The priest's portion.

Turning his attention away from Daniel, Brian looks through the window at the still-burning plant below.

—Isn't this the most amazing thing you've ever witnessed? he asks. I mean all of it. It's perfect.

Daniel tries to say something, but can't, only unintelligible little grunts coming out.

—What?

He wants to tell the monster that he failed to kill Ben, but straining as hard as he can, he can only get one comprehendible word out.

—Ben.

—What? Brian asks, a smile twitching at his lips. What'd you say?

—Ben.

—I'll remedy that, he says. Don't you worry.

Daniel tries to say something else, but can't.

—How does it feel? Brian asks. You've feared this so long and now it's here. What's it like?

—What?

—Knowing you're about to die.

Daniel wants to tell him he's okay, make him realize that he has no power over him, but he can only force out one word.

—Peace.

Brian turns from the window again.

—Really? You don't mind dying? What about knowing that I'm gonna burn Sam and Ben? What about knowing I'm gonna fuck her first, knowing I'm gonna hurt her? You got peace about that?

Daniel doesn't say anything.

—You don't deserve peace. You deserve to burn.

—Why? Why do I? Why did they?

—Turned on their own—or were born because their parents or grandparents did. They've so given in to the ignorant, hateful, backward. They hate themselves and those like them and so betray the very vulnerable people they should be protecting. It's the sick, demented cesspool that passes for culture around here. People don't even see it. Well, I'm forcing them to. Holding them before the brazen laver so they can see their iniquity. People betraying themselves and their own. *My* people working for the goddam Nazis. It's unimaginable. Unthinkable. I can't abide it—not a betrayal that goes so deep. The fire falls. Judges all.

—How have I—

—You're the worst offender of all.

—Me?

—Hell yes, *you*. You know better. You *are* better. But what do you do? You hide away from the world. Do you stand for anything? Do you do anything to help, to teach, to change the way things are? You read all those books and fill yourself with knowledge and information and then you don't do anything with it. I gave you a chance to do something with it, but it's too little, too late. You're gonna burn like the rest of them.

—But I—

—You know how the Nazis were able to kill six million of us so efficiently? Because of IBM. They supplied the punch card machines that enabled six million of my people to be murdered with precision. They didn't sell the machines, they leased them. They serviced them. They knew what their machines were being used for and still they profited from it. They'll claim they're not responsible for six million deaths, but aren't they? And what about you? How many good people are dead or are living in hell because of you? Like Burke said—all that is needed for evil to triumph is for good men to do nothing. You've been doing nothing. The world is crumbling in around you and you can't be bothered to lift a finger, to do your small little part to fight all this shit. Well, guess what? When you do nothing, you cease to be a good man. And you're gonna burn.

Brian turns to look down at the massacre below again, and Daniel attempts to open the box of matches with the fingers that hold it. It'd be a challenge with one hand if it were fully functional, but impossible in his current condition, and he drops the small box.

Feeling around, he manages to find it, and realizes that having it on the floor makes it easier for him to open.

With his thumb pressing down on the top of the box, he pushes the end with his forefinger and it slides open.

It takes a few moments, but eventually he withdraws a single match.

Holding the match with his thumb and forefinger, he presses down on the box with his other three fingers.

Brian looks down at him and begins to laugh.

—You have far more accelerant on you than I do, he says.

Daniel manages to strike the tip of the match across the box, the friction producing a spark—one tiny flame, one small chance.

Realizing the fiery potential of the small booth, Brian lunges for Daniel.

Daniel waits until the monster is nearly on top of him, then flicking his wrist just enough to get the match airborne, he slings it at Brian.

The match finds accelerant-soaked cloth and begins to run up Brian's body, spreading over him, licking, devouring, engulfing.

As Brian moves about, he spreads the fire through the tinderbox of the old booth and soon the entire station is burning, the flames quickly spreading to Daniel, consuming his shirt, eating his flesh. The skin of his chest begins to melt off, sliding from his torso in long, stringy sheets of molten flesh.

The pain is unbearable.

He screams.

And screams.

With every bit of strength he can muster, he begins rocking back and forth, a fraction of muscle control returning to him. When he's got enough momentum, he rolls into the opening and falls down the stairs, banging hard against the small landing.

Burning.

Melting.

Crying.

In a few moments, Sam is there, rolling him over, stamping out the flames. Screaming down for paramedics.

Weakly, Daniel nods toward the door.

—Close him in.

She jumps up, climbs the flight of stairs, pulls down the door and latches it, sealing the monster in his fiery fate.

Rejoining Daniel, she offers comfort and continues to yell for help.

Before the medics arrive, they hear breaking glass and screams, and turn to see Brian Katz, arcing like a signal flare, plunge two-hundred feet to his death, his body continuing to burn once it smashes into the earth.

Chapter Sixty

Shock.

Burn unit.

Pain.

Pain management.

Infection.

Intravenous fluids.

Skin grafts.

Dressings.

Time.

Healing.

—Is he really dead? Daniel asks.

—Dead, burned, buried, Sam says.

She has come back to his hospital room for the next to last time. Tomorrow he will be released to heal at home.

He glances down at his scarred, deformed chest.

—He'll never be dead for me, he says. He made good and goddam certain of that.

—You got him. You slayed the dragon. You saved Ben and so many future victims.

He looks down at the misshapen mass of his chest again.

—You look like me now, she says.

He looks up at her, his eyes moist, blinking.

—I do, don't I?

—We're twins.

—You say the sweetest things.

—Can't wait 'til you're better and our scars can make love to one another.

Home.

Together.

Settling in.

Healing.

Building a life.

It's cooler now, fall in full effect.

These days, in addition to gravel, autumn leaves crunch beneath their running shoes.

It's a Saturday morning in November, the day cool, clear, and bright. Sam is now assigned to the Tallahassee office, Daniel back teaching, consulting, and the two are inseparable.

—Fall is my favorite time of year, Sam says.

Daniel nods.

—Mine too.

The greens of the North Florida Wildlife Preserve are just beginning to brown, orange, and gold.

—Okay, Mr. Mind, she says. Who said 'Nature's first green is gold'?

He shrugs.

—Whitman?

She shakes her head.

—Frost, but he should've said, 'Autumn's first yellow is gold.'

—Doesn't quite have the same ring.

No longer running from death as much as toward life, Daniel can't stop smiling lately—and why not? He had done all those things Sam told him in the hospital—saved his friend, slayed the dragon, gotten the girl.

—You sure Ben doesn't mind me taking his place? she asks.

—You kidding? He told me he was gonna send you flowers.

There are no monsters to chase at the moment, only each other.

—You mind if we have Thanksgiving at my mom's?

—Of course not, he says.

—This'll be our first together.

—First of many.

—I was thinking just the two of us should go away together for Christmas.

He smiles.

—What? she asks, smiling back.

—Just like the way you think.

—You like the way I do other things too, she says.

—I was thinking we should cut our run short and go back and do some of them.

She smiles.

—What?

—I just like the way you think too.

You buy a book.

Chapter 7

I was in my room in the Cove Hotel at Wilson Avenue and Cherry Street. It was a two-story Spanish-style hotel, surrounded by an Edenic landscaping of trees and flowers, with a dock and dive platform out into the bay. My room, which I could not have afforded otherwise, was part of my pay for being the house detective.

In the dream, we were lying in between sand dunes looking up at the stars, listening to the unseen waves of the Gulf caress the shore. Beneath us, the sand was cool, above us, the sky was dark and clear and dotted with stars, and around us, the beach was empty for miles.

Harry was at his weekly poker game, and we were whiling away

...olt, in..........ht me up out of the ...b......ed.......of me remained.

W......door, Lauren rushe...side and closed it behind her.

In m......half-conscious condition, I took her in my arms and kissed......he resisted, but then kissed me......going limp inte...ne, my body responding to hers.

It was......she pulled away that I became fully aware of the waking w......is in now, and realized that I didn't have two arms to wrap......and that my body couldn't respond to hers.

"I'm......e said. "I didn't mean to—"

My s......f, my right shoulder and upper arm exposed. She stared at......he other gunshot wound scar...on my upper body.

Pulpwood Press
Where Books of Life become Trees of Life become Books of Life

We plant a tree.

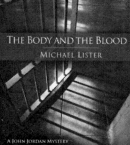

Michael Lister

A native Floridian, award-winning novelist, Michael Lister grew up in North Florida near the Gulf of Mexico and the Apalachicola River where most of his books are set.

In the early 90s, Lister became the youngest chaplain within the Florida Department of Corrections—a unique experience that led to his critically acclaimed mystery series featuring prison chaplain John Jordan: POWER IN THE BLOOD, BLOOD OF THE LAMB, FLESH AND BLOOD, THE BODY AND THE BLOOD, and BLOOD SACRIFICE.

Michael won a Florida Book Award for his literary thriller, DOUBLE EXPOSURE, a book, according to the *Panama City News Herald*, that "is lyrical and literary, written in a sparse but evocative prose reminiscent of Cormac McCarthy." His other novles include THUNDER BEACH, THE BIG GOODBYE, BUNRT OFFERINGS, and SEPARATION ANXIETY.

Michael's next book is a meditation on how to have the best life possible titled, LIVING IN THE HOT NOW.

His website is www.MichaelLister.com.

CPSIA information can be obtained at www.ICGtesting.com
Printed in the USA
LVOW111408050312

271662LV00001B/18/P